Gangadhar Gadgil was born on August 25, 1923, in Mumbai. He is an economist by profession and a leading Marathi writer who is recognized as the creator of the new Marathi short story. His work in the field of criticism, humour, travelogues, novels and personal essays is groundbreaking. His first short story was published in 1941. Since then, he has published over fifty books consisting of collections of short stories, humorous stories, travelogues, novels, plays, one act plays, literary criticism, stories and plays for children. Three collections of his short stories have already been published in English. These are, *The Woman and Other Stories, Crazy Bombay* and *The Throttled Street and Other Stories.*

He is the recipient of numerous State and other literary awards, including the Sahitya Akademi Award and the prestigious Janasthan Award. His writings, both in Marathi as well as in translations, have been published in leading newspapers and journals in India and abroad. His works are prescribed for study in the school and university level in Maharashtra. Some of his short stories and humorous writings have been selected for Australian and Canadian textbooks.

Gangadhar Gadgil was appointed as an Honorary Professor of Marathi for three years by the University of Bombay. He was the Vice-President of Sahitya Academy and of Mumbai Marathi Grantha Sangrahalaya. He is also in the committees of various literary bodies.

The US Library of Congress has recently chosen Gangadhar Gadgil as one of the writers whose voice it wishes to record and preserve.

Husbands and Pumpkins and Other Stories

Gangadhar Gadgil

Popular Prakashan

Popular Prakashan Pvt. Ltd.
35-C, Pt. Madan Mohan Malaviya Marg
Popular Press Bldg., Tardeo
Mumbai - 400 034

First Published in 2001
'The Big Silver Rupee' first
published in *The Throttled Street
and Other Stories*, 1994

(3626)

ISBN-81-7154-869-5

PRINTED IN INDIA
By Jyoti Printery
419, Milan Industrial Estate
Cotton Green, Mumbai - 400 033
Published by Ramdas Bhatkal for
Popular Prakashan Pvt. Ltd.
35-C, Pt. Madan Mohan Malaviya Marg
Tardeo, Mumbai - 400 034

To

My three-year-old grandson Arjun
who is universally acknowledged
to be the strong man of the family

Contents

Husbands and Pumpkins and Other Stories

TAGORE
SHAKESPEARE
KEATS
POETRY

1

Moms in the Good Old Days

Recently I had occasion to visit a poet. When I rang the doorbell her husband opened the door. When I went inside I found her lying on a sofa looking very pale and spent. Anguish was written all over her face and she was clutching her head in distress.

I was alarmed by what I saw and asked her, "What is the matter? You seem to be quite unwell."

"No! really! I am just utterly exhausted", she said in a low whimper.

I had heard that poets have to pour out their very souls to write a poem even if it consists of only a few lines. I, therefore, asked her, "Did you get up early in the morning and write a poem, or did you have to stay up the entire night to write it?"

She said with a wan smile, "No, I didn't write a poem. I have spent the last two hours and a half to get my daughter ready for school and send her off. I have just returned after pushing her into the school bus. I had to run frantically and wave my hands and scream in order to catch it. I am so fagged out after all this frantic activity that I will have to lie down and rest for half an hour before I can do anything at all."

"Do you mean to say", I asked in disbelief, "that you are so utterly tired after sending off one little daughter to school?"

"Well!" she said, "You seem to have no idea of the stressful and hectic work it involves. One has to wake up the girl, make her brush her teeth quickly without dawdling over it and beg of her again and again to drink a cup of milk. Bathing a reluctant girl is not easy and to brush her hair and push her into her uniform is a very onerous task. One has then to shove and squeeze her feet into her shoes amidst a lot of screams and protests. Mind you, that is not the end of it. One has to collect her books which are scattered around and check whether she has done her homework. If she hasn't one has to complete it in a hurry and then..." At this point the mere narration of her chores had exhausted the poet so completely that she had to gather enough strength to complete her tale of woe.

The long tale and the way she told it would have aroused anybody's sympathy. But it didn't arouse mine. On the contrary, what I felt was not sympathy but indignation. I barely managed to conceal my feelings with a sympathetic nod. But even as I gave her that sympathetic nod, I thought indignantly of how low the contemporary mothers had fallen as compared to their sturdy and dauntless predecessors, who handled mountains of work with nonchalant ease. As I thought of them, vivid memories of the moms in the good old days came back to me.

In those halcyon times a mother usually had atleast four or five children and it was not unusual to have as many as nine children. Why, I have seen with my own eyes moms who reared a dozen children. Mind you, it was not only children that mothers had to look after. Their households also included one or more mothers-in-law, three or four sisters as well as brothers of their husbands. It must be conceded that she also had the help of other women in the joint family. But, mind you, they too had children of their own, Morever, normally a baby was added to the woman's brood atleast every two years.

Everyday in this mom's life saw her wake up and get out of bed before dawn. Thereafter she quickly cleaned her teeth, combed her hair and took a quick bath. She then tucked her saree and started the day's chores. She lighted the chula or primus stove and placed on it a big pot of water to boil for the morning tea. Another pot full of milk was placed on the adjoining chula which heated it more gently. When the water steamed and was close to boil, she gave a call to the children to wake up and get out of bed. Her tone would be gentle and persuasive initially. But, if the children failed to respond, as they generally did, it became more and more demanding and strident. If words failed to get an errant child out of bed, it was pulled out of it unceremoniously. In this exercise, apart from urging children in general terms, she also urged and admonished each one of them separately.

Yamuna, the twelve-year-old girl was told that it was not at all proper for womankind to be in bed till sunrise. Balu, the ten-year-old boy was sharply reminded that he had to appear for a test in Geography that day and he had not been noticed preparing for it the previous evening. On the contrary, he had spent the afternoon romping and chattering with his buddies in the neighbourhood. Vaman was told angrily that sitting around doing nothing was a bad habit and worse still was the dirty habit of putting one's fingers in one's nose. The two little girls, Kamal and Sindhu, were told sternly not to get into a scrap and pull each other's hair immediately after getting out of bed. Finally, they were all sharply told not to wake up the baby and were threatened with dire consequences in the form of sore behinds and swollen cheeks if they didn't heed the warning.

The amazing part of it was that this was done while mom walked in a hurry towards the kitchen with her back turned towards the children. How she could see what her children were doing, while she looked the other way, has always remained a mystery to me. Moms in those good old days not only had eyes in their backs but could also see through walls.

Mom spent the next twenty minutes in the kitchen serving tea to the adults in the family and after finishing this chore her footsteps turned towards the big bedroom in which the numerous children slept in a row on the floor. The very sound of her footsteps had a magical effect. Balu, still lying spreadeagled in bed like the demon Ravana, quickly opened his eyes and sat up. He then jumped out of bed and began dutifully to roll up his bedding. Yamuna, lying curled up with her head hidden in her arms, jumped out of bed, rolled up her bedding and disappeared into the bathroom to brush her teeth. The two little girls Kamal and Sindhu stopped their fight and ran towards the bathroom to resume their unfinished tussle. Occasionally, however, a child or two were discovered in bed and administered sharp whacks on their behinds. Thereafter the mother rolled up the beddings of the children who were too young to do so themselves. She then stacked all the rolled up beddings tidily in a corner and repaired to the kitchen with quick steps to feed the children.

While she poured milk in their cups, her ears kept an eye on what was going on in the bathroom and her sharp tongue held the kids in leash.

"Brush your teeth thoroughly. Otherwise you will have germs crawling in your teeth," she cried and that was meant to be a general admonition, followed by warnings and threats to individual children based on their habits and proclivities.

"You there, Balu, don't roam all over the house while brushing your teeth and dirty the floor with your spittle."

"And you silly little goats, you don't have to look into the mirror with your noses pressed against it, while you are brushing your teeth."

"Yamuna, don't dawdle, brush your teeth quickly. If you conduct yourself that way in your husband's house your mother-in-law will be after you with a cudgel."

It was only because of her miraculous ability to see through the walls that she could know exactly what her children were doing out there, while she was still in the kitchen.

When the children went into the kitchen after brushing

their teeth, they found their individual cups full of milk waiting for them. In filling the cups every child's preference were considered. There was extra sugar in Vaman's cup, while the layer of cream was carefully removed from Yamuna's cup, who didn't like it. The mother, in the meanwhile, got busy cutting up vegetables to be cooked for the morning meal.

While in a rush to finish her chores on time, she was called out to the living room by the children's father. Tradition required that this was to be treated as a command to be complied with immediately. She, therefore, on hearing the call, put aside the vegetables, washed her hands and hurried towards the living room as she dried her wet hands on the pallu of her saree. She then did what her children's father wanted her to do and gave him his shirt and cap, so that he could go to the vegetables stalls at the street corner and buy fresh vegetables and other provisions for the daily meals. She also told him respectfully what needed to be bought. As she walked towards the kitchen after attending to her husband's needs, she cried, "You pests, why are you sitting there dawdling over your milk? Finish drinking it and get a move on."

Back in the kitchen, she noticed that little Kamal had a moustache of tooth powder on her face. She sent her to the bathroom to wash it off.

The children as usual, grumbled while they drank their milk. They found it too tiresome to drink milk every day. They craved for tea, which the adults drank. But they did not dare to grumble loudly.

However, Balu had entered his teens and started behaving like a young bull, with newly sprouted horns. So he stubbornly refused to drink milk and asked for tea. "I am not a baby any more," he protested. Mother told him sharply not to be overwise and drink his milk without any more fuss. When he persisted in being difficult and perverse, he was sharply pulled up and told, "Any more of this nonsense and I will catch you by your ear and drag you in the presence of your father." That threat was enough to put paid to Balu's tantrum. Arguments with children were a daily hassle and couldn't be allowed to interrupt work. So mom cut the vegetables and attended to other chores in the midst of the daily arguments and admonitions.

When the children had finished drinking milk they were shooed away to finish their other morning routines. They were told to go to the toilet, have their baths and comb their hair. As the girls were too young to comb their hair and tie them in braids properly, the mother did it for them. So while she busily made all the preparations for cooking the morning meal, she asked Yamu to bring the comb, the little kettle of coconut oil and the toilet box which had a mirror on its lid. Thereafter the girls were expected to open their braids of hair and get ready for the morning hairdo. The girls were in the habit of peering into the small mirror and preening themselves over and over again. Knowing this, they were sharply admonished not to dawdle and waste time in preening themselves. The boys, who were generally prone to ignore mother's instructions and admonitions, were asked much more sharply to go to the toilet and take their bath.

Vaman protested, "But, Aai, I don't need to go to the toilet."

He was told sharply "Who knows better, you do or I do? Now, no back talk, do as you are told."

Vaman obeyed reluctantly and discovered that he did need to go to the toilet. Mother, it seemed, always knew better.

While mom was in the midst of arguments with Vaman and greenhorn Balu, the girls had assembled all the articles needed for the morning hairdo.

Seeing this, mom set aside her other chores and walked into the adjoining room to comb and braid the girl's hair. As she walked in, she caught Yamu in the act of parting her hair at a rakish angle.

Mom cried, "Yamu, I am watching what you are upto.

Those are the ways of the dancing girls and in our kind of families, we don't rear dancing girls but decent women."

The admonition was accompanied by a not so gentle thump in the back. Mom then squatted on the floor and asked Yamu to squat in front facing her. The comb was thereafter used to wipe out the rakish parting of hair. Next, she poured out of the little kettle a generous amount of coconut oil on her hand and rubbed it into Yamu's properly groomed hair. This was done with robust vigour to ensure that Yamu's head was massaged and the oil rubbed deep thoroughly into the thick hair. Poor Yamu's head almost sank into her shoulders and she winced often while this was being done. She also emitted suppressed screams. But mother continued to rub the coconut oil thoroughly into Yamu's hair and at the same time scolded her for wincing, screaming and making faces at the slightest excuse. A woman, she was told, must be able to suffer silently discomfort and pain. When the oil was thoroughly rubbed in, Yamu was thumped on the back, which was a signal to turn around and sit with her back to the mother. Then followed a vigorous combing of hair. So vigorous was it that Yamu almost keeled over every time the comb was pulled backwards through the hair. This process was punctuated with screams and contortions on the part of Yamu.

"Comb the hair a little bit gently," whined Yamu.

"How can I," protested mom, "when you have tangled it so badly. I wonder what you girls do with each other's hair, when you are at school. It is a bad habit to play around and tangle up each other's hair to try some fancy hairdos."

At this juncture mom noticed that Yamu was squatting on the floor crosslegged like a man. The consequence was a sharp thump on the back. Yamu didn't have to be told what it was for. She understood and quickly changed her posture and pulled up her knees so close that her chin rested on them.

"When on earth are you going to learn how to sit properly like a woman should. Your mother-in-law will raise hell if she sees you sitting like that and call me names for not bringing up my daughter properly."

By this time the hair had been untangled and combed into a smooth tidy stream. It was then parted into three streams of equal size and thereafter mother pulled the hair back and began to knit them into a very tight braid. So tightly was the braid knit initially that Yamu almost keeled over and screamed, "You are killing me mom. Not so tight please. Let it be a little loose."

"Really Yamu! I have not pulled back your hair too tightly. If the braid is not tight, your hair will break loose and will be flying all over your face in a few hours. A woman's hair should be so combed that even at the end of a day of heavy work, it should not be dishevelled," said mom. Nonetheless, she loosened her grip on the hair and knit a slightly loose braid. She then tied the ends of the long braid with a thick woollen thread which could be untied easily.

Another thump on the back indicated that the braid was complete and the girl should make room for her sister. It was also a reminder that she should bow low to the woman who had combed her hair. This was the custom and it had to be drilled into the girls. Otherwise mother would get a bad name for not bringing up her daughters properly.

After Yamu had bowed properly to mom, she was asked, "Will you now put the red kumkum mark on your forehead? Or will mother have to do that for you? And mind you, the kumkum mark should not be so tiny as to be invisible. It should be of a proper size."

While Yamu's hair was being combed, Kamal, the other daughter, was asked to open her braid of hair and be quick about it. She was told, "You are not born in a princely household and no maids are running around here to open your hair. So do it quickly. And where is the piece of woollen thread with which I tied your braid yesterday? The way you girls lose hairpins and woollen threads, you will reduce even Kubera, the god of wealth, to penury. I pity the boys who are destined to marry you girls."

Mom used to be particularly eloquent about how her daughters would drive their mothers-in-law crazy and reduce their husbands to penury. She also wondered aloud as to who were the unfortunate boys who were destined to marry her daughters.

The eloquence was often interrupted by a child in the toilet who was so young that it needed to be washed by mother.

"Aai," it cried, "I am done."

"Wait," cried mother. "My hand is not free at the moment."

The hand however, generally remained tied up for too long and the child eventually began to howl. Mother then, had to leave unfinished a chore in hand and go and wash the child and wash herself thereafter.

Mom was very keen to finish her chores before her mother-in-law finished her morning worship of the family deities and came into the kitchen to take command of things. But with these frequent interruptions she never managed to finish them all in time. And once the mother-in-law entered the kitchen, mom had to be at her beck and call. At the same time the unfinished chores had to be attended to and they kept her constantly on the run. On entering the kitchen the mother-in-law took a look at the preparations the daughter-in-law had made for cooking the morning meal. It was rather unusual for her to find everything in order and to her taste. She noticed some lacunae somewhere and called, "Er Laxmi..."

On hearing this call, Laxmi dutifully set aside whatever she had in hand and rushed to the kitchen to do her mother-in-law's bidding.

After doing whatever she was asked to do, mom returned to take in hand the unfinished chore of combing and setting Kamal's hair.

Not infrequently the baby woke up at this juncture and began to cry. Mom knew that it would do no harm and in fact do some good to it if the baby cried lustily for a few minutes after it woke up. In any case, born in a family which had a large number of children, the baby had to get used to being ignored or neglected from time to time. But the men squatting in the living room and reading the morning paper found the shrill screams of the baby quite annoying and demanded that they be stopped immediately. Poor mom left the combing of Kamal's hair unfinished and rushed to quieten the baby. The simplest and quickest way of doing so was to give the baby a quick breast feed which she did. She then asked Yamu to keep the baby in good humour and rushed back to complete the hairdos of Kamal and Sindhu.

The little gap of time between these two chores was used to go to the bathroom and give a bucketful of warm water to Vaman so that he could have his bath. She then returned and attended to the hair of the girls. While doing so, she kept mouthing rapid fire instructions to Vaman to take a proper bath. This was because the boy was in the habit of taking a perfunctory bath. He particularly neglected to pour water over his head for fear of getting suffocated when it streamed down his face.

The bath as usual was over far too quickly. So mom left the chore in hand unfinished and once again went into the bathroom to find out what kind of bath Vaman had taken.

Overruling his protest, she felt his hair with her hands and cried, "Why, the hair is as dry as tinder. When on earth are you going to learn to wash your head properly. Why, your face is as oily as it was in the morning. What good is a bath if it doesn't even clean your hair and face? This only means that I will have to scrub you and wash you every morning henceforth. If I don't, lice will soon be crawling in your hair."

Thereafter, disdainfully ignoring his rowls she soaped, scrubbed and dried Vaman's head thoroughly and briskly returned to finish combing the girl's hair.

How moms in those good old days did such a variety of chores in the morning is a mystery I have never been able to unravel. A time and motion study I did showed that it was totally impossible. But I have seen moms achieve the impossible and at the same time keep an eye to ensure that the soapbox was drained of water.

After pushing the children through their morning chores and asking them to do their lessons diligently, mom made preparations for the morning worship of the family deities by the male head of the family.

In the midst of these preparations, mom didn't forget to shoo away the children to do their lessons. Being sharply observant she knew the failing of each of the children. The girls Yamu, Kamal and Sindhu were told not to waste time in tidying up their school books and sharpening their pencils and do their lessons instead, which was far more important. Balu was in the habit of rushing off for help and consultation to his classmate Sadu, who lived in the same neighbourhood. They then wasted time in jabbering and arguing with each other. Balu was therefore warned not to stir out of the house on any pretext and do the lessons all by himself. If he needed any help in doing his lessons, he was told to get it from his father. Mom knew that Balu avoided seeking father's help for fear of being scolded. He was, therefore, told that he shouldn't mind being scolded, for parental scolding was good for children.

Mom knew that her advice though sound would not be acted upon by Balu. So she went to the door of the living room and pleaded in whispers to the children's father to help them in doing their lessons. This soft and sweet persuasion in a subdued voice was a constant refrain of her daily life.

Thereafter, mom went into the kitchen to help mother-in-law to cook the morning meal. She had to give Grandma the utensils and other things needed in the course of preparing a meal. She also had to set the plates and serve the food.

While she did this quietly and deferentially for the adult men in the family, the children received rapid-fire dos and dont's along with their food. Balu was told that eating cooked vegetables was good for health and that grown up children were not expected to spill the curry and sprinkle rice around their plates. Vaman was told to keep his food at the centre of his plate and not to pile it up in a corner. He was also told that it was high time he grew out of the childhood habit of eating his chapati with a thick spread of jaggery and ghee on it.

While serving food to the family, she also managed to feed the baby rice crushed and soaked in milk. How she could do all these things at the same time, is something I have never been able to fathom.

The children were told to wash their hands thoroughly after they had eaten with their fingers and the hands were inspected to make sure that they had been properly washed.

After washing their hands and wiping them dry, the children were marched off to get ready for school. While they put on their clothes, the mom was often called upon to stitch buttons on shirts, hooks on blouses, find lost pencils and misplaced erasers and crayon boxes and tidy up the hair of the girls.

At last when the children streamed out of the house along with their school bags, mom cried, "Out and on your way! Now that you are out of my way, I will have respite to do a bit of honest housework."

Mom thus seemed to think that what she had done since early morning wasn't real honest housework! Can you beat that?

Those were the kind of moms we had in the good old days. As against them, the moms of today cut a sorry figure. Sending off one solitary child to school seems to do them in! The poor things have to lie in bed for an hour to recoup from that exhausting effort.

❑

2

The Travails of Mothers-in-law

I do not know how things stand today in this matter of daughters-in-law. But when I was a boy every elderly woman of my grandma's age had one or more daughters-in-law of her own. Why, auntie Bhagirathi had no less than four daughters-in-law. I don't know why but she never called them by their names. Instead she called one the older one and called another the younger one. She also used to speak of the in-between one. The trouble was that there were two in-between ones and she always found it difficult to identify the particular in-between daughter-in-law she was speaking about. My grandma suggested that things would be easy for all concerned if auntie Bhagirathi identified her daughters-in-law by their names. But somehow auntie Bhagirathi never got round to doing so. May be she couldn't remember their names or it could be that she did not approve of the fact that creatures like daughters-in-law, who constituted the lowest rungs in the ladder of family hierarchy, should have names of their own.

Well! Not all elderly women were so fortunate as to have four daughters-in-law of their own. But most of them did have two or atleast one daughter-in-law. Well, come to think of it not everybody was that lucky. Poor Yamuna auntie had seven daughters and not a single son. My grandma often wondered what sins Yamuna auntie had committed in her previous birth to invite this misfortune on her head in this present birth of hers. Yamuna auntie, however, blamed her misfortune squarely on her daughters. They were so perverse that each one of the seven of them insisted on being girls. She often cried, "They are none other than my enemies in a previous birth, who are now born as my daughters to wreak vengeance on me. They will not rest until they ruin their parents completely."

Although I was a mere boy who was not allowed to pass opinions on the affairs of my elders, I in my heart, tended to agree with Yamuna auntie. There was really no reason for Yamuna auntie's all seven daughters to be daughters. It would have done them no harm if three or even four of them had been born as sons. But I as a boy knew that girls are by nature perverse and stubborn. One could do absolutely nothing about it.

Anyway, let us not get drawn into a discussion of the perversity of girls about which I have a good deal to say. It was daughters-in-law that I was talking about and, as I said, most of my grandma's friends had atleast one or more of them. And each one of them proudly brought her new daughter-in-law along when she called on my grandma who blessed the girl and asked her own daughters-in-law to give the girl the customary presents. This was the privilege of my auntie who was older than my mother. She came out of the interior of the house carrying in a silver plate heaped up rice, a coconut and a blouse-piece. The daughter-in-law again bent low and bowed to my auntie who then gave these presents to her with appropriate ceremony. My mother made her appearance at his juncture to participate in the proceedings. On noticing her, the daughter-in-law again bowed low to her and was appropriately blessed. Sometimes other women, who were next door neighbours, also dropped in to see this new daughter-in-law and she bent low and bowed to each of them separately. I used to be amazed then, at the capacity of these daughters-in-law to bow so many times, without spraining their backs or breaking them altogether.

After having bowed umpteen times to all the assembled women, the daughter-in-law would stand in a corner with bent head, trying to be as inconspicuous and humble as possible. This convinced my grandma and other elderly women that the girl had a proper upbringing and the virtue of obedience had been instilled into her. My grandma then would invite her to sit down. But the girl would keep standing and bend her head even lower to show respect. That little gesture would satisfy her mother-in-law that the girl knew her place in the scheme of things and she would gruffly ask her to be seated. The daughter-in-law would then squat putting her arms around her knees and pulling them up close to her breast. She would then rest her chin on her knees and her face would become almost invisible as was demanded by the precepts of modesty. My grandma then would make conventional conversation and ask the girl about her parents or about the number of brothers and sisters she had. The daughter-in-law would look demurely at her mother-in-law to seek permission and when it was granted with a nod she would reply to my grandma's question in a voice so low that one wondered whether it was audible even to her knees. Her mother-in-law would then scold her and say, "Speak a little loudly, will you? What you say has to be audible, isn't it?"

The girl was no fool. She raised her voice just a wee bit. I wondered whether that made it more audible to my grandma. I, for one, didn't catch even a word of what she said.

How could I, when I watched these proceedings from an adjoining room peering surreptitiously through a chink in the door? I would have loved to watch them at close quarters. But if I ever tried to enter that room, my grandma shooed me away saying, "What are you a man doing here amidst women? Be gone."

After my grandma and other elderly women had asked the girl a few questions, the girl was asked to utter the name of her husband.

On hearing this the girl would shudder and blush profusely and hide her face behind her knees. This would tickle and amuse the elderly women and they broke into broad smiles. My mother and auntie being younger would smile more discreetly. The girl was then cajoled over and over again to utter the name of her husband. She would then blush profusely and that would cause a lot of merriment in the assembled womenfolk. Eventually, the mother-in-law would mildly admonish the girl and ask her to stop blushing and do what she was told to do.

In those good old days of obedient, respectful and devoted wives, custom didn't allow women to utter the names of their husbands. If a woman wanted to talk to her husband, she would never call him by name. She would ask demurely, "Am I being heard?" The husband would then turn around and say, "What is it? Out with it. Don't you see I am in a hurry?"

It was only the young bride who had the privilege of uttering the name of her husband, when called upon to do so by the elders in the family. This was no easy task, for the name of the husband had to be woven into a couplet which was expected to be both laudatory and entertaining. The bride had to have quite a stock of them. Happily her mother and aunts supplied her with quite a few of them and made her learn them by heart.

Ultimately after a lot of blushing the daughter-in-law recited the couplet with her husband's name woven into it and was duly complemented by the assembled women. However, seated as I was in the adjoining room, what the daughter-in-law said never reached my ears. How could it, when she talked in such a low whisper?

That used to annoy me terribly and I always wondered why marriage had such a deleterious effect on the vocal cords of girls. I knew for certain that before they got married, girls had strong voices that would be raucous and shrill and they often were exactly that. But marriage did strange things to their throats. Overnight their voices sank into almost inaudible whispers and they couldn't swallow not only big laddus but even tea.

Take for instance the case of Kamal who used to live

next door. That girl screamed and shrieked so loudly when she played with other girls that on hearing her babies woke up with a start and startled women dropped the brass cooking pots in their hands. That made her mother lose her temper and she yelled, "Why must you shriek like a demon every time you play? Has somebody shoved a pounding rod down your throat?"

I for one had no doubt that Kamal's mother's suspicions were well founded. That was because only a girl with an abnormally enlarged throat could swallow a big laddu as quickly and effortlessly as Kamal did. Why, I could barely dig my teeth into a laddu before hers vanished down her capacious throat.

Yet, I found this selfsame Kamal unbelievably transformed when she visited us after she was married. She was barely audible when she spoke and her bite into a laddu was no bigger than the peck of a sparrow. I suspected that the girl was gravely ill. But to my surprise my mother thought that marriage had done her a lot of good.

But that is another story. As far as daughters-in-law in general were concerned, I had a good opinion of that species. They appeared to me well-behaved, respectful and obedient. But I was totally disillusioned on that score in the next Diwali vacation. It so happened that being preoccupied with sharpening my skills in playing with marbles and scoring hits with my catapult, I had rather neglected my lessons and had performed somewhat poorly in the half yearly examination. Mothers being what they are, my mother stopped me altogether from going out and playing with my friends in the neighbourhood yard. Instead she made me spend my entire day in a room doing my lessons.

Luckily for me my grandma used to rest and meet her many cronies in the adjoining room. I could therefore relieve the tedium of long hours of study by listening to their talk. Mind you, although I heard their gossip, I didn't neglect, my lessons. I had my eyes dutifully riveted on my books and I memorized loudly whatever I had learnt.

I was learning the geography of Mumbai and had to memorize the various routes of the tramcars. In the course of the study I would chant, "Tramcar number eight starts from Opera House and stops at Portuguese Church, Thakurdwar, Chira Bazaar, Dhobi Talao, Esplanade and reaches Flora Fountain in a final stop."

It was while I diligently memorized the routes of tramcars in this manner that I learnt from the talk in the adjoining room how difficult and troublesome these innocent looking daughters-in-law could be and how they were a pain in the neck to their poor suffering mothers-in-law.

Take for instance the daughters-in-law of Radha auntie. She looked so innocent that it seemed to be beyond her even to hurt a fly. Yet that girl, it seemed, was nothing less than a domestic disaster and Radha auntie had to keep a close watch on her all the time to save her family from starvation and penury. She, it seemed, was a great spendthrift if ever there was one and left to herself would have spent all the salary of her husband and her father-in-law in barely the first two weeks of the month leaving nothing at all to live on in the remaining two weeks. If she was asked to fry chaklis, she poured oil in the deep-bottomed frying pan until it was filled to the very brim. Very little of that oil was used up in frying the chaklis and the daughter-in-law poured all the rest of it down the drain. Poor Radha auntie's heart raced pit-a-pat, pit-a-pat when she saw her daughter-in-law do that. If she was asked to cook two measures of rice, she ended up cooking at least three measures of rice, if not more. So a lot of rice was left over everyday. And do you know what she did with that large quantity of rice that was left over? She generously gave it all away to the maidservant. Radha auntie almost swooned when she saw her do that. Thereafter Radha auntie kept her eyes fixed on her daughter-in-law whenever she asked her to cook a meal. That spendthrift girl would use up a cake of washing soap in three days, while Radha auntie could make it last for as long as two weeks. When asked to give the customary present of a coconut and a blouse-piece to a visiting young bride, this daughter-in-law gave away the biggest coconut in the house along with a blouse piece decorated with gold thread.

That was absolutely the limit. Poor Radha auntie saw penury standing on the threshold of her house and staring in her face.

No wonder Radha auntie lost her temper and screamed, "Plague on you, girl! Do you think that your father-in-law is a millionaire to afford this kind of profligacy? Do you want all of us to stand in the street with begging bowls in our hands?"

A decent daughter-in-law would have been contrite and catching both her ears in acknowledgement of her guilt would have assured her mother-in-law to mend her ways. But do you know what this girl did? She burst into tears and that too when her father-in-law was looking.

The father-in-law had a heart as soft as butter and he had never understood the need of watching pennies, the way Radha auntie did. His heart melted when he saw his daughter-in-law in tears and being very simple-minded admonished Radha auntie in the presence of her daughter-in-law.

He said, "Why do you scold that girl? Surely a generous use of cooking oil is not going to put any strain on our family income."

Simpleton that he was, he didn't realize at all the enormity of what he had done. For to admonish and belittle a mother-in-law in the very presence of her daughter-in-law is the surest way to spoil the girl. Seeing how things stand, the daughter-in-law would lose no time in climbing on the head of her mother-in-law and would settle there for all time to come!

Radha auntie displayed her presence of mind and sharply observed, "Running the house is women's business. Men folk should keep out of it."

Her husband realized his error and said a little sheepishly, "Well! you can run the household the way you like. But I can't stand anybody in my family shedding tears."

That put paid to all efforts of Radha auntie to instill some sense into her spendthrift daughter-in-law. For the girl was in the habit of promptly breaking into tears whenever she was admonished and her father-in-law got quite agitated whenever he saw anybody in tears in his house. Well! Radha auntie could have shut her eyes and ignored the spendthrift ways of her daughter-in-law. But she just couldn't bring herself to do that. For every time the daughter-in-law poured a very generous quantity of cooking oil in the frying pan, poor Radha auntie's heart raced pit-a-pat, pit-a-pat and her mind reeled at the enormity of the waste. So the only alternative left for Radha auntie was to do all the household work herself exercising the skills of economizing she had honed over the years. So everyday the poor woman cooked, washed clothes and cleaned the house too to save the broom from getting worn out too fast. Well! If a woman had to slog like this, what good did it do her to have a daughter-in-law?

As poor Radha auntie narrated this tale of her woes and humilitation to my grandma, she must have been overcome by grief and shed a tear. For my grandma told her not to take these matters so much to heart and repeat the name of Lord Rama a thousand times with her rosary, to regain her peace of mind.

The next day I had to learn by heart the route of tramcar number six. It started from Dadar and travelled by stages to Parel. It would have proceeded further and terminated at Museum had it not been halted in its track by the arrival of Godavari auntie to spend an afternoon with my grandma.

Godavari auntie too had a daughter-in-law and I had seen her when she was brought to our house to bow to my grandma and get her blessings. She too had seemed to me to be a nice, obedient and respectful daughter-in-law. But soon enough I gathered from the talk between my grandma and Godavari auntie that this girl too wasn't at all as nice as I had thought she was.

Godavari auntie had decided that she didn't want any smart and pert city-bred girl as her daughter-in-law. Girls in cities like Mumbai and Pune were, she believed, brought up on a loose string. They were allowed to have their own way more often than was good for them. They also had far too much education and were prone to argue with their elders. Such girls obviously couldn't be good daughters-in-law. A daughter-in-law, if she was to be useful in her mother-in-law's house, had to be obedient and hardworking. It helped if she had not set her foot in a school and moreover was rather dumb. Such girls, Godavari auntie knew, could only be found in the remote villages of Konkan. So, she had scouted around and chosen as her daughter-in-law exactly the kind of girl she was looking for. That had made her particularly happy. She had then looked forward to years of happiness with just the right kind of daughter-in-law at her beck and call. But gods, who rule over the destinies of mere mortals, seemed to have ordained otherwise and poor Godavari auntie soon found herself mired in a heap of troubles.

She discovered that girls from rural Konkan are awfully ignorant of life in a city like Mumbai. Her daughter-in-law had never seen water flow out of a tap at the turn of a key. So whenever she had an opportunity, the daughter-in-law turned on the tap full blast and stared at it in wide-eyed wonder. The result was that Godavari auntie had water splattered all over her small kitchen. The girl was equally amazed to see a room bathed in bright electric light when she pressed a tiny button and she switched the lights on as often as she could to see the miracle. Godavari auntie kept a strict eye on her when she was at home. But whenever she went out, the girl switched on all the lights in the house and turned the tap on fully and watched those miracles with wide-eyed wonder. The result was that the electricity bill mounted and Godavari auntie lived in constant dread of slipping on the wet kitchen floor and breaking her bones. Godavari auntie scolded the girl sharply. When she did so, the girl was very remorseful and burst into tears. That was such a pitiful sight, that kind-hearted Godavari auntie couldn't scold her any more.

What amazed the girl the most was the constant flow of traffic in the streets of Mumbai. So she took every opportunity she could to go out into the common gallery of the chawl and watch the flow of traffic in the street below.

An excuse was needed to go out into the gallery and this she found in the tulsi plant that hung in a pot from a hook in the gallery. Every Maharashtrian household has a tulsi plant of its own. The women in the household water it and bow to it every day in the morning and in the evening. After all the plant is an abode of gods and the tulsi herself is a goddess. If therefore a daughter-in-law wants to water the tulsi plant and bow to it, a mother-in-law cannot or rather wouldn't stop her from doing so.

Realizing this the daughter-in-law, hailing as she did from deeply religious rural Konkan, made it a point to water the tulsi plant in the gallery. Once in the gallery her eyes were riveted with fascination on the stream of cars, taxis, tramcars, pushcarts, hawkers and marriage processions in the street below. She watched it with open-mouthed wonder and couldn't bring herself to tear away from that sight.

Inevitably, her household chores remained unattended and Godavari auntie found, to her horror, the rice burnt black on the kitchen fire while the vegetables remained half cut.

That naturally upset Godavari auntie and she cried, "Where are you? What on earth are you doing?"

She had to raise her voice to the very limit before she was heard. When at last her words penetrated her daughter-in-law's ears, the girl gave a start and rushed into the kitchen with a contrite expression on her face.

Godavari auntie asked angrily, "What on earth were you

doing out there in the gallery for so long?"

"I was watering the tulsi plant," explained the daughter-in-law.

"Why should that take so long? Were you feeding it water with a spoon, the way one feeds a baby?" asked Godavari auntie angrily.

Being obedient and respectful, the daughter-in-law kept mum and busied herself with her unfinished household chores.

On seeing that Godavari auntie went out to the washing place to take her bath and then got engaged in the ritual worship of the family deities.

The daughter-in-law then dutifully cut all the vegetables, put them in a brass container, which she put on the kitchen stove for cooking. The rice being burnt she would again take two measures of rice, in a brass pot and put that on the kitchen fire for cooking.

Having nothing to do except to wait for the vegetables and the rice to be cooked, the girl again felt drawn towards the gallery. So she took a pot of water and went out to water the tulsi plant.

When Godavari auntie walked into the kitchen after finishing her bath and ritual worship, she again found that the rice and the vegetable were overcooked if not charred and rendered unfit for eating.

That sight made Godavari auntie's blood boil and she yelled, "Now where on earth are you? And what are you doing?"

On hearing that, the daughter-in-law rushed back to the kitchen with the pitcher of water in her hand.

On seeing that Godavari auntie screamed "Don't tell me that you were watering the tulsi plant once again."

The daughter-in-law would then bend her head in acknowledgment of her guilt.

Godavari auntie then shook her head in disgust and said, "If you water the tulsi plant so often, it will die of too much water and your family will starve because they would have nothing to eat, except charred rice and burnt vegetables."

The girl certainly tried very hard to keep away from the gallery. But so fascinated was she by the busy and colourful street that after a few hours, she once again found herself dragged to the gallery and the only excuse the dumb girl could think of for doing so was that of watering the tulsi plant.

Godavari auntie screamed and yelled at her. The daughter-in-law bent her head and cried every time she was scolded. She nodded obediently when she was asked not to go out into the gallery. But after a few hours her feet once again dragged her to the gallery.

Godavari auntie was almost in tears when she told this tale of her woes.

My grandma sympathized with her and tried to reassure her that things do get better after a spell of misfortune. A downturn is followed by on upturn on the wheel of fortune.

That gave me the impression that Godavari auntie's tale of misery had ended and I set my tramcars in motion and they proceeded by stages from Parel to Byculla.

But it seemed that the worst of Godavari auntie's woes still remained to be told. For she said to my grandma. "Well! You haven't yet heard it all."

"Good heavens! I had thought that things couldn't get any worse," cried my grandma.

"Oh! They could and they did," cried Godavari auntie and then she told the story of the vanishing laddus. Godavari auntie took good care of her family and prepared for them regularly various sweets which they ate as snacks with relish. Once, after the daughter-in-law had become a part of the family, she prepared laddus. Godavari auntie was renowned in the neighbourhood as a good cook. Her laddus were known to be particularly delicious and her family always looked forward to eating them. So she had prepared some laddus which she put in a can with a tight-fitting lid. She then placed the can on a shelf, which could not be easily reached by children. With her laddus stored safely, she went to the Ganpati temple as she was wont to do every afternoon. The Ganpati temple, apart from being a place of worship, was also a meeting ground of womenfolk in the various neighbourhoods of Girgaum. There, messages were conveyed and received, happiness was shared and burdens of sorrow were lightened, and even marriages of daughters and sons were arranged. Like most other women, Godavari auntie spent an hour or so there and then proceeded home in a cheerful frame of mind. She then attended to household chores and tried to train her daughter-in-law to do a few things around the house. Soon it was evening and her husband and son returned from their places of work.

Intending to give them a pleasant surprise, Godavari auntie climbed on a stool and took down the can of laddus. She was a little surprised when she found that the can wasn't quite as full of laddus as she thought it was, when she had filled it. A suspicion flitted across her mind, but she ignored it. "One does sometimes form wrong impressions", she told herself and hastened to put two laddus in each of the two plates for the menfolk in her family to eat. After they had eaten laddus smacking their lips, she put one laddu apiece in two dishes. One of them she gave to her daughter-in-law and the other she ate herself. She was rather annoyed when the daughter-in-law smacked her lips and that too loudly when she ate her laddu. But knowing that she was but a girl and a dumb one at that, Godavari auntie did not scold her for that impropriety. If only she had known what those smacks portended, she would have been more stern and watchful.

As usual, Godavari auntie went to the Ganpati temple the next day in the afternoon and returned after a couple of hours. What she saw on her arrival surprised her no end. She saw her daughter-in-law holding her stomach and rushing to the toilet.

"What on earth is the matter?", cried Godavari auntie in amazement.

"My stomach! My stomach! Something strange is happening there," cried the daughter-in-law and vanished into the toilet.

Godavari auntie couldn't figure out why all of a sudden her young and robust daughter-in-law should have an upset stomach. But soon, she put two and two together and surmised what could have happened. So she climbed on a stool and took down the can of laddus. As she had expected it was amazingly light and when she opened it she understood why. A large number of laddus had disappeared from the can.

While she looked at the nearly empty can in stunned amazement, the daughter-in-law emerged from the toilet. When she saw her mother-in-law looking into the can of laddus, she burst into tears.

Godavari auntie wanted to say a great deal but she couldn't find words to express her feelings. She opened her mouth and closed it wordlessly. But that didn't really matter. For her daughter-in-law was in no condition to be engaged in conversation and be scolded. She clutched her stomach and rushed to the toilet once again.

Godavari auntie clutched her head. She was at her wits' end. It seemed that she was destined to do all the cooking and household chores herself. Her daughter-in-law, it seemed, was too dumb to do any of them. Moreover, she had to keep a watch on that girl constantly. Even a visit to the Ganpati temple could prove hazardous to her house and also to her daughter-in-law. It was terrible.

After staying almost imprisoned in her own house for ten days, Godavari auntie couldn't stand it anymore. So she had ventured to leave her house in the care of her daughter-in-law and visit my grandma to unburden herself of her woes.

She cried, "I have to slave in the house myself and stay imprisoned there to keep a watch on this girl. Why, I can't sleep in peace even at night for fear of what my daughter-in-law would be upto. Even if a mouse stirs, I sit up with a start."

My grandma was all sympathy for her and Godavari auntie needed it all. She had tried to avoid the troubles that mothers-in-law suffered when they had smart and slick city girls as daughters-in-law. She had chosen as a daughter-in-law not only a girl from a poor family in a Konkan village but also taken care to see that she was rather dumb. But this girl turned out to be far more dumb than what Godavari auntie had bargained for. In fact it had never occurred to her that a girl could be as dumb as that. But there was such a one and she was right there on her hands.

My grandma was a kind and helpful person and with her long experience of solving problems of relatives and friends could offer useful suggestions to women in trouble.

She said to Godavari auntie, "It might help if you keep the can on a shelf in the sacred corner of the house where the idols of family deities are kept."

It was a gem of a suggestion. Atleast I thought so, for only a person who had a bath and who wore a silk garment could touch anything in the sacred corner. It would have been a sacrilege for anybody else to touch anything in that corner.

I had expected Godavari auntie to accept the suggestion with alacrity. But she merely grimaced, "I had thought of that. But I am not sure that the girl with her uncontrollable craving for sweet things would not be tempted to break the religious rules. If she does that, not only will I lose the laddus but will also have sins heaped on my head."

My grandma was aghast when she heard this, "Are things that bad?"

"They certainly are", said Godavari auntie with laconic grimness.

"In that case", said grandma, "You better not keep the laddus on that shelf. For apart from committing sacrilege she may eat not only your laddus but also the very special jam which is generally kept in that corner."

"She is not a bad girl otherwise. She never talks back and does whatever she is asked to do. She is a good workhorse, strong and tireless. But she has an appetite as large as that of half a dozen girls and she is so crazy about watching the traffic in the street, that I have to keep my eyes open, if I want to get anything done from her at all.'

At that juncture my mother brought in cups of scalding hot tea which both the elderly women drank with noisy relish.

Guessing that the tale of woes had been fully told I set the tramcar number six in motion and it proceeded without any interruptions from Byculla to Girgaum and on to Museum.

Next day it was tramcar number nineteen that started its journey in the afternoon from Opera House to Ballard Pier. However, the tramcar had hardly reached Nul Bazaar when Bheema auntie called on my grandma for tea, sympathy and sage advice. She looked quite haggard and spent. Obviously, she had some pretty distressing problems of her own.

My grandma guessed this immediately and asked, "Bheema auntie, are you unwell? You look quite haggard and spent."

Bheema auntie's knee joints crackled as she settled down gingerly on the straw mattress with a heavy sigh. She then moaned and nursed her knee.

Grandma as usual was very understanding. She took no time at all to guess that Bheema auntie was in great distress. She asked, "What is eating you Bheema auntie? Why are you so distressed?"

Bheema auntie moaned and said, "Mathutai, I have no words to describe what I am going through. I am afraid that this daughter-in-law of mine will any day drive me over the fence. You shouldn't be surprised if you find me one of these days wandering around in the streets pulling my hair and tearing up my saree."

This seemed to be a tale which demanded my undivided attention. So tramcar number nineteen had to halt in its tracks near the Round Temple, until the tale unfolded.

"Really? Do you mean to say that you too have the same kind of problem that Godavari auntie has?" Asked grandma. She was obviously quite surprised. She continued, "But how can that be? You chose for your son a bride from the city of Pune. Moreover, she comes from a good family. She is fair-skinned, beautiful and quite a lively young girl. She also has had some education. Every woman I met at the Ganapati temple said that the girl is one in a hundred and that you were very fortunate and wise too to have chosen a girl like that as your daughter-in-law."

Bheema auntie moaned and said ruefully, "Oh, Mathutai! Unfortunately, choice of that girl from Pune, which everybody considers wise and happy, has turned out to be a blunder. If only I had not been so particular and chosen a simple run-of-the-mill kind of a girl as a daughter-in-law, I would have had peace and happiness in my old age. But that was not to be and I can only look forward to trouble and humiliation for the rest of my life."

Poor Bheema auntie looked a picture of misery and she snuffled several times.

My grandma was at a loss to understand why a lively, educated girl from Pune should cause so much distress to her mother-in-law. So she asked, "But what does that girl do to cause you so much distress?"

"What does she do indeed! What does she do! Why, this slip of a girl barely in her teens, offers, nay throws at me gratuitous and impudent advice about how to run my household and how to conduct myself in family gatherings."

My grandma was so stunned by what she heard that she stared at Bheema auntie in open-mouthed amazement for a long time. She then cried, "Good heavens! Have things come to that pass? Have they, really?"

Bheema auntie was obviously overwhelmed by the enormity of what was going on. It took her some time to recover from the shock. Thereafter she pondered over the situation and said haltingly, "Well ! we all know and so do you that the people from Pune tend to be a little uppity.

They think rather highly of themselves and look down their noses at people in the rest of the world. But I am sure that it never occurred to you, as it never had to me, that even daughters-in-law hailing from Pune would have the temerity to talk impudently to their mothers-in-law."

"Talk impudently? And that too to a mother-in-law? Can such thing be?" Exclaimed grandma in open-mouthed wonder.

"Yes and it is my misfortune to be that mother-in-law," said Bheema auntie in great anguish.

Bheema auntie then continued, "To tell you the truth, Mathutai, I was well aware of this proclivity of Puneities and I was particularly reluctant to have as my daughter-in-law a girl who had spent some years in a Pune school. I knew that in those schools they put all kind of pernicious ideas in the heads of girls. But my son Visoo, inspite of having a college education, is totally ignorant of the ways of the world and particularly of the ways of Puneites. On the contrary he thinks that the girls from Pune and particularly those who have studied at the Huzurpaga school are smart and pretty and marrying one of them is the best thing that can happen to a young man. So he insisted that he would only marry a girl from Pune, who had studied at the Huzurpaga school."

Grandma shook her head sadly and said, "I do not know what things are coming to! If a woman cannot choose her daughter-in-law, how can she run the family and hold it together! In the good old days a boy wouldn't have dared to tell his family that he wanted to marry a particular girl. But this is the dark age of the evil Kali and the world is falling to pieces."

There was a look of stony resignation on Bheema auntie's face and she said bitterly, "I must have committed a thousand sins in my previous birth to have to suffer this."

"At least his father should have scolded Visoo and dissuaded him from marrying an impertinent girl from Pune", observed my Grandma.

"That is what should have happened. But on the contrary the boy's father encouraged him to marry a girl who had studied at a school. Now, if one's own teeth bite one's own tongue, what can one do? Well! Who am I to complain against the dictates of the gods, who govern our lives." She said this in a resigned philosophical tone but that could not hide the bitterness in her voice.

These words seemed to indicate that as far as Bheema auntie was concerned, the topic was closed. But obviously she had a great deal more to say about her impertinent daughter-in-law and it all came out when my grandma asked sympathetically, "Is she making life too difficult for you? I hope she is not grinding red chillies with stone on your head, as some daughters-in-law seem to be doing these days?"

"Well! Yesterday she tried to teach me how I should cook suran. She said that the suran I had cooked was far too hard to bite and swallow. In Pune, she claimed, they cook a suran so that it becomes as soft as butter."

"Did she really say that? Oh, the temerity of these girls!" murmured grandma sadly.

Well! I wasn't the one to take that lying down. I told her that suran is naturally hard and it ought to stay hard when cooked. We folks from Konkan like it that way and eating it poses no problem for us, because we have strong and healthy teeth. Folks in Pune, it seems, do not have good teeth and that is why they cook suran till it becomes as soft as butter. We folks in Konkan need no lessons in cooking or anything else for that matter from folks in Pune."

This certainly was a blistering retort and the way Bheema auntie said it, made it sound like a knock-out blow.

"She certainly asked for it", said my grandma approvingly and added, "I hope she did not talk back, when she heard this."

"No she never talks back. Never says a word. But she covertly smiles and turns up her nose. The way she does it is very annoying. I feel like tweaking that impertinent nose, when she turns it up."

Grandma was aghast when she heard this. She cried, "What on earth are things coming to in this dark age of the evil Kali! We never even looked up into the eyes of our mothers-in-law when we talked to them."

Those words only added to Bheema auntie's anger which was very much on the boil. "That impertinent girl turns up her nose at everything in our house. Why, she even turned it up when she saw the peacock my daughter has embroidered. She considers us rustic because we have no radio in our house. Well! If she wanted radios and fans in the house, she should have married a rich nobleman Sardar from Pune."

"But doesn't Visoo pull up his uppity wife?" asked grandma, who was amazed that a husband should tolerate such impudence on the part of his wife.

"Ha! That indeed, is the root cause of these troubles. Do you know what this stupid son of mine does? He nods approvingly to whatever she says. He behaves like a man bewitched. I had never imagined that Visoo could sink so low", cried Bheema auntie. One could guess from her manner and tone that she was utterly disgusted.

Grandma couldn't believe this, She cried, "Don't tell me that Visoo has become such a softie, that she can crush him in her little fist."

"Why, he eats out of her hands like a poodle and I his mother have to watch it", cried Bheema auntie and she was so overwhelmed by her feelings that she burst into tears.

I was amazed and not a little confused by what I had heard. I had seen Visoo and he was a tall and hefty man with a big moustache while his wife was a relatively small and lean woman. I wondered how she could make a mouse out of this big man.

I realized that this was a riddle I could not solve. So I gave up. A good hot cup of tea assuaged Bheema auntie's feelings somewhat and after a while she left for the Ganapati temple along with my grandma.

I too had to set in motion tramcar number nineteen which had halted in its tracks and it proceeded by stages past Carnac Bunder to Ballard Pier.

Next day it was the turn of tramcar number one and it had travelled from Flora Fountain to Kalbadevi when Satyam auntie called on my grandma to spend an afternoon with her.

As she walked past me to grandma's room, I noticed right away that she was greatly agitated. As she settled down on the mat spread for grandma and her visitors, I heard loud agitated sighs which sounded alarmingly like sobs. She also pulled her nose over and over again, which was an indication that she was about to break into tears.

My grandma, noticing how worked up Satyam auntie was, felt greatly concerned and said, "Now, now, Satyam auntie, do sit down and relax. Laxmi, bring a glass of water right away and then quickly make some tea."

My auntie Laxmi, being a well-behaved and obedient daughter-in-law, rushed to do what she was asked to do.

On noticing the respectful behaviour of a daughter-in-law Satyam auntie heaved a heavy sigh which was indistinguishable from a sob and snorted.

Grandma was, as usual, full of consideration and sympathy. She put a hand on Satyam auntie's shoulder and said, "Now, now, do calm yourself. God is kind and everything will be all right."

Satyam auntie shook her head sadly and said, "You are very kindhearted, Mathutai. But I am unworthy of your kind blessings. I must have committed many sins in my previous birth and that is why I have to suffer this misery and humiliation and that too at the hands of a daughter-in-law. Almost every woman has a daughter-in-law and not all daughters-in-law are nice. Some are dumb and some are too clever and some are sly too. Very few are as respectful and obedient as yours are, Mathutai, and may you continue to enjoy this good fortune for all time to come. But even those that are not nice do atleast maintain appearances and outwardly show respect to their mothers-in-law. But in my house, everything is topsy turvey. Why, Mathutai, don't be surprised if one of these days you find my daughter-in-law lolling on the sofa and poor me standing behind her and fanning her."

At this juncture Satyam auntie was so overcome by her feelings that she couldn't say anything more and sat there sighing and snuffling loudly over and over again.

"What has that daughter-in-law of yours done lately to make you miserable?" asked grandma who knew too well how nasty daughters-in-law were becoming lately.

"What indeed!" exclaimed Satyam auntie, "Ask me what she hasn't done. After all, she is educated, isn't she? She has even studied at a college for two years, hasn't she? So nothing is now beyond her."

"Did she have the gumption to talk back to you, her mother-in-law?" asked grandma and I could sense the feeling of outrage in her voice.

"Well! She hasn't gone that far yet. But that can very well happen. And, remember Mathutai, talking back is not the only way of showing disrespect for and humiliating a mother-in-law. For instance, a daughter-in-law can pretend not to have heard the words of her mother-in-law. The poor mother-in-law may bid her to do certain things, forbid her to do other things and may even scold her. What good would it do, if her daughter-in-law pretends not to hear her at all. Can you think of anything more humiliating than that?" Satyam auntie's voice almost choked and she could not say anything more. All I could hear were sighs and snorts.

Grandma said nothing, to gives Satyam auntie enough time to regain her voice. Then she said, "Have things come to that pass?"

"Well! I will tell you what she does. Every morning this girl, instead of going into the kitchen to cook the morning meal, sits on a chair and reads the morning paper the way men do. Why, she sometimes sits in the favourite chair of her father-in-law. Nowadays she goes out for a walk with her husband walking with him instead of behind him as a wife should do. And what she did yesterday was the limit. She wore a six yard saree like the Gujarati women do and she had combed her hair in a fancy manner. All the residents of our chawl came out of their houses to watch her go out almost hand in hand with her husband.

After she left, I had to listen to the sharp-tongued comments of the women in our chawl. They all said, 'Satyam auntie, you have a daughter-in-law who is miles ahead of all of us in her ways and her clothes. We won't be surprised if one of these days we find her wearing a dress like English women do, baring her legs right up to her knee."

"I wanted to scream and tell everybody what I felt about this uppity daughter-in-law. But that would have been like biting one's tongue with one's own teeth. So I retired to the kitchen and hid there for the rest of the evening." Satyam auntie almost broke into tears at this point.

My grandma, who normally does not lose her cool, was outraged when she heard of the wanton, uppity behaviour of Satyam auntie's daughter-in-law. She therefore said sharply, "Well! If things have come to that pass, you should better ask her father-in-law to pull up both this girl and her husband. I know that young people are somewhat foolish and tend to run wild. But this is absolutely the limit. Why, this girl may cut her hair one of these days as the English women do. And you won't know where and when to hide your face, when she puts you to shame in that manner. Frankly, it is time the girl's father-in-law put his foot down."

Satyam auntie emitted a loud sigh which was almost a sob. She cried, "I wish my husband had done that. But he can be firm only with his poor wife. When it comes to scolding his son or his daughter-in-law, he becomes utterly tongue-tied. Well, he did draw my son aside and whisper a few things to him in almost an apologetic voice but that was the end of his asserting himself. So I took matters in hand and roundly scolded my son. And do you know the outcome of that? Why, he had the gumption to say to me, "Mother, if you are so unhappy about all these things, I would rather rent a separate apartment and live there. That would give you peace of mind."

My grandma almost keeled over when she heard that. She cried, "Have things gone that far? Then better be prepared for the worst. One of these days, you will certainly have to stand behind your daughter-in-law with a fan in hand."

It was inconceivable that a son properly brought up by a good mother like Satyam auntie would be guilty of such insolent behaviour. Obviously, some external influence was at work and where could it come from except from a girl spoilt by two years of college education. Satyam auntie considered it essential to point this out. She cried, "Mind you! My darling Madhu on his own wouldn't have thought of doing such a thing. He has been all along a decent, well-behaved son, who always did whatever his mother wanted him to do. But it is this spoilt girl who has put these wrong notions in his head. These are the things, it seems, she learnt in those two years at college and she pours them in his ears everybody. She is very coy and sweet, when she does so. And this silly son of mine laps up whatever she says."

Satyam auntie's voice choked as she told this tale of a proud mother being humiliated by an impertinent and uppity daughter-in-law. My grandma entirely concurred with Satyam auntie. She said indignantly, "Let me say this, Satyam auntie, our good old days were the best. In those days girls were married very young and mothers-in-law sternly disciplined them with a rod in hand. The daughters-in-law therefore, did as they were told. When mothers-in-law said get up, they got up and likewise sat down when asked to do so. None of them even dared to think of setting up a separate household of her own."

Satyam auntie took a deep breath and said, "Well! In any case, I didn't take this impertinent talk lying down. The moment I heard this talk of having a separate household. I picked up the heavy grinding stone and said, "If ever anybody tries to set up a separate household in my family, I will break my own head with this stone. It will be only over my dead body that my son and daughter-in-law would walk out of my house."

I was so engrossed in hearing this highly dramatic tale of an outraged mother-in-law that not only did my tramcar stay stalled in Nul Bazaar but I also did not notice my mother glowering at me with her hands on her hips.

Well! Thereafter events took their usual course. My mother pulled my ear and cried, "Is that the way you do your lessons? It is four days now since your tramcars started their journeys and none of them seems to reach its destination. You are a man, aren't you? What business then do you have listening to women's talk. Get up! Out with you. Sit in the living room and do your lessons.

Thereafter I couldn't hear any more the tales of uppity and errant daughters-in-law. But whatever I had heard till then was enough to convince me that daughters-in-law hailing from the Vidharbha region weren't any better than those that hailed from Konkan. Daughters-in-law hailing from the city of Pune were particularly nasty. But nastier still were daughters-in-law who had a couple of years of college education in Mumbai.

I, therefore, wondered where the good daughters-in-law came from. I needn't have wondered so really. But I was then too young to know that there was no such thing as a good daughter-in-law!

❑

& CO
SILKS
GIRGAUM

3

A Boy Without a Wadi

It all happened many years ago when I was a boy. Mothers in those days had an unpleasant habit of burdening children with various chores, whenever they found them playing or having a good time. My mother was no exception and on that particular day she nagged me continuously for being of no help at all in her household work.

I was used to being nagged, but I got really upset when she refused to give me a laddu to eat when I asked for it. Boys, as everybody knows, get hungry every hour or two and it is the business of mothers to give them something sweet and savoury to eat when they get hungry. What are mothers for anyway, if they don't. But mothers, as everybody knows, can be very perverse. My mother certainly was more than unusually perverse that day and stubbornly refused to give me anything at all to eat, if I wasn't going to be useful around the house. I protested vehemently and eloquently and even pretended to be in tears, but to no avail.

So ultimatley I gave in and cried in utter disgust, "All right, have it your way. Command, oh my master, and this slave will obey."

I was witheringly sarcastic but my sarcasm left mother unmoved.

Never at a loss when called upon to foist chores on me, mother promptly gave me a box to be delivered to Yamuna auntie who lived in Pimpalwadi, which was one of the numerous wadis in the Girgaum area where we lived. A wadi was a cluster of houses built around an open yard, where children could play and women could gossip and the Ganapati festival could be celebrated.

I delivered the box to Yamuna auntie and she gave me a couple of dates and some coconut candy. I knew that on returning home, I could demand from mother a laddu as a well deserved reward. So I tripped homeward cheerfully feeling that doing that chore for mother wasn't a bad bargain after all. As I walked through that wadi on my way out, the last thing I had in mind was to tangle with the kids who lived there. In fact, no kid was in sight. Yet all of a sudden I was hit on the head from behind with such force that my cap got knocked off my head and my head was in a whirl. I was so completely taken by surprise that it took me some time to look around for a culprit. When I turned around, I noticed a little urchin watching me with a broad grin.

When I noticed him, he twitted me holding a thumb to his nose and cried, "Ho, ho!"

Furious, I rushed at him. He grinned and ran, continuing to boo as he ran.

That put me on the boil and I followed him in hot pursuit. I caught hold of him soon enough and whacked him.

He screamed to high heavens. But I didn't let go of him and whacked him some more.

While I was feeling satisfied for having given the boy more than I had taken from him, there materialized out of every doorway and nook and corner of the wadi an incredibly large number of kids.

One of them noticed me and screamed, "Ho! Look! This boy is beating up a lad from our wadi. He is an outsider."

On hearing that all those kids rushed and pounced on me. One of them whacked me on my back so hard, that it made me double up backwards. I wondered how I didn't break into two. But there was no time to wonder. For, before I could pull myself together, I was thumped on my head with such force, that fireworks burst before my eyes and my feet wobbled under me. As I tried to steady them, another boy started pulling me from underneath. As I was falling to the ground, I somehow managed to get hold of a lamp post; and that enabled me to stand on my feet while I was being belaboured from all sides. In the midst of this melee a little boy had the temerity to sneak up to me and pinch me real hard, while a little girl jumped and danced on my cap and giggled very happily. I feared that if those boys managed to get me down to the ground, they would jump and dance all over me the way the girl was dancing on my cap.

Luckily, all the hullaboo disturbed the grown ups in the wadi. They therefore leaned out of the windows to see what was going on.

When they saw what was going on they cried, "What is going on? Are you trying to kill each other?"

On hearing their parents' strong reprimands, the kids disappeared as fast as they had appeared. I picked up my cap in a jiffy and streaked out of the wadi, so fast, that I wondered how and when I managed to do it.

When I was safely out of the wadi, I became aware of all the pains and aches in various parts of my body and my indignation at the indignities I had suffered knew no bounds. What I needed most at that time was a lot of sympathy and I knew that my mother was the last person from whom I could expect it.

She did not belie my expectations. In fact, instead of exuding sympathy, as she should have done, she began to scold me. She cried, "Plague on you. Must you always get into fights, when I send you out on any errand? Goodness me! It was only a week ago that I bought you this new cap. It now looks no different than the rag with which I wipe the kitchen floor. Oh my mother! Your shirt is torn too. What kind of a fight it was you got into? Did you use knives and scissors in your fight?"

I tried to explain to her that what happened was not my fault at all and that a bunch of kids both boys and girls had attacked and belaboured me without any provocation. But as was her wont, she didn't believe a word of what I said. She firmly believed that it was me, who started the trouble.

She shook her head and said, "No. I can't believe it. Why would kids attack a boy who is innocently and harmlessly passing by?"

Nowadays mothers drip with sympathy and pamper their kids if they get hurt. They are always convinced that if there is a fight, it is always the other kid who is at fault and believe whatever their kids tell them. When I was a kid, we kids were not that lucky. If a kid got into a fight and his mother got to know about it, she got convinced right away that it must have been his fault and thrashed him soundly. I didn't therefore expect my mother to believe me although what I told her was the god's truth. I therefore considered myself lucky that she merely pulled my ear instead of giving me a thrashing. Later on she applied some ointment to my bruises too.

Next day when I went to school, I met my friend Sadu. I told him the story of the unprovoked attack and the beating and indignities I had suffered. I looked forward to sympathy and offer of help. To my surprise and disappointment I got neither. On the contrary Sadu fixed me with a resentful stare and cried, "Indeed? Do you mean to say that you were beaten up black and blue and jeered at, and you took it all lying down?"

This was so unexpected that I stared at him in wide-eyed amazement. I then tried to explain. I said, "But what could I do, Sadu! There were seven of them and I had to face them all by myself."

Sadu, however, wouldn't buy my plea. He cried, "What do you mean, you were alone! Don't you have your own gang of boys in your wadi? You should have taken them along and given a sound hiding to those nasty brats. Well! I will tell you what I did in a similar situation. During the Ganapati festival I had gone to Khot's wadi to run some errand for my mother when a gang of boys there caught hold of me, put a basket upside down on my head so that

I couldn't see a thing and then marched me in a procession around the wadi. They beat me up, jeered at me and poked me with sticks too. I had to suffer it all. But I said to myself that I will teach them a lesson. I knew that those boys used to go to the Wilson College gymkhana ground to play cricket. So I collected a gang of boys from my Ambewadi and we beat them up until they had more than what they had given me. Had it not been for the watchman at the Gymkhana ground, those boys would have gone home bruised and limping. Why don't you do something like that? Or are the boys in your wadi sissys?"

I lowered my eyes and said in a tearful voice, "Poor me! I don't have a wadi of my own. I stay in a house which stands all by itself on a street."

Sadu was amazed. He cried, "Do you mean to say that this house of yours has no wadi around it? It stands alone all by itself?"

I nodded shamefacedly.

Sadu still couldn't believe it. He said, "A house without a wadi!"

I again nodded dejectedly.

"Do such houses exist?", cried Sadu and I knew that he wasn't putting a question to me but trying to convince himself.

I nodded shamefacedly and my lower lip jutted out in utter helplessness.

Sadu rolled his eyes as he mulled over the matter and then just threw up his hands. He cried, "In that case, you are sunk. If a boy doesn't have a wadi of his own, there is nothing that he or anybody else can do for him."

It was a bitter pill, particularly when it came from a chum, whom I expected to be of help. But I realized that what he had told me was the bitter truth. In those days not to have a wadi of one's own was the most demeaning thing that could happen to a boy in Girgaum. Why, every friend of mine had a wadi of his own. Sadu himself lived in the sprawling Zaoba's wadi. Nanu lived in the labyrinthine

Khot's wadi where a visitor couldn't help getting lost. Vasoo lived in Pandurang wadi, which had a renowned hututu team, while Vinoo was the undisputed 'Dada of the boys' in the Ganapati wadi. Even Balu had a minuscule wadi called Kakad wadi. It wasn't much of a wadi, but still he could get together nine kids if the need arose. Ramakant lived not in any wadi but Shantaram's chawl, which was so huge and had such a spacious yard in front, that it was nothing less than a genuine wadi. My friends Bandu and Vithoo lived in Angrewadi, which was in a different class altogether.

Have you ever seen Angrewadi, as it was in those days? If you haven't, you have missed something. That wadi was a paradise for kids. It was so big, that it looked like an entire village transplanted from Konkan. It had a sprawling old fashioned wada, which must have been once the residence of a zamindar. It also had more modest houses typical of a Konkan village, tiny bungalows of British colonial vintage, a few huts, cowsheds, a huge chawl that stood guard almost like a battlement at its entrance and also a huge school building. But somehow these incongruities existed cheek by jowl in that sprawling wadi. It had not one but many open yards and small open spaces hidden in its various nooks and corners. The nooks and corners were so many that it was an ideal place for children to play thieves and policemen. It had a well so huge that children could swim in it. It had a Pipal tree and a few tall coconut trees and an almond tree too. Kids had a wonderful time climbing up and down those trees and polishing their skills at bringing down almonds with big catapults. There were telephone cables too which made flying kites a very challenging adventure. To salvage kites caught in the branches of the trees or in telephone cables used to be a highly skilled operation. There were of course many spots where the kids could fly kites or play hututu or a game of marbles. School boys and college students played the new fangled games of volleyball or badminton there. In the rainy season the main dirt road that traversed the wadi from one end to another was transformed into a swollen stream that took the muddy rain water down the slope from Girgaum Backroad to Sandhurst Road. Water used to be knee-deep at some points on that dirt road. Kids could wade through that stream, push each other and have water fights or make paper boats and send them floating down the stream.

Crows, sparrows, pigeons and even a family of parrots built nests on various trees in the wadi, and climbing up trees and looking at little chicks in those nests used to be quite an adventure. If, however, a boy disturbed a crow's nest, they pecked hard not only on his head but even on the heads of the unsuspecting people who happened to walk past the tree. They were so annoyed once with my friend Vinoo that for several days he had to cover his head with a gunny bag when he ventured out of his house.

No other wadi offered more to kids than Angrewadi. The kids living in that wadi, therefore, developed a variety of skills to a far greater degree than denizens of other lesser wadis. There used to be fierce battles of kites in the sky during the kite flying season and the kites that got cut often floated across the wadi. To catch them with a long bamboo pole used to be a great adventure. To catch a kite one needed a quick eye, a long bamboo pole and the ability to run fast with it and manipulate it to catch a kite. One also needed a bunch of followers who played a supporting role. In this adventure one had to face competition and that many times resulted in fights in which the kite generally got torn. In such fights a gang of supporters was an absolute must. The kites often landed on roofs of houses or were caught in the branches of trees or telephone wires. To reach them and disentangle them required a variety of skills.

To master such varied skills was not easy. My friend Visoo had mastered them all and he had no equal not only in Angrewadi but several wadis surrounding it. To see Visoo carrying a big bamboo pole and running to catch a kite used to be a sight that I watched with awe and envy. No obstacles including fences and high compound walls stopped him, nor was he deterred by the prospect of climbing up trees or on to roofs. He had a retinue of followers who ran behind him carrying small sticks and branches of trees. Even four or five-year-olds used to follow him toppling often as they ran.

To me he looked like the legendary Shivaji charging into combat. I very much wanted to join his retinue. I was, however, hooted out because I was an outsider who did not live in the wadi. No wonder I had not learnt even the rudiments of catching a kite.

Jagoo was another boy in Angrewadi whom I adored. He was the undisputed champion in spinning tops. Spinning a top, I can tell you, is not an easy accomplishment. To wind a string tight around its sloping, grooved base is a pretty tricky thing to accomplish. Whenever I tried to do that, the string slid off the bottom of the top. If I managed to keep it in place and threw the top, it didn't stand on its sharp iron tip and spin around itself. It just dropped lifelessly on the floor. I tried it umpteen times and in umpteen different ways, but everytime the top stubbornly refused to spin. I obviously needed an older boy to be my guru in learning the abstruse lore of spinning a top. But how could I get such a guru if I did not live in a wadi.

Jagoo must have had no such problem and he had therefore become a champion top spinner. He did not have to struggle to wind his string around a top. It got wound easily and stayed there. And no matter how he threw it, the top stood on its sharp iron *ari* and spun at a terrific speed. He could make it go in circles or swing sideways or do a lot of other amazing feats. Sometimes he made it spin on its head and sometimes it kept spinning in mid-air until he held out a hand on which it could land.

But Jagoo's greatest skill lay in waging battles against other formidable tops and making them bite dust. His small top could leap from his hand and land on the head of a big heavy top, twice its size, with such force as to knock it down. It then used to spin with a joyous wobble to celebrate its victory. Sometimes his top knocked out the rival top in mid-air before the poor thing could land on its single foot. If, however, it was his turn to spin his top first, he made it rush around in such crazy patterns and at such a speed that his rival could never knock it down by a throw of his top. The story of his exploits with his top, though interesting, is too long, so I won't tell it. Suffice it to say that Jagoo was a genius when it came to spinning tops.

His fame had spread far and wide right upto Phanaswadi at one end and Shastri Hall colony at the other end. Renowned spinners of tops from distant corners of Mumbai came to enter into top spinning contests with him and went back humbled by egregious defeat.

The contests used to be acrimonious but the acrimony never went so far as to result in fights. But one hefty contestant, who hailed from the notorious Phanaswadi, was so irked by his defeat that he lunged at Jagoo to beat him up. As Jagoo was the champion all contests used to take place in Angrewadi. The two contestants were therefore surrounded by kids who belonged to Jagoo's own wadi. Naturally, when they saw that hefty chap from Phanas wadi jump at Jagoo, the entire crowd jumped on him.

Thereafter for some time there was such utter confusion that I for the life of me couldn't make out what was going on. Eventually, I saw the hefty contestant streaking away in ignominious flight, trying to hold his torn shirt in place.

"Ho, ho", jeered the boys from Angrewadi as they pursued him to the door of their wadi.

I too was delirious with joy like all the others and joined them in crying, "Ho."

But that annoyed the boys from Angrewadi and they said, "Why are you crying 'ho'? You don't belong to our wadi. You have no right whatsoever to do so."

"I will say 'ho' when I want to," I protested.

"You think so, do you?" said the boys advancing

menacingly. Having seen what had happened to the contestant from Phanaswadi, I quickly took to my heels and avoided unpleasantness.

The hefty lad from Phanaswadi and his mates were not likely to take this lying down.

"Step out of your wadi and I will make micemeat out of you", was his terse message to the boys in Angrewadi.

"Do try to do that and we will make chicken curry out of you", was the equally terse reply.

I don't know what those threats did to Jagoo, but I was scared out of my wits. I lived in constant fear of being caught between two formidable gangs of boys belonging to the two big wadis. The fact that I had no wadi of my own and no gang to support me did not make things easy. However, the crisis passed without a mishap.

If Jagoo was a champion top spinner of Angrewadi, Chandu, who lived in the same wadi, was an equally renowned expert in playing with marbles. He could hit from the base point any marble in the circle which as per the rules of the game was about ten feet away. Even if the ground was uneven and the marble awkwardly placed, he never missed a hit. Why, even if two marbles stood cheek by jowl in the circle, Chandu could hit one without disturbing the other. He could do it with a throw or by using his finger as a catapult. He could be seen going from one pitch to another winning marbles at every throw. His pockets always bulged with marbles which jingled at every step he took.

His mother was a very strict woman and she made it a point to confiscate all his marbles she could lay her hands on. She would scold him all the time and tell him to stop playing marbles and do his lessons instead.

Chandu, however, was not the kind of boy to be deterred by mother's threats. He used to give her the slip, sneak out of the house and be amongst the various groups playing marbles. He would then borrow five marbles from somebody and start playing. In no time at all, he won a lot of marbles and returned the five he had borrowed. Soon enough, thereafter, his pockets would bulge with marbles which jingled as he walked.

Nanu was a champion hututu player. But, I think, I have said enough. If I were to tell you all the stories of the exploits of the outstanding boys of Angrewadi, they would never end. And mind you, it was not only Angrewadi that could boast of boys who excelled in various games. My friends who lived in other wadis refused to acknowledge the superiority of the boys of Angrewadi and boasted of the star players of their own wadis. Visoo, I was told, was a great batsman. He used to hit tall sixes that broke windows on the top floors of houses in his wadi.

All in all, the kids in the other wadis of Girgaum had equally outstanding skills in important games like playing marbles, spinning tops and catching kites, I particularly mentioned Angrewadi only because I visited it often. I had to because my school was located in the wadi and so was my grandma's house. I mean my grandma on the mother's side. I, therefore, used to feel that I had a claim on that wadi and was keen on joining one of the gangs of kids in that wadi. But the kids in Angrewadi looked upon me as an outsider or a stranger and refused to have anything to do with me. They wouldn't let me participate in a game of marbles or of hututu. And if they had, I would have made a laughing stock of myself. For I was a dud when it came to playing these games. Why, I couldn't score a hit on a marble ten feet away, even if I tried for half an hour.

And let me tell you that this was no fault of mine at all. I bet I could have been atleast half as good as Jagoo in spinning a top, if I had but lived in a wadi and had grown up in the midst of boys spinning tops. But I hadn't and it was entirely my father's fault. I had pleaded with him that we should leave the apartment we lived in and move into a tenement in one of the wadis in Girgaum. In those days many wadis used to display 'tenements to rent' boards and we could have easily moved into a nice wadi. Why, Jagoo had told me that we could move into his next door tenement, from which the Ponkshes had moved out.

When I heard such good news, I promptly told my father. But when I did that, he just laughed and did nothing about it. That annoyed me greatly and I badgered him for letting go of such a golden opportunity.

When I did that, he told me, "This apartment we live in is very nice. We get plenty of light and fresh air and we do not have to share a common bathroom and toilet. It is spacious too and we have a big living room where I can meet my clients if they call on me at my house. And they don't have to search for my house in a labyrinthine wadi."

These arguments seemed to me quite beside the point. The clients visited our apartment for a few minutes or at the most for an hour, while I had to live there all the time. And what good was an airy, spacious apartment if there wasn't a wadi around it teeming with kids, with whom I could romp and play. And I can tell you that a common toilet can be a lot of fun. One could have company, even when one was squatting in it. A friend often waited outside to give company and one could chat with him. When I visited Sadu, he did exactly that, when I was in his chawl's common toilet. Why, one could even sing in a toilet, which my mother never allowed me to do at home. She thought that it was utterly improper to do so.

If being a lawyer deprived one's children of all the fun, fathers should not be lawyers.

I grew so desperate that I asked my father sharply, "Would you like your son to be a dud, who can't spin tops and fly kites? Well, even if you do, I certainly don't. And what is all this fuss about lawyers not being able to live in a wadi. Let us move into a wadi. I am sure your clients will greatly enjoy calling on you in a wadi, where a red ripe almond may drop right on their heads as they walk towards our house."

My father looked at me with amusement and laughed

and went off to the law court to argue his cases.

I was disappointed and quite upset. But what could I do, when I had a father like that? We continued to live in a house which was airy and spacious but which had no wadi around it.

The result was that I had to plead and beg with boys living in wadis to let me join them in playing various games. Sometimes they did, but when they found out what a dud I was on the playing ground, they threw me out. So I just stood and watched while they played and displayed their skills which made me look miserably small.

One day while I walked towards Angrewadi gloomily, I ran into a boy who was busy counting the empty cigarette packets he possessed and I could see that he had a lot of them.

Playing with cigarette packets was not quite as respectable as playing with marbles. For cigarette packets offered a bigger target than marbles at a distance of ten feet. It was, therefore, easier to score a hit on any one of them from a distance of ten feet. I wasn't good at doing that either. But I believed that I had a better chance of learning that game, than the game of marbles. And here was an opportunity. For the boy did not seem to have a gang of his own. I could also see from the large bundle of cigarette packets in his hand that he was an expert in that game. His hands, I knew, would be itching to play it.

So I sidled upto him and said, "How about the two of us playing together?"

He looked at me, shook his head and said, "No! Nothing doing!"

"Why not? Let us play for a little while until the boys of your wadi come down to join you."

He again scanned me from head to foot and said, "All right! Let us play until the boys of my wadi come down to join me. But how can you play? You don't seem to have any cigarertte packets?"

I nodded shamefacedly. It was but too true that I had no

empty cigarette packets. To win them in a game was out of the question. Nor was I good at picking them from the street. I was no good at spotting them and if I did spot one, more alert boys living in wadis pounced on it before I so much as bent to pick it up.

I said sheepishly, "No. I don't have any empty cigarette packets to wager in the game. Where can one get them? Can I buy them?"

The boy's countenance was suddenly transformed. He asked, "Did you say you want to buy them? Do you have money?"

In those days it was not customary to give money in the hands of children. That was considered to be a sure way of spoiling them. The boy, therefore, was surprised and looked at me in disbelief.

I said, "Yes! My father gives me one anna every day. So I could spend a paisa to buy empty cigarette packets. Do tell me where I can buy some."

The boy said hastily, "Oh no! You don't have to go anywhere to buy the cigarette packets. I could sell them to you. I have plenty."

I produced my nickel anna from my pocket and said, "I have this one anna coin. Do you have change to return three copper paise to me?"

The boy shook his head. This seemed to be the first occasion in his life when he had engaged in a financial transaction as big as this one.

I was disappointed. I asked, "What do we do now? If we go to that grocer across the street, would he give us change?"

"No! Grocers aren't helpful and kind. He wouldn't give us change just because we need it," said the boy and his face clouded with disappointment. Then suddenly it bringtened and he said, "But if you buy lemon drops worth one *paisa,* he would give you change."

I was so keen to play with him that I said, "Well! If that is the only way, we can get change, we will buy lemon drops."

The boy, whose name was Parsha, grinned broadly and catching me by my elbow almost dragged me to the grocer's shop in a hurry. He bought for me one paisa worth of lemon drops and gave me the little packet of lemon drops and three paise. He then put his arm around my shoulders and held me in a friendly hug as we walked back to his wadi.

When we reached there, I handed over a paisa to him and asked, "How many empty cigarette packets will this one paisa buy?"

Parsha stood staring with shining eyes at the one paisa in his hand and then put it carefully deep inside his pocket. He then asked me "Would it be okay if I give you ten?"

"Ten?", I asked, quite overwhelmed by his generosity, "Yes. That will be very nice."

Parsha noticed how pleased I was and said, "You know, one paisa normally fetches only eight cigarette packets. But because you are such a good friend, I have offered you ten."

He gave my shoulders a squeeze to show the warmth he felt for me.

That pleased me immensely and I said, "You can give me eight packets for one paisa if that is the proper thing to do. I wouldn't mind."

I offered to return two packets. But Parsha shook his head and said, "Forget it. What is done is done. Let us now play. Should we start with two packets each?"

So we got together four packets for the first throw. He then very generously offered me the first chance to throw. I was touched by that friendly gesture and was very pleased too. I was convinced that Parsha was the best friend I had made in a long time. I remembered that he had helped me to get change for one anna by buying one paisa worth of lemon drops and had not asked me to give him even one lemon drop. And now he had generously sold me ten cigarette packets instead of the usual eight for one paisa. He had done all this, even when I was an outsider intruding on his wadi.

I threw the four cigarette packets in the marked circle and tried to hit the one he had selected for a hit. Well! My hit stone missed that packet by more than a couple of feet. Parsha did not look down upon me with a supercilious smile. On the contrary he patted my shoulders in a friendly manner and then proceeded to win easily all the four packets in a single throw. So I took out two more for another round, which I lost too. But that didn't matter, because I had a friend who was prepared to play with me and was tolerant about my poor performance. So, although he won back from me in a short time all the ten cigarette packets he had sold me, I was in a very cheerful mood.

When I had run out of cigarette packets, Parsha laughed and said, "That ends our game."

I got quite worked up when he said that and protested, "What makes you think that it is the end of the game. I still have two paise with me. I wil buy one more paisa worth of cigarette packets from you."

Parsha was so amazed when he heard this, that he almost fell over backwards. He cried, "Do you mean to say that you will spend one more paisa to buy cigarette packets?"

However, at the same moment I saw other boys in the wadi coming out of their homes to play in the yard. That put me out. For I thought that Parsha would prefer to play with his friends who lived in the same wadi. But Parsha was a very generous and good friend, who remained loyal even when more attractive opportunities to play and have a good time came his way.

He put his arm around my shoulders and whispered in my ear, "Here they come, the other boys from my wadi. They wouldn't let me play with you. So come along. There is a quiet nook in the wadi, where we will go and play."

I was so moved by his kindness that I almost choked. I pressed another paisa into his palm and when he offered ten packets of cigarettes in exchange I firmly refused to accept them.

"No," I said, "I will accept only eight packets and not ten. I wouldn't let you suffer a loss on my account."

We haggled over the deal for a while and eventually Parsha very reluctantly agreed to give me only eight. I lost all the packets in four throws. However, that didn't put me out at all. In fact, I enjoyed those four rounds immensely and took a brave decision to part with my last paisa. I fished it out of my pocket and pressing it into Parsha's reluctant palm cried, "Sell me another eight packets and let me play some more."

Parsha looked at me in utter disbelief. He asked timidly, "Really! Do you want to spend all your money this way? Wouldn't your mother scold you if she learns about it? Would not she ask you what you did with one whole anna?"

I laughed, "She would, if she knew. But I wouldn't tell her."

Parsha looked at me hesitantly for a long time, but ultimately he took my paisa and gave me eight cigarette packets.

As we got ready to play, he said, "Four rounds are too many. Shall we now put in four packets each per round? Would you mind?"

I was reluctant to do so. But how could I say 'no' to such a wonderful friend? So I agreed and in no time at all I had lost one paisa worth of cigarette packets.

Parsha pushed those packets back into his bulging pocket and he laughed and said, "Well? We can't play any more, can we? So go back home and I will go and play with the boys of our wadi. Is that okay?"

I felt a little disappointed because I couldn't play any more. Nonetheless I felt very grateful and happy because Parsha had played with me without in any way running me down as a poor player. So I said, "Of course, it would be okay. I hope you win hands down when you play with those boys."

As I was walking back home, Parsha came running and caught up with me. He then put his arm around my shoulder and asked me in an intimate between-friends-only whisper, "Does your father give you one anna every day? I mean every single day?"

I smiled and nodded affirmatively.

He smiled and said in a more intimate and between-friends-only whisper, "In that case I will play with you tomorrow too. Come a little early so that only the two of us can play. That would be a lot of fun. Wouldn't it be?"

I was overwhelmed by his kindness and cried, "You have seen that I am not too good at playing this game. And yet you would play with me tomorrow too. Would you really?"

He tightened his arm around me in a very friendly hug that almost choked me and said, "Of course. I will play not only tomorrow, but every day."

I was so moved I almost had tears in my eyes. I fished the lemon drops out of my pocket and I pressed one into the palm of his hand and I too ate one. He accompanied me to the gate of his wadi, which made me feel real good.

As we parted at the gate, he put his arm around me, gave me a tight squeeze and said, "Well! You wouldn't mention my name, would you, if your mother asks how you spent your anna. I mean buying those empty cigarette packets was entirely your idea. Wasn't it?"

"Of course, it was my idea. I don't tell on my friends. I never did and would never do", I said proudly.

"You are a real friend", he said, thumping me affectionately on my back, and then rushed off to join his friends and I went home cheerfully as I had acquired a wonderful friend and a playmate too.

❑

BANDRA.

4

Mishaps That Trigger Agitations

Come to think of it, it was a minor incident and quite a few days have elapsed since it occurred. But I remember it distinctly as the immediate cause that triggered the separatist agitation in Marathwada region of our Maharashtra State.

It was five-thirty in the evening. The offices in the downtown Fort area were closing down and the people were on their way home in droves. I was to meet somebody in that area and was walking in a hurry to be on time.

I was more than a little surprised to find, standing at some distance, Mr. Anantrao Bhalerao, the editor of *Marathwada,* the leading newspaper of Marathwada region.

He seemed to be bewildered and distraught and that surprised me. For whenever I met him in his hometown Aurangabad, he used to be a picture of confidence and cheerful bonhomie. So I wondered what could be the cause of his distress.

I wanted to accost him, but as I approached him, he threw up his hands and began to walk with an angry gleam in his eyes.

Obviously he was too preoccupied to notice me and I too, being in a hurry, had no time to draw his attention. So I walked on with quick steps. But my steps slowed down and faltered as I began to realize the implications of what was happening. Anantrao, an important personage of the Marathwada region, was in Mumbai, the capital of Maharashtra and something had happened here that had caused him considerable distress and annoyance. This was an alarming development with an explosive potential.

I knew that deep discontent was brewing in the various regions of Maharashtra. The general feeling was that the people in the industrially advanced Western Maharashtra and particularly those in Mumbai rode roughshod over the interests and sentiments of people in the other regions of Maharashtra. They grabbed all the good things for themselves and threw crumbs at others. They were generally inconsiderate and often rude to people of other regions and even when they deigned to be nice they were annoyingly condescending or offensively patronizing. The discontentment had reached boiling point in the Vidarbha region, where people wanted to break away from Maharashtra and form a separate state of their own. There was every likelihood that similar separatist tendencies might gather strength and cause a conflagration in Marathwada. In such a situation, it was not at all advisable that a visit to Mumbai should cause distress and annoyance to the editor of the leading newspaper of Marathwada.

I wanted to do my bit to avoid such a development. I, therefore, stopped in my tracks, turned back and hurried to catch up with Anantrao.

"Hallo, hallo Anantrao...Anantrao", I called, to attract his attention.

I called so loudly that about fifty or more people around me turned and looked at me. But Anantrao was in such a huff that he heard nothing. I ultimately ran upto him and touched his shoulder.

Anantrao stopped sharply, spun around and gave me an angry questioning look.

I tried to soothe his ruffled feelings with the most pleasant and friendly smile I could muster and said, "Anantrao, what brings you here?"

"I never wanted to be here", said Anantrao angrily.

That stumped me and I ejaculated, "No? Then how come..."

Anantrao cut me short and said, "I boarded a bus that

promised to take me to Mahim and brought me here instead."

I was about to break into a guffaw but noticing how upset Anantrao was, I controlled myself instantly.

"And how did that come about?", I asked, pouring as much concern and sympathy in my voice as I could.

"How do I know? The ways of Mumbai's buses are strange indeed and too difficult for country bumpkins like us to understand", growled Anantrao.

I realized how correct my fears were and said, "Come, come, Anantrao, if you are a country bumpkin then I will have to describe myself as a village idiot. I know how upset you are. Do tell me what happened."

Anantrao cried, "Well! This bus of yours carried a board which said "Fort/Mahim". So I concluded that the bus was on its way from Fort to Mahim and boarded it, as I wanted to go to Mahim. But instead it travelled in the opposite direction; and so here I am in the Fort area where I don't want to be."

Anantrao grew more and more agitated as he told me the story and that alarmed me.

I looked at him guiltily and also apologetically and said, "I confess that such a mix up is a distinct possibility. This is because buses which travel in either direction carry the same board."

"But why on earth can't you people in Mumbai put a proper board on a bus indicating its destination?"

Anantrao almost thrust his angry questioning finger in my eye, when he flung that question at me.

I cowered guiltily and helplessly. The truth is that like every Mumbaite, I have no say at all in how the city's bus service is run. That is decided exclusively by the powerful workers' union and like all the other passengers I cower and suffer meekly the rough and rude treatment meted out to me. But there was no point in telling this bitter truth to Anantrao, who was then in a very uncharitable frame of mind.

So I said, "I entirely agree with you Anantrao. In fact for many years our buses did carry boards indicating their destinations. These new boards have been introduced only recently as an improvement."

"Improvement, did you say? What kind of improvement is that?"

I merely pursed my lips and shook my head in a manner which could mean anything at all. There was an error in Anantrao's reasoning, but it would have been unwise to point it out to him particularly at that juncture. He had assumed that the bus service in Mumbai is run for the benefit of the passengers. That was so in the old days, when a decadent capitalist order prevailed in the country. But now we have a new brave and equitable socialist order, in which public services are operated primarily for the benefit of the erstwhile exploited working class. There is, therefore, a constant effort to increase their emoluments and minimize their workload. Viewed in this context, it would be readily understood that to be called upon to change the indicator board at the end of every one way trip is a very tiresome and onerous burden on the employees. Moreover, the city transport undertaking has to spend money on preparing a separate indicator board for every destination. This reduces the amount available for raising the emoluments of workers. To overcome this difficulty, the city transport service has decided to use one indicator board for both destinations. This might cause some slight inconvenience to commuters, but that disadvantage, it will be agreed, far outweighs the benefits flowing to the working class from this decision.

I knew that Anantrao was a veteran socialist of revolutionary vintage. He would, therefore, have appreciated this decision of our transport undertaking, were he in a reasonable frame of mind. Unfortunately, this was not the case. So I desisted from explaining the situation to him.

Instead, to pacify his anger I said as pleasantly and

persuasively as I could, "Well, we can easily sort out this mix up. What I will do is that I will put you on a bus that takes you to Mahim."

I offered to help because there was a distinct possibility that Anantrao may board the bus which, instead of going North to Mahim, might be on its way to Colaba, the Southern tip of our island.

Anantrao, however, turned down my offer of help with a dismissive gesture of his hand and said, "No. That is not necessary. I have now got the hang of the set up here and will board the correct bus." He then paused and pondered a little and said, "Supposing I now do not want to go all the way to Mahim, but want to get off midway at Parel, how do I do that?"

I didn't quite understand his problem. So I gave him a questioning look and asked, "Parel? Did you say Parel?"

"Yes. Parel!", said Anantrao, getting a trifle annoyed all over again. "What I want to know is how do I know that the bus has arrived at Parel, where I want to get off?"

I understood Anantrao's problem. A Mumbaite knows the Parel area and can make out that he is there. But a visitor can't do that. I smiled and said, "It is simple. Ask the bus conductor."

Instead of feeling happy that his problem had a simple solution, Anantrao erupted and cried, "But, why should I have to do that? Your conductors on buses are so rude that I want to have as little to do with them as possible. But why on earth don't you put up boards at every stop indicating its location? I see a lot of hoardings at every bus stop advertising everything from toothpaste to bras. Why don't you take the trouble to put up just one more hoarding giving the location of the bus stop?"

I realized that Anantrao was still under the erroneous impression that bus services are run for the convenience of commuters. It was time he got rid of these reactonary capitalist ideas. But he was not at all in a proper frame of mind to listen to such sane advice.

I, therefore, wanted to offer him a cup of tea and explain things to him in a relaxed atmosphere. But Anantrao didn't give me an opportunity to do so. He took leave of me with a dismissive wave of his hand and walked away, waving his arms and muttering angrily to himself.

I realized that this spelt trouble but unfortunately could do nothing about it.

I have no idea whether and when Anantrao reached Parel that day. But he certainly did return to Aurangabad in a few days. For soon enough anger erupted all over Marathwada region and there was an angry agitation for the secession of Marathwada region from the state of Maharashtra.

A few days after this unfortunate episode, I ran into a writer from the Vidarbha region. I greeted him most warmly and invited him to have dinner with me at my home. Being familiar with all the regions of Maharashtra, I am particularly careful not to offend the people of Vidarbha, who are very proud of their lavish hospitality. They naturally get terribly annoyed if the same hospitality is not lavished on them when they visit other regions of Maharashtra. I had heard from them sharp comments about people of the city of Pune, who in their view are penny pinchers, have poor manners and are extremely remiss in returning hospitality extended to them. I, therefore, always took great care to extend warm welcome and hospitality to my friends from Vidarbha, many of whom were distinguished editors and writers.

I was happy that I was to get an opportunity to show that the people of Mumbai could be as warm and hospitable as the people of Vidarbha and asked my wife to put together a lavish meal. I wanted friends in Vidarbha to understand that Mumbai was not Pune.

Good food cannot be enjoyed unless there is good company. I, therefore, invited three of my writer friends, who could enliven an evening with lively talk, spiced with wit and interesting anecdotes.

My guest was expected to arrive at seven-thirty in the evening and I told my friends, who were prone to be late, to be on time at least for once. Having realized that Mumbai's fair name as a hospitable city was at stake, they tried their best to do so. One of them was only fifteen minutes late and the other one arrived ten minutes later.

We soon got engaged in such a lively exchange of pleasantries that we lost track of time. But soon my wife emerged from the kitchen, wiping her hands on the kitchen towel and told me that the dinner was ready and could be served at a few minutes notice. She then looked around and asked, "Ha! But where is our guest from Vidarbha?"

That made me look at the clock. It was fifteen minutes past eight and I began to feel somewhat concerned.

My wife gave me a sharp look. I could see that she had begun to suspect, as she normally did, that I had bungled in extending the invitation. She asked, "You didn't forget, did you, to give him our full address with detailed instructions on how to reach here?"

"Of course, I did that and I also drew a detailed map for his benefit", I protested.

"What good would that do?" asked my wife, "If you haven't told him which bus or suburban train to take?"

"Now, now, don't give me that look", I cried, wagging my finger at her, "I actually wrote out for him on a piece of paper the detailed instructions about which bus he should take or alternatively the train he should catch to reach here. I also wrote where he should get off. I then remembered our friend Anantrao's unpleasant experience and suggested that he should preferably take a train. I did tell you what happened to Anantrao, didn't I?"

"Yes, yes. You did that thrice", said my wife hurriedly and began to think of what further fault she could find in the way I had handled things.

"Are you sure," she asked, "That you told him to be here at seven-thirty, or was it..."

"Seven-thirty it was, and I am dead certain about it", I

cried, and thumped the teapoy thrice to remove any shreds of doubt lingering in her mind.

Such persistent probing questions do shake one's confidence and although I was dead certain that I had given him seven-thirty as the time, I began to wonder whether there was a slip of tongue and I had said eight-thirty.

These doubts were, however, completely dispelled when the clock showed nine-thirty and the guest from Vidarbha hadn't turned up.

My other guests had by now lost patience and I began to hear critical observations about the manners and habits of the people of Vidarbha. I tried my very best to assuage their anger and to speak up for the people of Vidarbha.

But my voice was drowned as voices got raised and more and more unpleasant things began to be said about the way the people of Vidarbha conduct themselves.

"I suspect that this friend of yours on his way here ran into another gentleman from Vidarbha. So they greeted each other effusively and walked to a paanwala's shop to chew a paan with a liberal helping of choice tobacco in it. And you know how it is with the people of Vidarbha. One paan leads to another and friendly talk begets more friendly talk. It is very likely that they decided to forget about today's dinner and have it with you tomorrow", said a friend in a barbed voice.

"No, no," I protested, "they wouldn't do that. I know that the people of Vidarbha don't like to make a fetish of punctuality, but they are never late by a whole day."

"Aren't they? Is that what you think?", asked my other friend mockingly and said, "Well! A friend of mine from Vidarbha turned up one whole week late for dinner at my house."

My wife was quite alarmed by the prospect of a guest dropping in without notice for dinner a day or a week later.

At this juncture the doorbell rang sharply. So I rushed to open the door and in walked our guest from Vidarbha.

I expected him to be apologetic and wanted to assure him with a broad smile that no apology was called for between good friends.

But instead of an apology, I was stabbed with an angry stare. He waved us aside peremptorily and flopped noisily on a chair.

"Ha!" He cried, "Ha!"

Distress and outrage were creating turmoil on his face.

"What? What is the matter?", I asked.

He brushed aside my query with an impatient sweep of his arm and cried, "Water! A big flask of water! Right away!"

I ran to get the water for him.

He cried, "It has to be ice cold. Understand, ice cold!"

I quickly took a bottle of water from the fridge and began to pour it hurriedly in a glass.

But he snatched the bottle from my hand and began to pour it in his mouth. He stopped only when the bottle was empty.

He then cried, "Ho!" and looked at all of us.

I took this as an invitation to open conversation and asked, "Whatever happened? What went wrong?"

But he ignored my question and began to unbutton his shirt.

I gaped at him wondering what he was upto.

He gave me a sharp look and asked belligerently, "I propose to take this wet shirt off my back. Do you have any objection?"

I was confused and scared and said hurriedly, "Oh. No! Not at all."

The shirt was taken off.

The guest from Vidarbha again looked at me and said in the same belligerent tone, "Now I propose to take off this sticky vest."

I was so taken aback that I didn't even manage to nod my consent.

The guest from Vidarbha took off the vest.

My wife vanished into the kitchen in a hurry and my

friends from Mumbai stood looking askance at what was going on.

The guest from Vidarbha then said in a threatening voice that dared me to object, "I now propose to lie down on this divan and rest."

He then lay down on the divan as comfortably as he could and said, "Ha!"

I quickly turned the regulator knob and increased the speed of the ceiling fan to add to the guest's comfort.

I had heard that in Vidarbha a guest is invited generously to treat the hosts' house as his own. While I have always appreciated this gesture of warm and generous hospitality, I had no idea that the invitation was accepted so fully and literally by the guests.

The guest from Vidarbha closed his eyes and took a snooze lasting for about twenty minutes. He then opened his eyes and seemed to be in a somewhat relaxed state of mind.

So I asked, "What happened? What went wrong?"

The guest from Vidarbha sat up and said, "Oh, nothing went wrong—nothing at all! I followed your advice, took a local train and arrived here tired and perspiring like a sponge. Oh! This Mumbai weather."

There was a distinct touch of sarcasm in his voice and the words "I followed your advice" were uttered with a particular emphasis.

I said, "Had I...had I made any mistake?"

"Oh no! Not at all! You had merely omitted to tell me that the railway stations and local train in Mumbai are so overcrowded, that it is virtually impossible for ordinary human beings like us to travel on trains and stay alive and sane. I was shoved, kicked, stepped on, butted, strangled and battered in the course of the journey. I was also about to be pushed out of a running train."

"I am so sorry. But that is how things are..."

The friend from Vidarbha cut me short and cried, "It took me half an hour to manage to board a train. I missed seven trains in a row and could mange to get into the eighth one because of a mighty shove by a bunch of burly Punjabis who were behind me. In the process all my breath was squeezed out of me and I am unable even now to breathe properly."

I apologized to him guiltily for what he had to go through and asked, "I understand, I understand! But why did it take you so much time to reach here?"

This question resulted in another outburst of anger. The guest from Vidarbha cried, "What else can happen if I have to travel all the way to Andheri?"

"What made you do that? Did you have to meet anybody there?", I asked.

"No. No! I was on my way here and wanted to get off at Bandra. But I was carried over to Andheri."

"How did that happen?", I asked.

"I was not allowed to get off at Bandra station. I pleaded, begged, shouted, screamed and pushed too, but to no avail. Nobody budged and made way for me and so I travelled on and on until I reached Andheri, which was the terminus. I have never seen people as inconsiderate as those in this city of yours."

"I am terribly sorry. But I must say that people in Mumbai aren't all that bad. The trouble is that in an overcrowded train sometimes one can't move and make way even if one wants to."

The guest from Vidarbha rejected my argument with an angry sweep of his hand. He cried, "I would have believed that, if what followed hadn't happened."

"Good gracious! What happened?", I asked, alarmed by the prospect of being confronted by another disaster.

"I will certainly tell you what happened. You ought to know it", continued the guest from Vidarbha angrily. "When I got off at Andheri, I was stopped by a mean looking ticket checker and he fined me for travelling from Bandra to Andheri without ticket. I tried to explain to him how I was overcarried. But he wouldn't believe it. He forced me to pay the fare and a heavy fine too. When I protested, he said that instead of protesting, I should thank him for only collecting a fine and not sending me to the lockup. If this is how the people of Vidarbha are to be treated in the capital city of Maharashtra..."

I knew what was coming and so intervened and said with a guilty and apologetic smile, "It was terrible. That ticket checker ought to be reprimanded. We will persuade the suburban passengers' association to make a strong representation in the matter. You don't have to worry about that. But I do hope that thereafter you had a smooth sailing, when you travelled back from Andheri to Bandra."

"Yes, it was smooth. I had no difficulty in getting off at Bandra", said the guest from Vidarbha in a voice loaded with sarcasm.

"Did anything go wrong again?" I asked, "I hope you could quickly get a taxi to travel from the station to my house."

"No. I couldn't take a taxi. I walked."

"Oh poor you! Wasn't there any taxi at the taxi stand?"

"There was a taxi. But I couldn't take it."

"Why?", I asked.

"Because I had no money to pay for it!"

"No money to pay for the taxi?", I exclaimed. "The fare isn't high."

"But I had no money at all. One of your expert pickpockets in Mumbai had robbed me of my purse, while I travelled from Andheri to Bandra."

That one man should have had to suffer so many calamities was terrible.

All of us were full of sympathy for our guest. My wife suggested, "Even if you lost your purse, you need not have walked. You could have taken a taxi and we would have paid its fare."

"Well! I thought of that and had I been in Vidarbha I would have certainly done that. But I wasn't sure of how I would be treated by people in Mumbai. I am told that in

Mumbai people make a fetish of punctuality. If a guest is late, you don't wait for him, but eat your dinner and go out to see a movie. Had that happened, I would have landed in a soup. The cabbie would have then taken me to the police station and I would have found myself in a lockup."

"Oh, really! We wouldn't let such things happen to you. Whatever made you think that we would do that? In any case, dinner is ready. Shall I serve it right away or would you like to relax for a while before you have it?" My wife's heart was dripping with sympathy and she wanted to take good care of our guest.

But our guest from Vidarbha was still in a huff. He said, "Dinner can wait. What I need the most right now is paan with strong Vidarbha tobacco in it. It is only after I chew such a paan that I will be in a proper frame of mind to do other things and be sociable. So get a paan for me if you can."

Unfortunately, we people of Mumbai are not in the habit of keeping the elaborate paraphernelia for preparing a paan in our houses. We have no time for such things. So all I could do was to look at him helplessly with a guilty feeling.

Our guest noticed my predicament and cried, "Sorry! My most humble apologies. I should have remembered that one doesn't get a paan in the house of a Mumbaite. It didn't occur to me because, even the poorest man in Vidarbha offers a paan to his guest."

"But I will get it for you from the paan shop which is not far away. I will do so right away", I assured him and opened the door to leave.

"Oh, don't bother. It was wrong of me to expect to be offered a paan in Mumbai", he said and put his hand on my shoulder to stop me.

But I insisted and ultimately he relented and said, "All right! You can go and get a paan for me if you insist. But you know what, really good paans are just not available in the city of Mumbai. I am afraid, I will be able to eat a really good paan only after I return to Vidarbha."

He shook his head sadly and despondently. When a man from Vidarbha shakes his head like that, it means that he has written you off—washed his hands off you.

I did go to the paan shop though and brought for him the best paan I could get. But I knew that even the best paan in Mumbai wouldn't be good enough for a man from Vidarbha, and nothing upsets a man from Vidarbha more than being denied a good paan to eat.

I knew that this could lead to parting of ways, and my expectation proved to be right.

Soon after the gentleman from Vidarbha returned home, an angry and violent agitation for a separate Vidarbha state was launched.

❑

5

Husbands and Pumpkins

It had never occured to me even in my dreams that such a thing would happen. But it did. I had believed that as in the case of most of my friends, my marriage too would be arranged in the traditional manner. After all I wasn't the handsome and dashing kind of guy who sweeps pretty girls off their feet. But to my utter astonishment I met a pretty girl and before I knew what was happening, I was smitten with love for her. I was in it right upto my neck. What was even more astonishing was that she, a pretty girl, fell in love with a prosaic guy like me, who was prone to become tongue–tied in the presence of young girls.

It was altogether romantic. What added a whiff of spice and adventure to the romance was the fact that she belonged to another caste. Thus I suddenly found myself cast in the heroic role of a social rebel defiantly challenging the traditional Hindu social order. It was a role that I relished immensely.

I, therefore, looked forward to defying my father and other elders in the family. I wanted to be counted among the social reformers like Karve and Agarkar who had carved their names in glowing letters in the history of Hindu society.

But to my utter disappointment nobody opposed my inter-caste love marriage. Not even my father. When I told him what I proposed to do, he just shrugged and grunted. As regards the rest of the family, they received the news with pleasant smiles. They didn't even shun attending the marriage reception. On the contrary they attended it in all their finery and ate the dinner with great relish.

Their behaviour annoyed me. It wan't fair, I thought, to deny me the credit for being a social reformer. I had hoped that atleast the elderly women in the family and the community would express disapproval. But they too disappointed me. I found that instead of being angry, they were curious. They wanted to see this daughter-in-law who belonged to another caste. So my aunt took the lead and invited the new daughter-in-law to visit my family on the mother's side. I was not invited as men are considered a hindrance to the proper inspection of a daughter-in-law.

I was ready or rather looking forward to facing hostility. But as I was not invited, I didn't want to expose my wife to any unpleasantness. I, therefore, said to her, "Maybe one of these elderly aunties will say something that will hurt you. I would, therefore, suggest that you decline the invitation under one pretext or another."

"Don't you worry," said my wife, "I think I can handle them tactfully and if need be firmly."

Being in love with her, I had not noticed this side of her personality. But I was soon to realize that her family hailed from the Sindhudurg district of Konkan and the folks who hail from that district can be equally pleasant or nasty according to the demands of the occasion. In any case they are not intimidated by folks from our Ratnagiri district.

So my wife went to my aunt's house ready for all eventualities. But there was no unpleasantness at all. The elderly women stood with their hands on their hips and inspected my wife from head to foot. But they were curious and distant rather than hostile.

To break the ice my aunt suggested to my wife in a sweet affectionate tone, "Bow to them, Vasanti."

This was the proper thing to do and my wife wanted to show these women from a Chitpavan Brahmin family that when it came to observing proprieties, the Saraswat girls are as good as any in the world, including those from the Chitpavan Brahmin community. So she complied and did a thorough job of it by bowing so low that her nose almost touched the ground.

This was a sign of good breeding, which pleased those elderly women. Their expressions thawed and they broke into smiles. Their experience was that educated girls do not respect their elders. They were, therefore, particularly pleased with the respectful behaviour of my wife, who, they knew, was a graduate.

The ice was broken and the talk became free and easy and expansive. The more elderly among the aunties said, "Your husband may be a professor, but he cannot give himself any airs when he meets me. For, I have seen him since he was a naked baby no taller than my knee and washed his behind too. So you have to bow to me a second time."

My wife was amused, as women generally are when they hear anything that puts their husbands in a ridiculous light. So she laughed and bowed to that auntie once again. All the other elderly women too had seen me as a baby and had many interesting memories about how silly and perverse I was as a baby. They amused my wife with those stories and laughingly demanded one more bow from her. She complied with their demands cheerfully.

This pleased the old women no end and they went home pleasantly astonished that a girl belonging to another caste and educated at a college should be so respectful to elders and observe all the traditional proprieties, which were the hallmark of good breeding, While appreciating her, they did not forget to tell her how silly, difficult, obstinate and perverse I was as a boy.

This appreciation by the elderly women in my family pleased my wife immensely and she was tickled no end by the stories she had heard about my silly and perverse behaviour as a boy. She recounted to her family, with relish, those stories about me. I suspect that she added more than a little spice to the stories as she told them.

I was relieved that the meeting of my wife and elderly

relatives passed off so smoothly. But I must confess that I was a trifle disappointed that I was denied the opportunity of bravely defying social orthodoxy. It seems that it had vanished altogether before I decided to defy it.

I must say that a friend of mine was luckier in this matter. He married a Parsi girl and that led to a series of dramatic hair raising episodes in his life.

There was fierce and violent opposition to his marriage from the family of the girl and the Parsi community. He received angry and abusive anonymous letters that threatened him with gruesome consequences if he dared to marry that girl. Being a hot–headed guy he did just that. Soon afterwards he was confronted by a mob of irate Parsis wielding cudgels and hockeysticks and screaming vile imprecations. My friend was all alone and he did with alacrity the most sensible thing to do in such a situation. He turned away and took to his heels. The irate mob pursued him waving hockeysticks and cudgels. Luckily he had a strong and nimble pair of feet and he barely escaped with the skin of his teeth.

My friend wasn't the kind of person who would take such a thing lying down. He collected a big gang of his college mates who rushed into the Parsi colony and meted out rough treatment to the unsuspecting Parsis before the police arrived on the scene. At the sight of the first policeman my friend's gang melted and vanished like the guerilla army of the legendary Shivaji.

When I heard of this dramatic confrontation, I was very, very upset with my friend for having left me out of it.

"Why didn't you ask me to join when all of you went to rough up the Parsis? I would have borrowed a hockeystick and joined you", I asked in righteous indignation.

Any decent guy would have sheepishly mumbled apologies for being so unfair to a friend.

But do you know what my friend did? He guffawed loudly and said, "Now, now! You should know that you aren't the kind of guy who can be of any use in such situations. The only thing you seem to be able to do is to write stories."

That wasn't quite fair. If confronted with such a situation, I am sure, I would have proved equal to it. But I was denied the opportunity. No irate mobs, no anonymous abusive letters, not even angry words and looks. Nothing at all.

Well! Not quite. For slowly but surely a wave of indignation and resentment was building up in the Saraswat community of Girgaum, where I lived.

As everyone knows, the Saraswats live on fish. A Saraswat doesn't feel that he or she has eaten a meal unless there is fish in it. It would be an exaggeration to say that a Saraswat cannot survive even for a day without eating fish. For they do abstain from eating fish on the holy day of Ganesh Chaturthi. But one can see from their grim visages and general lack of bonhomie and good humour on that day that their capacity for self-control is being sorely tested and that it would be an unbearable hardship for them to continue the abstinence for another day.

One of the main responsibilities of a Saraswat husband is to go to the fish market in the morning and buy fresh fish. He has to be an expert in selecting really fresh and tasty fish for the day's meal. Naturally Saraswats in our Girgaum area used to meet each other in the fish market every morning and exchange tips about the quality of fish available on that day.

It was there in the fish market that the wave of indignation and resentment against me began to build up.

It seems that one Mr. Kamath, a Saraswat, met Mr. Nadkarni, another Saraswat, in the market. Mr. Kamath was in a very happy frame of mind because he had purchased Bangda fish which was extremely fresh and of excellent quality. He gave useful tips to Mr. Nadkarni about where in the market he would get the best fish. Naturally, there was some earnest talk about fish and they both agreed that the fish available in Mumbai was no match to the fish they could get in Konkan. They were about to part with smiles, when the face of Mr. Nadkarni got clouded over and wrinkles etched deep concern on his brow. He put a restraining hand on the shoulder of Mr. Kamath and said, "You know what, I am getting worried about that girl Vasanti."

"Oh! You mean Vasanti from the village of Shiroda, don't you? The one who got married to a Bhat by caste the other day."

"Yes. She is the one I am worried about. How on earth would that girl ever get any fish to eat in that Bhat's household, where they eat only grass."

"Good Heavens!", cried Mr. Kamath and stopped dead in his tracks with consternation writ large on his face. He couldn't stomach the idea that while he and other Saraswats gorged on mouth-watering fish curry in their houses, this poor Saraswat girl would be trying hard to swallow insipid curry of alu leaves in a Bhat household. He knew how difficult it was to abstain from eating fish even on the Ganesh Chaturthi day and this poor girl would not savour fish for the rest of her life. It was an outrage.

This sense of outrage found strong expression when Mr. Kamath met Mr. Rajadhyaksha and it got seasoned with hot chilly sauce when Mr. Rajadhyaksha met Mr. Dalvi. Dalvi got so worked up that he walked half a mile and climbed four stairs to express his strong feelings in the matter to Mr. Mantri. The news thus spread like fire all over Girgaum and beyond to Talmaki Wadi, which was a Saraswat stronghold.

Soon enough I found myself confronted with angry stares, wherever I walked in the streets of Girgaum. The women stared so hard that they almost bore holes in me. Some of them even pointed fingers at me and exchanged angry whispers. The whispers were so sharp as to be clearly audible. It took me some time to understand why it was so, but soon enough I realized that they were loud because they were meant for my ears.

Finally, one Saraswat gentleman could not contain his resentment any more. He accosted me in the street and asked, "Are we to understand that having married this girl of ours, you propose to make her eat insipid dal and rice for the rest of her life?"

I was amazed at this sudden outburst of a stranger and couldn't make head or tail of it.

Noticing the confusion on my face, he explained to me the import of what he had said. He said, "Look here! You Bhats might be able to survive on an insipid diet of dal, vegetable of alu leaves and rice. But if this girl doesn't get fish to eat, she would starve."

Suddenly the meaning of those angry stares and uncomplimentary whispers became clear to me and I felt as guilty as hell. I cowered and hid my face, whenever I was out in the streets of Girgaum. I had hoped to be counted among the liberal social reformers by marrying a Saraswat girl. But I found myself placed in the ranks of villainous men subjecting poor helpless women to cruelty and torture.

Unfortunately, there seemed to be no way out of this predicament. I used to stay in my father's house those days and fish and meat were not cooked in our kitchen. It was just not done.

All I could do, therefore, was to continue to feel guilty and cower under the withering looks of angry Saraswat women. I feared that the editor of the popular weekly in the town of Malwan would pen an angry editorial against me and on reading that the annoyed Saraswats of Girgaum would sally forth and beat me up with cudgels.

But a friend of mine, who was a Saraswat, explained my difficulty and helplessness to other Saraswats and being basically peace-loving and kind-hearted people they let me off the hook and found a peaceful solution to the problem.

My wife started receiving invitations to lunches and dinners. In fact, she received so many of them that she hardly ever shared a meal with me.

Often when I sat down to a meal, I asked my wife, "How about you? Aren't you eating with me?"

My wife responded with a smile and said, "I have been invited to lunch by Kamath auntie."

Next day she had an invitation from Nadkarni auntie and the day after the Rajadhyakshas were keen to have her for lunch.

So she was invited by one Saraswat family after another and in the belief that she was starving, she was fed fish until she was about to burst.

I sheepishly told her Saraswat hosts that my family and I didn't mind Vasanti eating fish even in our house. It was just that we were not used to cooking and eating meat. Having learnt this, her hosts fed her fish for lunch and gave her a tinful of fish to carry home for dinner.

I was very appreciative of this gesture. For although my family didn't eat meat, I used to eat it in restaurants in the company of my meat-eating friends. So I shared the fish with my wife and soon learnt all about eating various kinds of fish cooked in diverse ways. In fact, I became so good at it that I could eat a meal with Saraswat hosts without causing amusement and arousing laughter.

It was nice but embarassing and the embarrassment grew as days and weeks elapsed. This made me set up a separate home of my own, much sooner than I would have done otherwise. When that happened, I no longer had to cower and avert my eyes when I ran into a Saraswat. I could look them in the eye and talk to them knowledgeably about Bangdas, Pomfrets, Surmais and other diverse varieties of fish.

I was thus a happy man, at peace with myself, my wife and the rest of the world. But not for long. Soon enough I met a Brahmin friend of mine.

After the usual friendly greetings and recounting of happy childhood memories, the talk turned to our transition from being carefree school boys to being married men. In the course of our exchange of notes, he observed, "Ah, somebody told me that you married a Saraswat girl. Naturally, nobody thinks of caste and things like that any more and certainly not when one is in love with a girl. Naturally you were no exception to this. At the same time the hard realities of life are always with us and we have to come to terms with them. Well! Looking at things from that angle, I would suggest that you better be careful about the rupees, annas and pies you earn and spend."

"What makes you say that?", I asked, not quite realizing what he was driving at.

"Well! You know, these Saraswat are a very nice people, friendly and all that. Moreover, their women are pretty and affectionate. However, they like the good things of life more than most people do and do not hesitate to spend money to get them."

"Do you mean to say that they are spendthrifts?", I asked. His observation had made me a trifle uneasy as it seemed to crystallize the misgivings that were slowly taking shape in my mind.

We, Chitpavan Brahmins tend to be careful when it comes to spending money, We are not tight-fisted, mind you, but we do not spend an anna if a paisa would do and if something is very expensive and costs a whole rupee, we rather do without it. We feel uncomfortable not only when we are called upon to spend large sums of money, say like five rupees or ten rupees but we also don't like to see other people spending their own money.

When my friend noticed my worried look, he hastened to reassure me.

"No! no!", he said. "Saying that they are spendthrifts would be going too far. I would only say that they spend rather generously."

"For instance?", I asked.

"Well! I wouldn't like to cite instances and make a big fuss about small things. I think, therefore, that we should now talk about other things", said my friend, with his eyes scanning the distant horizon.

"But surely, you can cite one instance, you know, just one instance to give me a broad idea", I said coaxingly.

My friend said with a resigned air, "Well! Take for instance cashewnuts. They are rather expensive, aren't they?"

"They certainly are. Well! Not too much so, but expensive nonetheless", I said hesitantly.

"Would you now cook them in a big pot as beans are cooked and serve them with a meal as a side dish?", my friend asked, suppressing a smile as he spoke.

"A large pot full of cashewnuts? Cooked and eaten with a meal as a side dish? That can't be. I suspect you mistook peas for cashewnuts", I said shaking my head in disbelief.

"No. I did not", said my friend sharply. "Why, I ate a plateful of these cooked cashewnuts myself when I visited a Saraswat friend of mine."

"Really!" I exclaimed.

"Yes, of course—and frankly—that seemed to me like going much too far. I can understand adding a fistful of cashewnuts to chiwada to make it more tasty. But if one eats a potful of cashewnuts with one's meal, it won't take long to be pennyless."

I nodded and hastily began to calculate the amount of money one would have to spend in a month, if one was to eat cooked cashewnuts as a side dish every day. I realized that this single item alone would eat up a large chunk of my meagre salary.

My friend noticed the alarm on my face and added with a furrowed brow, "And mind you, that is not the end of the story. A coconut may not be as expensive as cashewnuts, but if a woman uses a whole coconut to season every meal, one would have to buy sixty coconuts every month and in some months the tally may rise to sixty two coconuts. Coconuts are certainly not very expensive but sixty coconuts can make a hole in one's pocket."

"Yes! I can see that", I exclaimed, and a quick calculation of the price of sixty-two coconuts made me realize that the hole, though not large, would not be insignificant.

I couldn't help remembering that my frugal Chitpavan mother used only half a coconut everyday to season both the meals.

"And that, mind you, is not the end of the story."

"Is it not? What else do these Saraswat women do?" I asked with bated breath.

"Well! We are used to our womenfolk getting up and starting the day's household work in the dark hours of the morning. But the Saraswat women are different. They don't get out of bed until the sun's rays hit their closed eyes", explained my friend.

"Does that mean that no Saraswat woman gets out of bed before seven o'clock in the morning?" I asked, wondering how I could get a meal before I left home for work.

"Well! That's about it, give or take half an hour or more", said my friend and I could see that he was leaning over backward to be fair to Saraswat women.

I mulled over the prospect of going to work everyday in the morning with an empty stomach and told myself that it was no use getting scared. So I said brightly, "I am sure I can persuade Vasanti to get out of bed at least half an hour earlier".

"Yes. You certainly could if you think so. But what good would that do?", my friend asked.

"Why? That certainly would give her enough time to cook a meal for me in the morning", I said and put as much confidence in my words as I could.

"Maybe she could do that at a pinch", said my friend and added, "but I suspect that it would be rather difficult if she goes about cooking a meal the way an average Saraswat woman does."

"What do you mean?", I asked narrowing my eyes with suspicion and alarm.

"Well! As far as I know, the first thing a Saraswat woman does in the morning is to crack open a coconut, remove its flesh and start grinding it with a rolling stone. She keeps on doing so until the flesh becomes a smooth pulp. I can tell you from experience that this is a very noisy process which goes on for not less than an hour", said my friend, pausing a little to get the time element right.

"One hour? How can that be?", I cried in disbelief.

"Well! All I can say is that I am being conservative. And mind you I am telling you this on the basis of first-hand experience."

"Rubbish! where on earth did you have this first-hand experience?", I asked.

"Yes, my friend, I am as a matter of fact speaking from first hand experience. A Saraswat family lives on the floor above ours in our multi-storyed apartment house and every day in the morning I have to listen to this ceaseless rattle-tattle of the stone roller on the grinding stone. It is terrible."

"And does this go on for one hour?", I asked, shuddering at the prospect of this sort of thing happening in the kitchen of my own house.

"I think two hours may be nearer the mark. The way she carries on, this Saraswat neighbour of ours will any day fall through the celling of our apartment on top of our heads, and along with her the grinding stone will also crash on our heads." My friend seethed with righteous indignation at the mere memory of his daily ordeal.

The prospect of this sort of thing happening in my house was frightening. I certainly didn't want to believe this story. So I protested, "Come, come! How can a woman spend two hours grinding a coconut, if she wants to serve a meal to her husband before he goes off to work?"

My friend responded with a loud guffaw, "Ha, ha!, ho, ho! Feed a husband, did you say? Oh, no! They don't worry about that. No, not the Saraswat women! Once married, a Saraswat man is no better than a big round pumpkin in the kitchen closet."

"Rubbish!" I cried, "You are highly prejudiced against Saraswat women. They are very sweet and charming and affectionate."

"Have it your way", said my friend nonchalantly, "But truth will dawn on you soon enough."

Although I had dismissed my friend's observations as so much piffle, I was more than a little apprehensive by the time I returned home and my heart missed a beat when Vasanti welcomed me with a big plateful of cooked spicy cashewnuts.

It seemed to me that my friend's forebodings were only too true. If this was the way my wife was going to spend money, I had no doubt that I would be sitting in the street soon enough with a begging bowl.

I wanted to give Vasanti a piece of my mind. But she had disappeared into the kitchen. So as I waited for her to return I began to compose in my mind a sharp and eloquently telling admonition.

"It seems that you are under the impression that you have married a Maharaja who can scatter pearls as he walks down the street..." So my admonition went.

It would have been a very eloquent admonition, if I could have completed it. But I was disturbed by the aroma of that dish of cashewnuts. I looked at that disturbing dish disdainfully. But it had such an innocent and inviting look that my disdain melted away.

I wanted to leave those cashewnuts untouched to underline my strong disapproval of my wife's spendthrift ways. On second thoughts, a Chitpavan Brahmin's down to earth realism prevailed. After all, the money had already been spent and there was no way I could recover it. Therefore, not to eat those nice-looking cashewnuts would have been a sheer waste. And having spent so much money, I certainly didn't want to waste it too.

So I put a spoonful of those spicy cashewnuts in my mouth. They were so soft, luscious and delicious that along with them my anger melted in my mouth. The trick was to cook and spice them before they were fried and dried and in the process deprived of their natural softness, taste and flavour.

By the time I had eaten my plateful, Vasanti came out of the kitchen smiling and asked, 'Did you like the cashewnut usal?"

"It was delicious - simply out of this world", I raved and asked, "Can I have some more?"

"Yes, you can," she said with a smile, "but mind you, one can't eat heaps of them. They are expensive, you know."

"Yes, yes. They certainly are expensive", I said shamefacedly.

But I ate another plateful of the cashewnut usal with great relish. I knew that I was hurtling down the path of penury. But to sit in the street with a begging bowl was a small price to pay for eating a dish so divine.

Later on in the evening, while busy with my books, I was disturbed by the loud rattle-tattle of a rolling stone on a grinding stone.

I peeped in the kitchen and saw the demise of a big coconut.

I realized that my friend's forebodings were coming true. So I placed my hands on my hips and said, "Now, now, are we using one whole coconut for seasoning a single meal? Aren't we going a little too far?"

Vasanti put down the stone roller in hand and stared at me wide-eyed, "Did I hear that one coconut for a meal is too many? What do you expect me to do? Season our food with a pinch of scraped coconut?"

I said, "Not really! But..."

She cut me short and cried, "How on earth can I prepare a tasty meal if I don't season it properly with coconut and spices. We can't eat tasteless food the way some people do. Can we?"

"Oh no! Not at all!", I said hastily, "I don't mind really, After all you know best."

It was no use pursuing the matter any further. So I left it at that. But I was convinced that one begging bowl wouldn't be enough and that I would have to sit in the street with two begging bowls.

When, however, Vasanti served dinner it was so delicious that I was full of admiration for my perspicacity in marrying a Saraswat girl.

The sour sol curry was particularly delicious and I drank a whole bowl of it. I said to myself that if this was the kind of food I was going to eat, I wouldn't mind sitting in the street with two begging bowls.

I complimented her for the wonderful meal she had served and humbly suggested that she should occasionally prepare some of my favourite dishes in the Brahmin cuisine.

She had no objection to that and she agreed to do so with a smile. I smiled too and for a while we were full of happy smiles. Then suddenly suspicion darkened her face and narrowed her eyes. She said, "Now tell me, is it true?"

"What are you talking about?" I asked, being completely in the dark about what she had in mind.

"This matter about sarees, I mean," said Vasanti puckering her brow, "a girl, who has been my closest friend since I was a kid, told me things that have got me worried."

"And what did she tell you?" I asked, being still unable to fathom what she had in mind.

"She told me," said Vasanti, peering deep into my eyes, "that a Brahmin buys only two sarees for his wife every year."

"Good heaven! Did she say that?", I asked sharply. I was quite offended by the canards being spread about us Brahmins.

My annoyance, however, did not reach my wife who was preoccupied with the weighty problem of the sarees. She continued, "And do you know what else she said? She said that the sarees they buy are about the roughest and cheapest that one can get in the market."

"Nonsense!", I protested.

"That is what I said too," said Vasanti, "but she said that she had seen with her own eyes a Brahmin woman in tears on seeing the sarees her husband had brought for her. That has got me worried."

"Forget those worries and don't you believe a word of the canards being spread about us Chitpavan Brahmins. We are no doubt careful or rather judicious when we spend money. But we are not penny pinchers. You will soon find that out when I buy you sarees. Incidentally, how many sarees would you expect me to buy for you in a year?"

"Certainly not two", she said with warmth. "Now, let me see. You will certainly buy me one for my birthday and you will not feel happy if you don't buy me one on your birthday. We cannot obviously let our marriage anniversary pass without a new saree for me and sarees have to be brought at all our major festivals like Diwali, Padva, Sankranti and all the other ones."

I gulped. I am not, as I have said, a penny pincher. In fact, I wanted everybody to know how generous we Brahmins can be. But what my wife seemed to be expecting went far beyond the most generous interpretation of generosity. I remembered my friend's warning about how expensive a Saraswat wife is likely to be. It seemed to me that begging bowls won't solve my problem. I would have to rob a bank to buy all those sarees.

However, I thought it wise to keep my own counsel on this matter and to delicately bring to Vasanti's notice the hard realities of life in due course. I wondered though how far I would be able to persuade her to be understanding and reasonable.

So I said in a tone of light-hearted banter, "I have a close friend too who has been my buddy since I was a kid. He told me that for a Saraswat woman a husband is no better than a pumpkin which hangs in a basket tied to the ceiling in the kitchen."

"A pumpkin, did you say?", exclaimed Vasanti and burst into laughter.

"Yes," I said, "the poor pumpkin, which is ignored and left hanging until the need arises to cut it and cook a piece of it for a meal."

"Nonsense," cried Vasanti, "in all the Saraswat families I

know of, husbands are treated very nicely. In fact, they are pampered, although quite a few of them are utterly lazy and perverse."

"Ha!", I said, "That is what things look like to you. But my friend has seen with his own eyes a poor Saraswat husband being treated no better than a pumpkin."

"And this he saw happening in a Saraswat family, did you say? That can't be. Did your friend tell you the name of that family?", she asked.

"I am not too sure but I think it was Muzumdar", I said not quite gathering the purpose behind the query.

"Ha!', she cried, "That explains it. Muzumdars are Saraswats from the Karwar region down South. We are Saraswats from the Sindhudurg region. I can tell you that Saraswats from the Karwar region are as different from us as mangoes are from onions. The women from Karwar run their households their own way and their husbands hardly ever get even a hearing. As you friend observed, those husbands are treated no better than pumpkins which are hung up harmlessly in the kitchen to be cut, cooked and eaten when necessary. But we girls from Sindhudurg region are as different from those women as mangoes are from onions."

Vasanti put all this across so persuasively that I felt greatly relieved that I had married a girl from Sindhudurg district and not from the Karwar region.

Vasanti was absorbed in thought for some time. She then looked at me in the eye and said, "I wonder though why you should worry about husbands being treated no better than pumpkins, because I have been told that pumpkins get a better deal from Brahmin women than do their husbands."

"Nonsense!", I cried, "Do you think that we Brahmin men would allow ourselves to be treated in this manner? We can put our foot down and squash uppity behaviour."

I discovered that Saraswat women have a way of remaining totally unimpressed by the strong words that husbands use. Atleast that seemed to be true of Vasanti who totally ignored my belligerent retort and said, "No! Bluster cannot conceal the truth. A friend of mine has a Brahmin family as her neighbours. She told me that the poor husband gets up early. He then goes out quietly without making any noise and brings milk. He then wakes up the children, makes them drink a glass of milk, gives them a bath and then..."

"Utter rubbnish! Your friend is a very imaginative woman, who seems to be in the habit of spinning yarns which do not contain an iota of truth. I can tell you we Brahmin men are made of sterner stuff."

While I searched for words to adequately express my strong feelings in the matter, my wife said with a smile, "My friend also told me that Brahmin men are in the habit of making a lot of fuss about being strong and masters of their households. Such talk, she told me, had to be ignored."

"Ha!", I cried indignantly, "You seem to have the wrong kind of friends. But you will soon find out for yourself."

My wife cocked her head and looked at me with an amused look. She then said with a smirk, "You know what? You look very very funny when you are angry."

I walked away in a huff when I heard that. But somewhere inside me I had an eerie feeling that I was well on the way to becoming a pumpkin like the general run of husbands, be they Brahmins or Saraswats.

❑

6

Woes of the Grandfathers of Today

"This is absolutely the limit. Real, absolute limit! She is going too far, much too far. And I am not going to take it any more", cried my friend Baloo, and the way his eyes flashed and he clenched and shook his fist, showed that he was terribly upset indeed.

Baloo and I have been friends since we were kids. We were buddies at school and so thick were we that when at the age of twelve we fell madly in love with the same movie star, Baloo very generously made a great sacrifice and said, "Well, if you love her so much, you can have her all for yourself." He went even further and handed over to me her picture, which he had kept for so long under his pillow. We are now old and retired, but still continue to be close friends. I, therefore, could guess right away that it was Baloo's wife, who was at the bottom of this explosion of temper.

Baloo really had no reason to be so terribly upset. He was leading a quiet, comfortable retired life. He had enough money for him and his wife to be able to do that. His two children had grown up and,were settled in the United States. He and his wife both enjoyed good health. Everything was as nice and comfortable as could be.

Of course, there was a little problem as there always is in any family. The problem was that his daughter was about to have a baby and Baloo's wife proposed to go and stay with her for a few months to help her with the newborn. However, in my opinion, that didn't call for all this fuss.

So I pleaded, "Now, look here Baloo, there is no reason

for you to be so upset. If a baby is due to arrive, your wife has to go and help your daughter, and particularly so, when it happens to be the first baby."

"But why is the baby arriving now? Babies have no business arriving any time they like. There has to be some orderliness about it. I had thought they did things in an orderly manner in the United States. But it seems they don't. Things seem to be as chaotic there as they were here in the lawless days of the Mughals", cried Baloo. He was so worked up that he sputtered rather than spoke.

I could see that Baloo was far too worked up to be able to see reason.

So I said, "Tut, Tut, Baloo. Don't be silly!"

Baloo turned sharply on his heels, caught me by my shoulder and fixed me with a piercing stare, "So, you think I am the one who is silly, do you? Well! Have you forgotten that my daughter-in-law had a baby barely three to four months ago. At that time my wife had rushed to Los Angeles to help her with the baby. She had said that she would stay there for just a month. But she actually stayed for three months and two weeks more."

"I know! I know! That was certainly hard on you. But your daughter-in-law very sorely needed help and so, I suppose, she persuaded your wife to stay on a little longer", I pleaded, trying to free my shoulder from his vice-like grip.

"Just a little longer, was it? She had assured me on oath that she would not stay a day longer than two months. And she stayed full six weeks and two days longer", asserted Baloo and tightened his vice-like grip on my shoulder to bring home his point.

"Come now Baloo! It is difficult to be so damned precise about these things. When a first baby arrives, there can always be complications and the inexperienced parents find it hard to cope with them", I pleaded once again, trying, at the same time, to loosen his grip of my shoulder.

"Rubbish!" cried Baloo. "I have been told that when babies

are due, American women themselves drive to the hospital, have their babies and drive back steering the cars with one hand and holding the babies in the other. They stay home for barely a week thereafter and then go back to work, while our Indian girls want their mothers-in-law to care for them and their babies for months together. Why don't they learn something from the American women amongst whom they live?"

Baloo could be very eloquent when he was angry, and his anger lent an edge to his eloquence.

Happily for me he had released the vice-like grip on my shoulder and instead, to drive home his point, thrust his finger in my eye.

I avoided the thrust of his finger with a deft maneuver and replied, "Now, now, Baloo, don't you tell me about American women. I have had an occasion to talk with an American woman on this matter. And she said that if she had an Indian mother-in-law, she would have persuaded her to stay for not only three but six months to help her with the baby. These American women are not as nice and innocent as you think they are."

But Baloo was in no mood to concede a point or yield even an inch of ground. He brushed aside American women with an angry sweep of his arm. "Forget American women", he cried, "I don't care what kind of mothers-in-law they have. Let us talk about our own Indian women. What business did this silly daughter of mine have to deliver a baby smack within four months of my daughter-in-law having a baby? Shouldn't these things be done in an orderly manner? And this wife of mine is always waiting for an excuse to pack her bags and go away, leaving poor me to fend for myself. She returned a week ago and has barely unpacked her bags. And yet, the moment she receives a call from her daughter, she starts packing her bags again. She seems to have forgotten that she has a husband too, who has to be fed and cared for."

To drive home his point, he thumped me on my back so

hard that I winced. I then moved to a safe distance and said reassuringly, "I know how affectionate your wife is and I am sure she will make arrangements for you to be taken care of."

"That is what you think. You might as well know that she has already left for the United States without doing anything of that sort," cried Baloo and his words and tone dripped with poisonous sarcasm.

"Is that so?", I asked, unable to conceal my surprise. While doing so, I involuntarily took a couple of steps backward.

"It certainly is so, so let us hear what you have to say about that", asserted Baloo in a tone both triumphant and challenging.

"Knowing your wife, as I do Baloo, I am sure she wouldn't leave in such a hurry unless there was a good reason for it. Maybe your daughter is likely to have a baby any moment", I tried once again to pour oil on troubled water and restore conjugal harmony.

"Hah!", cried Baloo and continued to fume and seethe.

So in another effort to soothe his highly ruffled feelings, I said, "In any case, Baloo, this sort of thing is unlikely to happen again at least for a few years more or maybe never. For women these days do not have babies too often. In fact, many of them put an end to that sort of thing after having just one baby."

But Baloo was in no mood to see any silver linings. He growled, "Maybe they do. But there are too many of them, who are likely to seek my wife's help. Do you know that she has two nieces who live in Atlanta and Chicago? Their mother, as luck would have it, is quite unwell and cannot go to the United States. So when they decide to have their quota of babies, as they may soon do, they would call up their auntie, who happens to be my wife and tearfully beg of her to come and help. And off my wife will go and leave me alone here again to fend for myself. The only way I can make her stay here seems to be to have a baby myself."

"Now, now, Baloo. Don't get so worked up. Don't forget

that you have a problem of high blood pressure and if you carry on like this, it will shoot up dangerously. Take it easy. You already have a maidservant, who brings you packed meals twice a day from your favourite eating house. And you are always welcome at our, all your friend's, dinner tables. And you can have a good time watching movies, plays and cricket matches."

"Hah! Good time, indeed! And how am I supposed to do that, when the milkman rings the bell in the morning when I am in the toilet. And he is always in such a desperate hurry that he keeps ringing it until I rush out of the toilet and open the door and take the milk. The newspaper arrives when the milk is getting warm on the stove and by the time I go and get it, the milk boils over. I then have to clean up the stove and the cooking platform. When I light the stove again and put the teapot on it, the stove flutters and dies. The gas cylinder decides to empty itself just at the moment. So no gas and no tea. In fact, it puts paid to my efforts at cooking for that day and perhaps for a few days more. For generally the new gas cylinder is not readily available. Thereafter, I go to the bathroom to have my bath and as soon as I turn on the shower and get wet, the telephone rings. So I have to rush out to take the call. It is not uncommon on such occasions for my wet feet to slip and bring me crashing to the floor. And by the time I manage to piece myself together, the telephone stops rining and very likely an important call goes unanswered. It is terrible. This woman, this wife of mine, is inflicting on me more torture than the cruel Emperor Aurangazeb inflicted on the gallant and brave Maratha king Sambhaji."

"You shouldn't say things like that. After all she is your wife", I said, speaking up for the absent party.

"And isn't a wife supposed to take care of her husband? What good is a wife if one has to rush out of toilets to take the milk?", growled Baloo belligerently.

I could see that Baloo was in a very unreasonable frame of mind. So I said, "I can see, Baloo, that you are finding it very taxing and annoying to run a household all by yourself. So why don't you too go to the United States and stay with your daughter? Your wife can then help your daughter with the baby and you can lean back in an armchair and relax. After all you have now retired and can do what you want with your time."

"Hah!", snarled Baloo, You don't have to tell me that. That was the first thing that occurred to me when the urgent call came from my daughter. But my wife turned down the proposal peremptorily. She cried, "No. I won't have it. I don't want you there bugging me and making me run around, while I have my hands full taking care of the baby. I am too old to be able to attend to two babies."

"Did she say that?", I exclaimed. I couldn't quite believe that a woman as affectionate as Baloo's wife would say things like that.

"She certainly did! That is what things have come to", said Baloo, seething with indignation, "And mind you, the selfsame woman was at one time in love with me and married me against her parents' will. Why, she used to spend hours then talking to me and looking at me with melting eyes. Now that selfsame woman thinks that I bother and nag her all the time. That is the limit, absolutely the limit."

Baloo threw up his hands in disgust and gave me a nasty piercing look which was obviously meant for his wife.

Things were getting far too difficult but I considered it my duty to try once again to pour oil on troubled waters and restore peace and tranquillity in a friend's household. So I said, "I don't think she really meant what she said. After all, we all say such things, when we lose our tempers."

But Baloo was in no mood to listen to reason. He snorted rejection of my plea, narrowed his eyes and pinning me with a sharp thrust of his finger into my chest cried, "Raghu! It is your enormous ignorance of women that is making you talk such rubbish. But I have now learned the bitter and naked truth about women. They are dissembling cheats and inveterate liars. They are full of honeyed talk and ooze love and affection when they want to trap an innocent young man into marriage. But once the man is trapped they reveal their sharp fangs. I told my wife as much and said, "Had I known this, I wouldn't have married you at all. That would have meant no daughter and no granddaughter and nowhere to go to in Boston, Chicago or Atlanta."

It was wild talk and it was amusing to hear it from Baloo, who was so helplessly dependant on his wife that she had to tell him which dishes he enjoyed when they went to a restaurant. But I suppressed my amusement and said, "Baloo, I am sure you will deal with this situation very firmly. But as little can be done right now, why don't we go out, have a nice cup of tea at our favourite restaurant round the corner and have a quiet relaxed walk. We will then call on our schoolmate Vasoo, who lives near Shivaji Park and three of us will then go to the beach and eat bhelpuri."

That is what we used to do, when we were young college students and even though he was very angry, Baloo couldn't turn down such an attractive proposition, particularly because it reminded him of the days when there were no wives to muddy our carefree lives.

So we both set out and called on Vasoo. He was very happy to see us and welcomed us effusively. I told him of our plan to take a walk around Shivaji Park and then go to the beach and eat bhelpuri. I then added, "But before we set out we could do with a nice energizing cup of tea. Come to think of it, just a cup of tea may not be enough to put us in a cheerful frame of mind. Your wife, I remember, prepares some delicious batataphohas and maybe we could persuade her to prepare them for us."

Vasoo and his wife were very hospitable and I expected him to welcome my proposal enthusiastically. But instead of doing so, he gave me a long quizzical look and then burst into hollow, mirthless laughter.

"Ha-ha-ha!", he laughed and said, "Well! Eating those batataphoas is going to be a wee bit difficult. You will have to go all the way to Washington to savour them."

"Washington! Washington, did you say? Is your wife now in Washington? What on earth is she doing there?" I wasn't prepared for a repetition of the same story in every friend's house.

"Don't you know?", Vasoo asked, "Don't you know that this story is being repeated in all the middle-class households from one end of Mumbai to another? Mothers and grandmothers are leaving their homes in droves and planeloads of them are going to United States and Canada or coming back from there."

"But why? What is the cause of this heavy traffic?", I asked.

"Well! It is the basic economic principle of supply and demand that is at work here. Mothers and grandmothers are in great demand abroad. That is because they serve many needs. They help the arrival of babies, take care of them in the initial months and they also cook tasty Indian meals which are so difficult to get or cook in those foreign lands", explained Vasoo, and it was a very neat and comprehensive explanation.

"And where does that leave the father and grandfathers? Don't they sweat and toil for the family? Are they absolutely redundant and useless? Who holds the baby when its diaper is being changed by its mother? I can still remember at least six different occasions when I have done it. And I am sure that you and Raghu have done it too. And if you women consider us to be redundant and useless, why do you marry us? Don't do it. But if you do, we won't let you treat us like dirt", cried Baloo, rolling his eyes and striking his most belligerent stance.

Vasoo said, "I know how you feel, Baloo, and my sympathies are fully with you. But let me tell you that to live in a house where a mother and a grandmother are engaged in taking care of a newly arrived baby is not at all a pleasant experience. It is neither pleasant here, nor in the United States, where all you have to do in life is to push a few buttons. I have gone through that experience once. And I don't want to do that ever again."

Baloo was quite surprised to hear that and asked, "Why do you say that? Did your wife nag you when you were there? Or did she make you change diapers all the time?"

Vasoo said, "Oh, she was itching to do that, but I put my foot down and said that I will have nothing - absolutely nothing to do with diapers. It was neither my wife and daughter, nor the newly arrived baby who drove me crazy. That was done by the three-year-old elder sister of the baby."

"A little child? A three-year-old child? And it drove you crazy? How could it?", I asked and laughed in disbelief.

"Let me tell you, Raghu, a little three-year-old child can drive you crazy and cause sprains, aches and even fractures", said Vasoo. It not only walks but runs, climbs up and down steps, pushes and pulls chairs, pulls down heavy boxes from shelves and swallows coins and pins too. Therefore, one has to be constantly alert and run like a gazelle to prevent it from falling, toppling, getting crushed under a chair or getting choked. In those frequent mad dashes one is in imminent danger of spraining one's ankle or neck or even fracturing one's arm or leg or both", Vasoo explained to me the dangers of accompanying one's wife who goes abroad to help with a new baby.

I shook my head in disbelief and asked, "How come none of our children caused me any such trouble when they were little?"

Vasoo laughed and said, "That is what you think. But actually they did all these things. However, in those days, there used to be grandmothers and other elderly women around, who looked after our children. That is not so any more. Looking after children is no longer considered to be a lifelong occupation by elderly women. They go to women's clubs or on Himalayan treks. So it is now the grandfathers who are expected to look after children."

"But they do have day care centres in United States, don't they?", I asked, seeing a ray of hope.

"Yes. But they look after a child for eight hours or so. It is very much on the fathers' and grandfathers' hands for the rest of the sixteen hours", Vasoo quickly smothered the ray of hope. He then added, "And our women no longer respect the menfolk as they used to do in the good old days. They nag and badger them until they start doing the household chores. And there is not the slightest sympathy for the hardships he has to suffer. I distinctly remember two instances of such callous lack of sympathy. In one instance my little granddaughter bit me so hard that she drew blood and I screamed. On another occasion, while I was asleep, she knocked her head against my nose. That made me scream too. But on both the occasions I didn't have even an iota of sympathy from my wife. On the contrary she admonished me for making a fuss over such trivial things."

Baloo had initially responded most enthusiastically to my suggestion that he should follow his wife and go and stay with his daughter abroad. But on hearing Vasoo's dire warnings he had second thoughts. It seemed to him that his life would be a tale of woes whether he stayed on here or went abroad to stay with his daughter.

I pondered over the problem and said, "It seems to me that the root cause of our troubles is the lack of patriotic love for the country in our younger generation. That is why they rush off to foreign countries looking for better jobs. The consequence is that their babies are born there and their mothers fly there to help with the babies. And we are left here to fend for ourselves and suffer all kinds of miseries. If only they had been patriotic and stayed on in their own country, we could have lived trouble-free and happy lives."

Both Baloo and Vasoo nodded in agreement and sighed. We sat there quietly for a while thinking nostalgically of the good old days when grandfathers enjoyed a long and happy old age. I saw myself as a grandfather in the good old days relaxing in an armchair and enjoying respectful attention lavished on me by my wife and children. I was particularly tickled to see my wife massaging my feet with oil. While she did so, my daughter-in-law came respectfully with a nice tasty snack which she had specially prepared for me. The grandchildren busily crushed betelnut with a pestle, so that I could eat it with my toothless mouth. My son then came in and dutifully handed over his salary to me for it to be spent wisely on the household and took instructions about writing letters to relatives. The nephews called on me later to pay respects and seek guidance on important matters. Later in the afternoon the postman brought letters from my younger brother and cousin. My brother lived in Belgaum, while my cousin lived in Kolhapur. In their letters they paid their respects and invited me and my wife to Belgaum and Kolhapur both of which had a salubrious climate.

I then looked with an indulgent smile at my wife who was dutifully massaging my feet and asked, "So, where would you like to go? Will it be Belgaum or Kolhapur? We have invitations to both these places."

Seeing how much I was respected by my relatives, she looked at me with worshipful eyes.

I smiled and said, "You have not answered my question. Shall we go to Belgaum or to Kolhapur?"

She was quite flustered and confused and said, "I, poor thing, will follow in your footsteps wherever you go."

The poor woman was not used to taking decisions. They were all taken for her by me. She blushed and looked at the floor.

I laughed heartily at her confusion and said, "Well, well! I think we will go to Belgaum this time. During our stay there, we will hire a car and visit all the temples in Goa, which you have been wanting to do."

My wife was so amazed that her mouth fell open and she quickly covered it with the palm of her hand. She cried, "You mean, we will not take a bus but hire a car all for ourselves? Wouldn't it cost a fortune? Can we really afford it?"

I passed my hand over my ample moustache and said, "Why do you worry about expenses? You don't have to, when I am there to take care of all these things. All you have to do is to enjoy all the good things that come your way."

My wife pulled the pallu of her saree, wrapped it more neatly around her and looking down said nothing. She felt very abashed and happy too.

I enjoyed seeing her so abashed and confused. So I laughed loudly and said, "Don't you worry about money. I will take care of that. You only have to make up your mind about what nice things you would buy in Belgaum and Goa. On that matter, I won't be able to help you. You will have to decide for yourself."

Pleased with my little joke, I laughed uproariously.

My little grandson stood there clinging to his grandmother for protection. I looked at him and being in a very generous mood, asked him, "And how about you? Would you like to accompany your grandma to Belgaum? You can then do all the running around for her. So she won't have to attend to all the little chores. She can then sit quietly and read the holy Dnyaneshwari."

My grandson clung still more closely to his grandmother and said dutifully, "Yes, Grandpa."

At this point my wife wiped with a piece of cloth the foot she had massaged for so long and then motioned me to extend the other foot to be massaged. I was in a jolly mood so I extended the other foot and mischievously put it right on her lap. She blushed and bent her head in embarassment and that made me burst into uproarious laughter.

I had wandered deep into a dreamland that was as removed from reality as a frog is from a lion. And when my friend Baloo shook me and brought me back into the real world, I felt quite embarrassed and foolish. Had my wife come to know about my fantasies, she would have poured a bucket of water on my head.

Baloo shook me and said, "What makes you smile? What are you thinking of? Come on, let us go out and sit on the sands in the Dadar beach."

"Yes. Yes. Let us go", I said and told myself that the kind of princely life my grandfather lived was not for me.

I no doubt have a handful of nephews and nieces. But none of them lives in Belgaum or Kolhapur. Why, one of them lives in Toronto and the other is settled in Geneva. They do send letters to us. But those letters invite not me but my wife, who frequently goes abroad.

When such a letter is received, she sends a reply assuring that she would spend a few days in Geneva, on her way to Detroit.

That makes me give a start and I ask, "Eh? Are you planning to go to Detroit? When is that?"

"What do you mean, when? I have to be there in June", she asserts, warning me with a stern look that she doesn't want to hear any arguments over the matter.

But that talk of a visit to Detroit gets me quite worried and I ask hesitantly, "I...err...I mean, the plane fare. It is quite a tidy amount, isn't it? I wonder whether we can afford it."

My wife glares at me and says, "Of course, we can't afford it. I won't be able to travel beyond the nearby hill stations of Lonavala and Matheran if I have to depend on your for my travel expenses. But don't you worry. Don't worry at all. My daughter will send me an air ticket."

I then look away shamefacedly and keep quiet. Oh, how things have changed since the days of my grandpa!

I sighed and followed Vasoo and Baloo down the stairs of Vasoo's flat into the street.

As we walked around the Shivaji Park, Vasoo said, "Can you see that house? That is where our college mate Madhu lives. He used to be always with us when we were at college. Let us see if he is at home. We, all four of us, will then go to the beach and have a good time and forget our wives who seem to be bent on deserting us."

It was a good idea and we all concurred with him.

As we walked towards Madhu's house, Vasoo observed, "Well! This guy Madhu is the luckiest of us all. Unlike our children, his children have not gone and settled abroad. His daughter, who is married, lives in the steel town of Jamshedpur, while his son lives with him right here in Mumbai. The son works for a German company, while his daughter-in-law is employed in the Atomic Energy Commission. Thus, this lucky guy Madhu has two women in his house. Sometimes his daughter comes to visit him and then he has three women in the house. They run the household, and he doesn't have to worry about a thing. Well, he buys vegetables and runs a few errands. But apart from that he generally leads a relaxed, retired life."

Baloo got a little peeved on hearing this tale of Madhu's good fortune. He said, "Since we were boys, this guy Madhu has been having a good time while we poor chaps have had to slog and toil. That is not fair. I mean it is pretty mean and selfish of Madhu to enjoy all the good luck that there is."

Soon we reached Madhu's house and rang the doorbell. We were expecting the effusive welcome which is extended to all school-mates and we looked forward to being served hot tea and tasty bhajias by his hospitable wife. But instead the door was opened by an irate Madhu who had an admonishing shh...on his lips and a threatening look in his eyes.

This took us quite by surprise and Baloo cried, "Madhu what on earth is the matter with you? What has gone wrong?"

"Shhh...", said Madhu in a tone that was even more hushed and more intimidating.

We couldn't make out at all the reason for his strange and unfriendly behaviour. So Vasoo opened his mouth to say something.

But he never managed to say it. For Madhu's hand shot out and was tightly clamped on Vasoo's mouth. He then said in a voice that was as threatening as it was hushed, "Be quiet! Don't make any noise."

So Baloo too lowered his voice to a hoarse whisper and asked, "Why?"

Vasoo wanted to articulate a question but he thought better of it and asked it with a clumsy movement of his hand.

I too expressed my surprise at this strange behaviour with lifted eyebrows and dilated eyes.

"My grandchildren...they are asleep", he answered in a strangled voice.

"Asleep!", I exclaimed, still not getting a hang of the situation.

"I have at last managed to put them to sleep with great difficulty", he whispered in my ear with cupped hands.

That tickled my ear and I broke into a rather loud giggle.

Madhu promptly gagged my mouth with his hand.

Baloo wisely decided to use not speech but gestures to carry on the conversation and asked how many grandchildren Madhu had.

Madhu spoke with his fingers and wiggled two of them to answer the query.

"How old are they?", I asked, gesturing with my hands and lip-syncing the words.

Madhu replied with gestures that gave us to understand that one of them was three-year-old and the other was six-month-old. He had to make quite an effort to remove Baloo's misunderstanding that the second one was six-years-old.

"And where is your wife?", I asked again in a language of gestures and unarticulated words.

Madhu lifted his hand and pointed skywards.

"Good heavens!" cried Baloo, "Is she...?"

He then choked his voice by clamping his own hand on his mouth and pointed with his finger heavenwards to indicate what he feared had happened to Madhu's wife.

Madhu shook his head in annoyance to remove the misunderstanding and shook his finger in the northerly direction.

I nodded to indicate that I had understood what he meant and explained to Baloo in a strangled whisper, "She has gone downstairs to the grocery store."

Madhu struck his head with his palm in exasperation and cried in my ear in an angry and almost inaudible whisper, "Jamshedpur, Jamshedpur! You idiots!"

As I was the only one who had heard him, I whispered in Baloo's ear, "She has gone to visit her daughter in Jamshedpur!"

Baloo then repeated those words in Vasoo's ears.

Madu confirmed with several nods that at last he had been correctly understood.

We were all relieved to know that nothing untoward had happened and expressed our feelings with nods and silent smiles.

Suddenly a loud wail shattered the silence, which we had taken so much trouble to maintain and it was followed by a loud bawling of a child.

Soon another child joined in a voice that was initially weak but gathered strength with every wail.

Madhu clutched his head and rushed inside in a frenzied run. We then followed him fearing that we may have to witness some gruesome disaster.

There was happily no disaster but two children, one a three year-old boy and the other a six-month-old baby girl, who were awake and seemed to be utterly miserable about it.

They were not accusing us in so many words but nonetheless making us feel very guilty. Children, I have observed, are extremely good at this.

Madhu picked up the little girl, held her in a gentle embrace and began to sway sideways like a waddling bear. But that did not at all have the expected soothing effect on the baby.

Baloo, it seemed, had some experience in pacifying wailing babies. He said, "You know what, when my granddaughter was once crying without respite, I covered myself with a bedsheet. She was so amazed by the transformation in me, that she stopped crying and watched me in astonishment."

Vasoo quickly pulled a bedsheet off a bed and threw it over Baloo's head. But that had no effect at all on Madhu's granddaughter, who refused to take notice of it. She was one of the babies who close their eyes to concentrate entirely on the business of crying lustily.

When both Madhu and Baloo's recipes for pacifying crying children failed, Vasoo suggested an alternative stratagem. He said, "My experience is that if you give a child a sweet laddu to eat it stops crying and begins eating it. That is what my mother used to do when I cried as a boy."

Madhu took his advice with alacrity. He rushed into the kitchen and came back with a sweet.

However, the baby wouldn't even look at it. It seemed that she had not yet developed a taste for laddus.

But Madhu's three-year-old grandson took hold of it preemptorily, stopped crying and started eating it in large mouthfuls.

We were pleased by the result of Vasoo's stratagem and expected Madhu to be pleased too. Instead he began to pummel his own head with both his fists in dire distress.

He then tried to snatch the laddu from his grandson's hand. The grandson tightened his grip on the laddu and shrieked so loudly in protest that we all fell back.

Madhu's behaviour made no sense to me. So I said, "Why do you want to do that? Let him eat the laddu. He has stopped crying, hasn't he?"

Madhu cried, "Stop him! Stop him! That boy has been eating various kinds of sweets for all of the last twenty-four hours and, you know what, he has not puked even once. At this rate, I am terribly afraid that his tummy may burst like an overblown tyre tube."

We looked at the boy's tummy and it looked so overdistended that Madhu's fears seemed to be well founded.

In fact, we too got quite worried and eyed each other with wrinkled brows. Baloo felt the boy's tummy and said, "This seems to me alarming and I think that emergency measures are called for."

"Don't I know it? I am scared to death," cried Madhu, "why, I have sent a terse fax to Houston "Eats constantly and hasn't puked in twenty-four hours. Will the tummy burst? Advise immediately."

"A fax? To Houston? What for?" We all cried in bewilderment, "What on earth has Houston to do with pukes of babies? Have the Americans established a specialized medical centre there to handle this specific problem?"

That, we found, was not the case. Madhu explained, "I faxed to Houston, because my daughter-in-law, the mother of these two kids, is there."

"There? At Houston? But she works right here in Mumbai for the Atomic Energy Establishment, doesn't she? How come she is there?"

"She is there, because she has been sent there by her employers, the Atomic Energy Establishment. She is participating in a week-long conference there", explained Madhu.

"And she has left the children here, with you, has she?", we asked.

"She pleaded and begged that I should take care of the children for eight days! She said that it was very important that she should attend the conference. She was in tears", explained Madhu further.

"And your heart melted with those tears, did it?", asked Baloo sternly.

"That is a very bad habit", said Vasoo, "If you let women melt your heart with their tears, you will never know where you will end up."

I said, "You should have brushed aside those tears and firmly said, 'No. I won't do it.'"

"Yes, I did! But she wasn't there to hear what I said. She had swooshed out of the house and vanished", said Madhu.

"Good God", cried Baloo, "These young women are getting quite out of hand."

"Well, well! Now that she is gone, nothing can be done about it", Vasoo observed in a resigned voice.

"Ha!", cried Baloo, "Poor Madhu! And we thought that he was a lucky guy because his son and daughter-in-law are living right here in Mumbai!"

I could see that although he was full of sympathy for Madhu, he was not altogether displeased to find Madhu in the same boat as himself.

Vasoo continued to be preoccupied with the serious problem in hand and asked impatiently, "Forget everything else. What reply did you get from Houston?"

"My daughter-in-law sent a reply via satellite communication. It said tersely, "Don't know. Ask mother-in-law."

Vasoo was furious. He cried, "This stupid girl doesn't know the answer to such a simple problem. How is it that she has been appointed by the Atomic Energy Commission to produce, maybe, an atom bomb? She ought to be..."

"Oh, cut that out", Baloo cried impatiently and asked Madhu, "Did you then manage to contact your wife and get her advice on this matter, which seems to be of great urgency?"

"I have been trying since morning but the telephone lines seem to be out of order", said Madhu, who was a picture of misery and distress.

Baloo said, "Do you know how to get round this kind of problem? You should ring up somebody in London and ask him to ring up Jamshedpur, get the advice and communicate it to us. It is strange. But it seems to be easier to reach any place in our country via London rather than directly."

Madhu said, "I did exactly that. I rang up my nephew who lives in London and I am waiting for him to call back."

While we were frantically trying to find a solution to the emergency he had created, the little boy ate the big laddu and demanded another. When Madhu refused to give it to him, he threw a tantrum so terrible that it scared us out of our wits.

Madhu was at his wit's end and began to pummel his head with both fists. That distressed us but had no effect whatsoever on that boy.

The little girl had for some unknown reason stopped crying and was savouring a toy tiger. The boy's tantrum, however, scared her and she began to emit a series of ear-piercing screams.

To pacify her, Baloo picked her up and began to sway and dance and sing a lullaby.

I can't say whether it was the effect of his weird dancing or the hoarse lullaby but the little girl opened her eyes and began to look at him in round-eyed astonishment.

Baloo was pleased with the results of his efforts and seeing that the girl was quiet tried to reason with her. He said, "Oh little darling, why do you cry? It is not good for you, you know. If you cry, your throat will be sore and even your ear may begin to hurt."

Madhu's granddaughter listened to Baloo attentively, looking at him steadily and with interest.

That pleased Baloo even more. He looked at us and said, "Look! How quietly and attentively she listens. Children, I believe, are very reasonable. One has only to explain things to them properly."

At that moment, Madhu's granddaughter suddenly caught hold of Baloo's glasses and pulled them off his nose.

"My glasses! Oh, my glasses! They will break", cried Baloo and tried to pull them out of the girl's hand.

But she clamped her fingers on them like a vice and began to scream at the top of her voice.

At this juncture, Madhu intervened decisively. He took hold of his granddaughter and pushed Baloo away.

Baloo's glasses were still in her hands and her fingers were clamped around them.

Baloo wailed plaintively, "My glasses! My glasses!"

Madhu admonished him and said sternly, "Now, now, Baloo, don't be absurd. Grown-up chaps like you and me ought not to quarrel with little babies. You can see that she has taken a fancy for your glasses. She is holding them firmly and trying to eat them. The main thing is she has stopped crying. So let her have the glasses."

"But I can't see a thing without them", pleaded Baloo plaintively.

"In that case, buy new glasses. I will pay for them", said Madhu in a tone which was quite unsympathetic.

"But that will take at least a couple of days. How on earth will I carry on in the meanwhile?", Baloo was almost in tears.

Madhu cried, "So you are worried only about yourself, are you? I have to take care of these two kids for two more days all by myself and that is driving me crazy. What am I supposed to do, if chaps like you snatch things out of the kids' hands and make them cry?"

At this juncture I asked a very pertinent question which had been bothering me for some time. I asked Madhu, "Why on earth are you doing this single-handedly? Your son, these kids' father, is here in Mumbai, isn't he? Why don't you ask him to take a couple of days off and share this onerous burden, which incidentally is entirely of his making."

Madhu cried, "That is precisely what I told him. 'They are your children so you have to look after them', I said, But his employers have chosen precisely this moment to confer on him a promotion and asked him to go immediately to Germany on an important assignment. He rushed to me and begged of me to take care of the kids for two days. 'I will finish my work and will be back in two days', he pleaded. Under the circumstances, I couldn't possibly say 'no'. Could I?"

"Well! I can see that you couldn't refuse. But in that case, why don't you send the children to your daughter-in-law's mother. Isn't she supposed to pitch in and help in a situation like this?"

Madhu stared at me like a man demented and laughed bitterly. He cried, "Do you think I am such a nitwit that this didn't occur to me? But you know what. That woman is now in Philadelphia taking care of her other daughter's new-born baby."

"In that case, at least your daughter-in-law's father should have come here to help. What on earth is he doing? Where is he?", I protested angrily.

Madhu cried, "Ha, Ha! Being a sensible guy, he is up there in heavens, far from all these troubles."

That stumped us all. Mind you Baloo, Vasoo and I have held important positions and dealt with very complex and difficult problems, when we were working. But we could find no solution to the predicament in which Madhu had been placed by his grandchildren. All we could do was to offer to spend the night with him and help him as best as we could.

Poor Baloo couldn't see properly without his glasses and stumbled as he walked. So Vasoo and I took him to an optician and ordered new glasses for him. We then shepherded him to his home and wended our way housewards pondering over the intractable problems with which Madhu was faced.

As we walked, Vasoo suddenly stopped, gripped my shoulder and said, "There is really a simple solution to this problem. Madhu should marry again right away and have a second wife, as our wise ancestors used to do. She would then take care of the grandchildren."

Absurd though it looked, it was a brilliant and yet very simple solution to an intractable situation. Our wise ancestors knew this and always had an extra wife or two to deal with such eventualities.

The trouble was that this sensible practice had been declared illegal by an Act of Parliament. And that is considered to be progress.

❑

7

Trouble Brews in Girgaum Kitchens

We kids in the Madhavji chawl always looked forward to the Sunday lunch, which used to be a sumptuous meal with a mouth-watering sweet dish as its highlight. The women in our households took a while to cook it and we romped and played while they were busy at it. That and the long wait whetted our appetites which made the lunch even more delicious.

Unfortunately on that Sunday, things went wrong in almost all the twenty kitchens in our chawl. My mother had planned to cook for us sweet rice seasoned with raisins, sliced almonds and saffron and I licked my lips as I looked forward to eating it. But it got burnt and was ruined. Bapu's mother got so worked up that she added salt and chilli powder thrice to the vegetable on the stove. The big pot in which Madhu's mother was preparing kheer was overturned, while at Nana's home...but, it is too painful to recount the disasters in the various kitchens in our chawl. The upshot was that mothers were upset, fathers were annoyed and hot words flew around in the various households.

When this sort of thing happens in a family, all the anger is taken out on the poor kids. So Bapu, Madhu, I and all the other kids had a hard time on that Sunday. My father had promised to buy me new shoes that weekend. But when I reminded him about it, his eyes became so big that I hastily beat a retreat. Had I tarried a wee bit longer hoping that he would change his mind, I would have received a stinging slap on my behind. Sensing how annoyed his father was, Vinoo was quietly slinking out of the house. But unfortunately, he caught his father's eye. The result was that he was scolded for neglecting his lessons and asked to solve fifteen tedious examples in the arithmetic textbook. Poor Visoo struggled with those examples till it was dark. Madhu wanted his father to buy him a lead pencil and a rubber. He got a whack on his back instead, and his father cried, "I have asked you umpteen times to learn by heart the hymns of adoration of Lord Ram. Have you done that?"

Madhu hadn't, so the poor lad swotted till dinner time. Poor Sadu.... But I think I have told you enough to make my point.

Well, everybody knows that mothers have a habit of rushing around doing a lot of other things when they cook. Things, therefore, do go wrong in the kitchen occasionally. But you might wonder how things went wrong in all the twenty kitchens in our chawl. In fact, the impression might get around that the mothers of all of us kids were poor cooks. I won't deny that mothers in our chawl had their failings as cooks. Some baked chapatis that were difficult to bite and chew. Some were prone to add too much chilli powder to the curry and some were pretty stingy when serving mango jam. But by and large they cooked food that was reasonably tasty.

What was it then that caused disasters in all the kitchens that Sunday? Did anything happen in our chawl that upset all the womenfolk? Was there a big quarrel? No, there wasn't. Then truth of the matter is that nothing untoward had happened in our chawl that weekend. The source of the trouble, as I came to know later, was in the Ismail chawl located in distant Thakurdwar area. At least a mile separated our chawl from this Ismail chawl and it wasn't at all easy for women in our chawl to visit it. For instance, Grandma Bhagirathi in our chawl found it extremely difficult to visit her niece who lived in Ismail chawl. After every visit her feet ached so much that she whined and grunted no end and complained so loudly that nobody could live in peace in her house. The daugher-in law had to massage grandma's feet with oil and a hot water bag so that the household could sleep in peace. My friend Nana's grandfather also insisted on visiting his cousin who lived there. After each visit, he sat in his doorway nursing his knees and told every passerby in great detail of the shooting pain in each of his two knees. Even my mother... but I think I have said enough to make my point; which is that communication between our two chawls was not easy. How then, you might wonder, could something that happened in Ismail chawl have such a catastrophic effect on the festive Sunday lunch in our chawl?

Well, I think that the best thing to do would be to tell you about all the things that happened that day since early morning.

I believe it all started when our Narmada auntie called on my mother that morning. This was unusual and so I pricked my ears, although I was busy doing my homework.

I said that this visit of Narmada auntie was unusual; because in those good old days, women did not call on each other on holidays. This was because menfolk were at home on those days, and a woman had to walk past them in the living room before she reached the kitchen to meet the women in the household. This was considered improper and women therefore avoided it. Things have changed now and women aren't bothered any more about men being around when they visit each other. My mother, who is now old, resents this. She says, "Women in these days don't care to observe the proprieties. They walk past menfolk even without caring to wrap the pallus of their saree properly and modestly around their shoulders. Women used to observe these proprieties in the days of my youth."

In those days, not only were men at home on Sunday but made demands that kept women busy in the kitchen all through the day. They had to prepare some savoury snacks like pohe and shira to go with the morning tea. Thereafter they were kept extremely busy preparing the elaborate holiday lunch. Relatives and friends customarily called on each other on holidays and they were customarily welcomed with tea and savoury snacks. This inevitably delayed the lunch well past midday and it was nearly three o'clock in the afternoon by the time the women cleaned up the kitchen after the lunch. Thereafter, they had hardly any time for a catnap, before menfolk woke up from their post-lunch siesta. So the women were up again and busy preparing tea for the menfolk. By the time the leisurely afternoon tea was over, the women had to get busy preparing dinner. With such a hectic schedule, it was impossible for a women to visit a neighbour or a relative on a Sunday even if she wanted to.

If, therefore, Narmada auntie had come over to our house on a Sunday morning, something really important was on the boil. She lived in a chawl across the small yard in our wadi (neighbourhood). It was, therefore, a short walk for her to our house and she used to visit us not infrequently. And if she had called on mother on any other day, I would have hardly noticed it. But when she came on a busy Sunday morning, as I said earlier, I pricked my ears.

Auntie had wrapped the pallu of her saree over her shoulders and covered herself fully. So the little pot she carried in her hand underneath the pallu was not noticed. But we kids had a keen eye for whatever mothers and aunties were upto. For those bits of information came in handy to us in more ways than one.

Mother saw auntie Narmada enter the kitchen. She, therefore, wiped her busy hands on the pallu of her saree and stepping forward said, "What made you find time for us so early on a busy Sunday morning?"

Auntie held out the pot which was so far concealed underneath the pallu of her saree and said, "I really don't know how I managed it. Why, I haven't had time even to breathe since I got out of bed. But I remembered that I had forgotten for far too many days to return the potful of chapati flour I had borrowed from you. So I decided to return it right away, before I forgot about it all over again."

Mother protested, "Ha! There was really no reason to rush to return a mere potful of flour. After all it would not have run away and vanished, if it had remained in your kitchen a few days more."

Narmada auntie said, "I have so many things to remember that I keep forgetting them all the time. I remembered today that I had remembered and forgotten about that potful of flour no less than five times. I absolutely did not want to forget about it a sixth time. So I decided to get it over with right away."

Mother took the pot auntie Narmada had brought and after a quick glance at it put it on the cooking platform. Nobody else would have noticed that quick glance of hers. But I knew why she did that. She wanted to check whether the pot was as full as it was when she had given it to Narmada auntie. Often it wasn't.

Narmada Auntie too had noticed that glance of hers and said, "I hope I have returned as much as I took. The pot was full upto its neck when I took it and so I think it is now."

"Oh really", protested mother, "After all it is all within the family. So a little bit here or a little bit there doesn't really matter."

Narmada auntie said, "That is all very true. But after all we have our households to run and we have to watch every penny to make ends meet. We are not like some folks, who can throw away fifty and seventy-five rupees to buy things that catch their fancy."

That last sentence was loaded with a lot of meaning and that was brought out by the tone of auntie's voice and a meaningful thrust of her chin. Her eyes became big too and she stared at mother to find out if the full import of what she had said had sunk in.

My mother, like most women in our *chawl* was quick on the uptake in such matters and in any case the way Narmada auntie had put it, she couldn't have missed the hidden import even if she had wanted to. So her eyes became big too and she said, "Throw away fifty or even seventy-five rupees? As if they are mere pieces of paper? Is there such a wealthy woman in our midst?"

"Hasn't this reached your ears?", Narmada auntie stared at mother in disbelief. Her mouth opened so wide in astonishment that she cupped it with the palm of her hand.

Mother moved a couple of steps closer to Narmada auntie and said in a confidential whisper, "No! I must confess that I know nothing about this matter, what on earth happened? Who are your talking about?"

I, for the life of me, couldn't gather where this talk which started with a potful of flour was heading. But I could see in it a spicy tale. I had heard women's talk in our chawl since I was a baby following my mother wherever she went and I could smell a good story when it was coming. So I stopped cramming the list of India's imports and moved a little closer to hear the whispered conversation. Naturally I did it unobstrusively without letting my mother notice it.

Narmada auntie was almost choking with astonishment when she gasped, "Goodness me! Do you mean to say that she has kept even you in the dark? You who are so close to her! It seems that some women are so secretive that they wouldn't let even buttermilk know that salt is being added to it."

My mother was pretty good at noticing the hidden import of what was being said. But even she couldn't make head or tail of what she was being told. This seemed to give a little pleasure to Narmada auntie, who watched her with wide-eyed interest and amusement.

My mother continued to flounder and said, "Who could that be — I mean this person who you say is very close to me? And what has she done? Which is the buttermilk and which is the salt? I cannot make head or tail of what you are saying."

Narmada auntie said, "Oh really! It is Vatsalabai I am talking about!"

Mother was still confused. "Vatsalabai? Do you mean the one that lives in Shastri apartments in the distant Grant Road area?"

I had heard women's talk so often, that I had become quite clever in putting two and two together. In fact, I was better at it than mother was. So I knew, therefore, who Narmada auntie was talking about, and I didn't want my mother to flounder any more. So I impatiently butted into the conversation without realizing what I was doing. I cried, "It is simple, Mom! The Vatsalabai she is talking about is the one who lives in the Ismail chawl at Thakurdwar."

Narmada auntie nodded approvingly and said, "He is right. The Vatsalabai I am talking about is the one who lives at Thakurdwar."

I grinned and said, "Do your see, Mom? I never make a mistake in such matters."

That did it. Mother gave me a sharp look and cried, "You meddlesome boy! You have formed a bad habit of poking your nose in women's talk. That, I must tell you, is none of your business. You better keep out of it and do your lessons properly. You would then not be scolded by your father and your teachers for your poor grades."

That is what mothers were like when we were kids. I had been of help to her and instead of being appreciated I was being scolded. I was, therefore, naturally disgusted and decided to have nothing to do with Mom's affairs any more. I took my book in hand and began to swot the exports of India, "Oilseeds, hides and skins, tea..."

After scolding me, mother turned towards Narmada auntie and said, "So it is that Vatsalabai you were talking about. I certainly know her very well. How could I not, when she happens to be the sister-in-law of my sister? I know that she is a...bit different. Does things that are, well, odd."

"Odd, did you say? Well! What she has done now goes well beyond being odd", said Narmada auntie.

"Is that so? What has she done now? I hope she hasn't taken to those new fangled ways of draping her saree. Some of the girls, studying in colleges, have gone overboard in these matters. I hang my head in shame, when I see them running wild."

"Well! I wouldn't be surprised if one of these days, she is seen wearing an English style skirt exposing her legs right upto her knees But what she has done only the other day is something altogether crazy."

"What could that be? Do tell me right away," cried mother.

Narmada auntie lowered her voice and said in an awed voice, "Do you know what? She went out and bought a machine, as casually as one buys vegetables!"

"Machine? What sort of machine? What does a woman have to to with a machine?", Mother asked in bewilderment.

Mother was being real dumb and I couldn't stand it. So I cried, "Mom, do you really have to ask that? That machine could only be a sewing machine, nothing else."

Mother looked at me to fully absorb what I said and then turning to Narmada auntie asked, "Is that so?"

Narmada auntie nodded to say yes and I couldn't help saying, "Look, Mom! Didn't I tell you so?"

Mother looked at me again and this time big angry furrows appeared on her brow. She cried, "There you go again, meddler. Now will you pay attention to your lessons, or do you want me to pull your ears?"

That did it - I said to myself, "Never again" and began to swot India's exports. I recounted loudly, "India exports mineral oil, machinery, textiles..."

But my lessons were again interrupted by women's talk. Mother said in a hushed voice, "Is that what she has done? Bought a sewing machine? And a brand new one at that? As casually as one buys vegetables? You mean she just walked into a shop and bought a whole new sewing machine? These machines cost nothing less than a fortune, I am told!"

"Of course, they do. Do you know how much a new sewing machine costs? Nothing less than seventy-five rupees. Do you get it? Seventy rupees and five rupees more on the top of that!" Narmada auntie was so overwhelmed by the enormous amount she mentioned, that she lowered her voice and whispered it in mother's ears.

My mother's eyes became so big that it seemed they would pop out any moment. She cried out and then quickly lowered her voice to say, "Seventy-five, did you say? Good heavens, that almost amounts to two months' salary paid by the Great Indian Peninsula Railway. And such a big amount she just threw away at one go, did she? Didn't she flinch and panic when she did that? I can't even imagine anybody doing that and least of all a woman."

At this juncture my nostrils sensed that something was burning. I sniffed and realized that the burning smell came from our kitchen. I had decided not to meddle in mother's affairs any more. But this was a serious matter. So I said, "Mom!"

Mother didn't like the interruption at all. She cried, "Shut up! No. Not a word from you any more. Keep quiet and do your lessons."

Narmada auntie continued to tell her story with great relish. She said, "It was madness — sheer and enormous. Usually when one decides on such a big buy, one ponders and talks the matter over with elders, relatives and friends It is also customary to go to a temple and find out if the gods favour such a purchase. The astrologer and family priest have to be consulted too to find out whether the stars favour the purchase and also about an auspicious day for making it."

My mother nodded agreement and said, "Yes! That is how such things are done. But she has gone and bought the sewing machine very secretively all by herself. She seems to be the kind of person who doesn't let the left ear know what the right ear has heard. I wonder how you came to know about it."

"My neighbour Ganga auntie came to know about it, when she called on her cousin who lives there."

At this juncture, the burning smell became so strong that

it stung Narmada auntie's nose too and she asked mother, "Is anything cooking on the stove?"

Mother's nose wrinkled too and she screamed, "Oh my mother! That is the end of my sweet rice!"

This reminded Narmada auntie that she had put on the stove three seers of milk to prepare kheer which was uncle's favourite dish.

She clutched her head and screamed, "My mother! My kheer."

She then ran out of the house as if she was on fire.

At the same time my mother rushed out of the kitchen pounding her head with her fists, "It's all over. The sweet rice is ruined."

She then noticed me and as is usual with mothers pinned it all on me. She cried, "You stupid boy! You always poke your nose into things that are none of your business Why then didn't you meddle when my sweet rice was getting burnt?"

I protested, "But, Mom, I did tell you as soon as I smelt something burning. But you asked me to shut up."

She screamed, "And on the top of it, you are talking back, are you? A whack on your back, that is what..."

I knew what was coming and took to my heels in a flash. I then spent some time in the long verandah of the chawl, brooding over the unfairness of women in general and my mother in particular.

After a while I saw mother walking out of our house. She had, as propriety demanded, wrapped the pallu of her saree over her shoulders and covered herself to her finger tips. Knowing the ways of women I looked at her closely and noticed that she was carrying a bowl in her right hand underneath the pallu. I guessed that she was going to one of our neighbours to give her something. As she walked with hurried steps, my friend Madhu's mother emerged out of her house in a great hurry.

She paused when she saw my mother and said, "Goodness me! Are you going out somewhere?"

"Well! It was you I wanted to meet", said mother.

"And I was on my way to visit you", exclaimed Madhu's mother and added with a smile, "What a coincidence!"

So they both walked back smiling to our house. I smelled right away that something was brewing, That was none of my business and I wanted to keep as far away from it as possible. However, I had to go into our house because I had geography lessons to do. So I went into the house, quickly picked up my geography book and began to swot India's exports, "Oilseeds, cotton, hides and skins, tea..."

I was concentrating on my lessons but couldn't help overhearing the talk in the kitchen. Madhu's mother said, "Ganpatrao has had a big raise recently and it is being said that he now earns one hundred and seventy-five rupees a month. That is a lot of money and it is spilling out of his pockets into Vatsalabai's hands. Her hands have an itch and they itch all the more because of all that money pouring into them. So she goes about throwing that money around. The whole Ismail chawl is agog with stories about how she spends fistful of rupees on this and that and anything else."

My mother simply gaped at what she heard. "One hundred and seventy-five rupees, did you say? All of the one hundred and seventy-five rupees?"

"Yes. Could be even more. Well! You know, don't you, how people like to pretend that they are earning much less than what they really do", asserted Madhu's mother.

Eventually mother recovered from the shock of surprise and said, "But even for Ganapatrao seventy-five rupees is not peanuts and to throw it away on buying a new fangled sewing machine doesn't seem right. After all, there is the family to be looked after and children to be reared. Inevitably, there will be thread ceremonies and marriages to celebrate. Moreover, sensible people do provide for their old age. Take our case. We may not be earning all that much. But the money that comes into our home every month is not something to be sniffed at. Yet we don't go throwing it around.

Madhu's mother nodded agreement "With us too things aren't any different. This year we had a biggish promotion. But we did not let even the left ear hear what the right ear was told. A saree was bought for me and a set of new clothes for the children. That was the end of it. Not a penny more was spent. Morever, new clothes were bought on the eve of Diwali festival where everybody buys new clothes. We didn't want our purchases to stick out and hurt other people's eyes. One's good fortune rouses peoples' bile and makes their mouths bitter."

Mother said, "Yes, indeed! One can't be careful enough in these matters. But this Vatsalabai seems not to care about what other people might think. She has cast discretion to the winds. That apart, I wonder why she felt she needed a sewing machine. All that she has to stich are a few blouses for herself and skirts and blouses for her daughter. One doesn't need a sewing machine for such a small amount of stitching. It can be done with a thread and needle. Don't we do it? One needn't spend a huge sum of a hundred rupees and buy a machine to get that done."

Mom was prone to be careless when it came to numbers and amounts used to grow every time she mentioned them. I, therefore, said, "Mom, the price of the sewing machine is seventy-five and not hundred."

"Mother said, "Oh! Seventy-five or hundred are all the same. In any case, hundred is a nice round number, easy to remember."

Madhu's mother ignored my interruption and put the talk back on the rails. She said, "This Vatsalabai is a lazybones. Poor Ganpatrao hardly ever gets his morning meal on time and often he rushes away with an empty stomach to reach his office on time. Sometimes, he has even to hire a taxi to be on time. You know how expensive taxis are."

"Don't I know it?", said mother. "It costs a full silver rupee to reach the Fort area in a taxi."

I knew that uncle Nana had once hired a taxi to go to the

Fort area and he had to pay fourteen annas to the taxi driver. I, therefore, had to again correct mother and tell her, "No, mom! It costs only fourteen annas."

Mother gave a start, looked at me and said, "And how do you know that it costs only fourteen annas! Did you ever hire a taxi to go the Fort area?"

I patiently explained to her that it was not me but uncle Nana who had hired a taxi to go to the Fort area and paid all of fourteen annas as fare.

Mother, however, stubbornly refused to agree. She cried, "No. I won't take that from you. Why, your father himself told me that a taxi ride to the Fort area costs a whole rupee."

I patiently said, "But mother..."

But mother lost her temper as she usually did when we had an argument. She cried, "Stop it. I won't have you meddling in every littly thing in the house. We will settle between ourselves whether the taxi fare is fourteen annas or one rupee. You keep out of it. And now go and sit in that far corner and do your lessons."

Knowing how perverse mother can be, I quietly picked up my book and went to the far corner to study it. I left mother no ground at all to say that I was being meddlesome. However, our two room tenement was so small and my ears were so sharp that I could still hear the coversation of my mother and Saguna auntie.

Having got me out of the way, mother took up the thread of the conversation. She said, "But shouldn't the master of the house pull up his wife sharply if he finds her throwing away good money like this?"

Saguna auntie smiled sadly and said with a knowing nod, "If the house really had a firm master things wouldn't have come to such a pass. But Vatsalabai's husband is like putty in her hand. What her ladyship says goes in that household. If she says that this should be done that is done; and if she says that something else be done then that is done."

Mother was amazed. She cried, "But shouldn't the man

in the family hold the reins tight in his hands? A sharp word from him would be enough to stop his silly wife from running wild."

Saguna auntie nodded and said, "That is how things are in all households, but not in that one."

Mother said resignedly, "If it is so then it is so. One can do nothing about it. But hasn't she a mother-in-law, who can firmly put her in her place? Or has this woman tied her up in a neat bundle and put her in the storage loft?"

Saguna auntie said, "Oh no! I know the mother-in-law and she is a firm, no-nonsense woman. But she lives far away in their native village in Konkan. She would therefore know nothing of what is going on here in her son's house. But eventually the news will reach her and then she will pull up this woman and put her in her place. I can assure you that she will do that and some more."

"Good to hear that," said mother, "although it should have been done yesterday."

At this juncture my mother heard a hissing sound from the kitchen and rushed to see what was amiss.

At the same time Madhu ran panting into our house and cried, "Mom, mom, there is a fire in the kitchen."

Saguna auntie rushed excitedly out of our house Never before had I seen her run so fast.

I tried to recollect India's exports, but I found that I couldn't. I then realized that I had studied for too long and couldn't concentrate any more. I obviously needed a break. So I put away my gerography book and went downstairs to Visoo's house to spend some time with him.

I found him sitting bent over his book. When I went nearer, I found that he had acquired a peacock's feather and he was putting it carefully between the pages of a book and spreading red kumkum powder on it."

"What are you doing that for?", I asked.

"Don't you know?", asked Visoo and added, "If you put kumkum on a peacock's feather it grows bigger and bigger day by day."

"Really?", I asked.

"Of course it does", cried Visoo, "Why, Shamu's peacock feather has now become as big as the page of his big Algebra book."

Our talk was interrupted by the loud creaking of sandals in the lobby of the chawl. Nagutatya was the only man who wore such loudly creaking sandals and so intimidating used to be the creaking sound that women stopped talking and the babies stopped crying when they heard it. Nagutatya was as proud of those sandals as he was of his thick walking stick. He used to get those sandals made in Konkan by a shoemaker who was renowned for his ability to make sandals that were thick, strong and durable and creaked loudly to announce their formidable presence.

Nagutatya himself was as formidable as his thick creaking sandals and he inspired respect and fear by his mere presence. He had retired after thirty-five years of devoted service to the British Raj. The white sahib who was his boss was extremely pleased by his total devotion and trusted him so completely that his word used to be the law in his department. He had risen to be an office superintendent, which was the highest position an Indian could reach in Government service those days. He had retired on a big fat pension of one hundred and twenty rupees, which was almost princely in those days. He had the robust health of a man hailing from Konkan and his spartan habits had kept him as strong and erect as his big walking stick even after fifteen years of retirement. He took long walks every morning and evening at the end of which he visited relatives, friends and acquaintances and berated them for their follies and weaknesses. He was heard respectfully with bent heads because of his age and the influence he wielded in the Government circles. I always wondered how he came to know of the foibles and follies of everybody and how he could express himself so authoritatively on every subject under the sun. He held forth in such a loud stentorian voice that I couldn't help listening to him although I really wanted to go back home and concentrate on my geography lesson.

That day he visited my friend Visoo's home, where he was welcomed respectfully by Nana, Visoo's father. Nagutatya settled down on the steel bedstead in the living room, which also doubled as a divan for visitors. Nagutatya always sat ramrod erect and never leaned against a backrest.

When he had settled down, Nana asked politely, "How are you Nagutatya?"

Nagutatya said, "I am fine. There is nothing the matter with me. God has given me a robust physique and our traditional spartan habits have kept me fit. The benign British Raj has given me an adequate pension to eat two square meals a day. I have, therefore, no reason to complain as far as I am concerned. But it is the follies and stupidities of other people that annoy and upset me. I tell all of you young people that you should take some advice and learn a few things from this old man. I have seen life and learnt a few things from it. So come to me, tell me what your problems are and I will tell you what to do. But nobody listens. Folks think that they are wise enough to know what to do and then commit egregious follies. I have then to get them out of trouble. If I had the time I could tell you hundreds of stories of such follies."

Nana said, "Nagutatya, you seem to be particularly upset today. Whose folly it is that has annoyed you so?"

I pricked my ears because I knew that I would now hear a juicy, spicy tale.

Nagutatya said, "Oh, there are umpteen things I could tell you about. But the thing that has upset me most is what that overwise Ganpatrao has done."

"Have you in mind the Ganpatrao who lives in Phanaswadi?", asked Nana.

Nagutatya said, "No. The one who lives in Phanaswadi belongs to the Deodhar family. He is not a lesser fool than others. But the Ganpatrao I am talking about is one who lives in Ismail chawl and belongs to the Nene family. Now don't mix them up again. Otherwise every time I mention Ganpatrao, you will ask me whether it is the Ganpatrao who lives in Phanaswadi or the one who lives at Thakurdwar."

Nana, like everybody else, was used to being put in the wrong and admonished by Nagutatya. So he said, "So this Ganpatrao of Thakurdwar, what did he do?"

Nasgutatya said, "Well, the usual folly. It is the same old story. He has got a promotion recently and as usually happens, his head has got swollen. He thinks no end of himself. He now throws around his money and worse still allows his silly pampered wife to do so too. The last thing one should do is to pamper women and to let them throw away money any way they like. So this silly woman went to a shop and threw away seventy-five rupees to buy a sewing machine. Seventy-five rupees! That is not peanuts. If she runs through his money thus, it will not be long before he would have to go around with a begging bowl in hand."

Nana said, "But Nagutatya, I am told that this Ganpatrao earns a fat salary. He can afford to buy a sewing machine if he wants to."

"Ha! Fat salary indeed! Well! I earned a fat salary myself and I can tell you it was fatter than his salary. But I never threw money around so foolishly. Nor did I allow my wife and children to do so. There used to be some grumbling in the kitchen. But I firmly put my foot down and said, "Let me make it absolutely clear that I will not allow money to be squandered on a lot of expensive sarees and jewellery. I want my family to eat well, wear decent clothes, have two or three expensive sarees for special occasions and a couple of pieces of jewellery which tell people where we stand. But no other funny stuff to satisfy women's whims and fancies. I firmly believe that women, like shoes, have to be kept in their place."

When I realized that Naguatya was holding forth on the purchase of the sewing machine, I pricked my ears and listened intently to what was being said. Visoo too hastily finished feeding kumkum powder to the peacock's multicoloured feather and joined me in listening to the talk on the hot topic. At the same time Visoo's mother came hastily out of the kitchen and stood with her ear to the wall to hear the men's talk.

Nana tried to get in a word edgewise.

But Nagutatya brushed him aside with an emphatic sweep of his hand and said, "I will hear no crowing about his fat salary. He works in the same office as I did and I know his salary grade. His salary now wouldn't be more than on hundred and ten rupees. One hundred and twenty is the outside limit. That is not the kind of income that permits throwing away large sums like seventy-five rupees to satisfy a pampered wife's silly whims and fancies."

Nana hastily said, "Well! It is his money and his wife. So we have nothing to do with it, have we?"

We all knew that Nagutatya wouldn't be silenced so easily. For he never stopped talking about anything until he had his full say and that was what happened on that occasion too. He shook his finger to reject Nana's timid suggestion. "No. I don't agree. If a man is committing a folly, it ought to be brought to his attention and convincingly at that. This has to be done for his own good. And I must tell you that apart from squandering money, Ganapatrao has committed another serious folly. Do you know what he has done? He has gone and bought a sewing machine of German make."

Nana couldn't make out what was the folly in buying a German sewing machine. Nor could we. He asked, "Why? Are the German machines of poor quality?"

Nagutatya was amazed that Nana couldn't perceive something that was so obvious to him. He said, "Ha! What a question to ask? That is the trouble. People can't see something that is as obvious as the palm of one's hand. If the Germans could have made sewing machines as good as our British sahibs do in England, would they have lost the World War? I hope everybody knows that it was the Germans and not our British sahibs who were defeated in the World War. That is reason enough to avoid buying a German sewing machine But there is another reason and that is very very important indeed!"

Here Nagutatya paused and looked at Nana to find out if he had caught the point. Having satisfied himself that he hadn't, he lowered his voice and said, "Well! I don't want to let the whole world know about it. But this Ganpatrao is in Government Service, isn't he? Is it then wise on his part to buy a machine made by an enemy country? Would the sahibs like it?"

Nana gave a start and exclamied, "Do you mean to say that the Government frowns on the purchase of even a sewing machine made by the Germans. Is there a law that forbids it?"

Nagutatya said, "Now, now! The Government wouldn't openly ban such things. After all there are certain proprieties to be observed. Nonetheless the Government keeps an eye on how people behave and what they do. This is particularly so in the case of Government servants. For instance, there is no law against wearing a Gandhi cap. However, if this Ganpatrao goes to his office wearing a Gandhi cap, do you think he will get away with it? You can be sure that he will be soon out of a job."

While Visoo's mother heard Nagutatya with bated breath, suddenly black smoke blew out of the kitchen and with it came a burning smell. That made Visoo's mother jump and she rushed into the kitchen screaming, "Oh my mother! The eggplant. It has been reduced to cinders."

Eventually Nagutatya got up and as usual his sandals creaked loudly and authoritatively as he left. Soon I saw Visoo's mother slip out carrying a small bowl underneath the pallu of her saree. She was met in the lobby of the chawl by Sadu's mother hurriedly proceeding towards Visoo's house.

They both stopped and Visoo's mother said, "It's nice

that you came along. I was on my way to your house. I wanted to return the groundnut chutney I had borrowed from you the other day."

Sadu's mother said, "Well! I have prepared some lemon pickle and I thought I would give a bowl of it to you. You had told me that Sadu's father likes lemon pickle."

You might wonder how I came to know what the two women said to each other. It so happened that when they met, I too was going back to our home. These two women, however, blocked my way in the lobby. So I waited and watched a kite caught in the telephone cable and fluttering in the wind. I thought that with Sadu's help the kite could be retrieved and we could fly it and have fun. While I stood there, I couldn't help hearing the excited whispers of Visoo's and Sadu's mothers.

Visoo's mother said, "You know what? Nagutatya called on us a while ago and told us the story of Vatsalabai who lives in the Ismail chawl..."

Sadu's mother said, "Oh, I know it, for I heard it too. I am amazed at the kind of things that are going on. Why, the latest stories I have heard makes my head whirl."

Visoo's mother cried, "Latest stories, did you say? What more has she done now?"

Sadu's mother said, "Why, it is developing into a story as big as the Ramayan. Well, her sister-in-law came to know that she had bought a sewing machine. She was annoyed that the sewing machine had been bought without so much as letting her know, while proprieties demanded that she, as the husband's sister, should have been consulted. So she called on Vatsalabai to see the machine and let Vatsalabai know her feelings in the matter. After some argument the sister-in-law declared her intention to take away the machine for a few days as she had to stitch some clothes for herself and her children. Vatsalabai wouldn't let her do that. However, to avoid exchange of hot words she told the sister-in-law that she could bring along the cloth and stitch the clothes in Vatsalabai's house. On hearing this, the sister-in-law flew into a temper and cried, "Who on earth do you think you are to tell me what to do. The machine is my brother's property. After all we two are close blood relatives, children of the same parents. You are an outsider. You have no business to tell me what to do. If my brother doesn't want me to take away the machine, let him say so. He won't do that. But if he does, I will know what to do."

However, Vatsalabai was equally adamant. She stood defiantly near the sewing manchine and cried, "I won't let you touch that machine..."

Visoo's mother heard this sensational story with wide-eyed amazement and exclaimed, "Goodness! Why, it seems they fought nothing less than a *Mahabharat* war. Well! I had a gut feeling that something like that would inevitably happen. Such foolhardy actions..."

Sadu's mother was so eager to complete the interesting story that she broke in and cried, "That wasn't the end of the story. Things went from bad to worse. For while the two almost came to blows, the sister-in-law's four-year-old daughter pushed her hand under the needle and turned the wheel. And then the needle pierced straight through the girl's finger.

Visoo's mother pushed the pallu of her saree in her mouth to suppress a scream and said in a choked voice, "Oh my mother! That must have led to a full-fledged Mahabharat war."

Sadu's mother said, "Yes. Indeed! I hear that blood streamed out of the girl's finger and it couldn't be stopped. The sister-in-law flew into hysterics and began to dash her head against the wall..."

I knew that this was something that mother had to know. So I dashed past the two women in the lobby and said to mother, "Mom, do you know what Nagutatya said at Visoo's house?"

Mother was rolling a chapati. She said, "I don't want to hear what Nagutatya said. Every time he opens his mouth he says that he is the wisest man in the world and everybody else is an egregious fool."

"Yes. That he did. But he also said something very interesting about Vatsalabai's sewing machine. He said that the white sahib, who is Ganpatrao's boss, is very much upset with him and Ganpatrao, therefore, is likely to lose his job."

Mother stopped rolling the chapati and kept staring at me. I could see that she felt completely lost with the turn that events had taken. She said, "Oh my mother! What strange turns events take! I am feeling completely lost. Now tell me clearly and slowly how one thing followed another, so that I can make sense out of your jumbled talk."

I patiently explained to mother what had happened. She put the chapati on the frying pan and listened to me intently. I expected her to be pleased with me for giving her such information. But such is the perversity of mothers that she scolded me for poking my nose in women's talk instead of concentrating on doing my lessons. She was holding forth on this matter at length, when she suddenly noticed that the chapati had got burned and blamed me for it.

I was amazed at how ungrateful and perverse mothers can be and decided there and then and once and for all not to ever again tell mother any of the interesting things I happened to hear.

I took my Geography book in hand and began to learn by rote exports of India. Cotton, oilseeds, hides and skins, tea.

I suddenly remembered that I had forgotten to tell mother about the sister-in-law's visit and about the needle of the sewing machine piercing straight through the finger of her daughter.

"Why should I", I said to myself thinking of how perverse and unfair she had been. But as I swotted the exports of India, I realized how small and uninformed my mother would look among the women in the chawl, if she alone did not know the story of the sister-in-law and the needle of the sewing machine. I just didn't have the heart to see my mother belittled. So I decided to break my vow to tell her nothing just once.

I said, "Mom, I haven't yet told you the most interesting part of the story. Sadu's mother said..."

Mother flared up and cried, "There you go again. I have told you not once but umpteen times to stop meddling in women's affairs. But...oh well! What was it that Sadu's mother said?"

So I told her the whole story, which so fascinated mother that she stopped rolling the chapati and stared at me wide-eyed.

When I finished the story, she and I both looked at the hot pan on which the rolled chapati was burnt to cinders. She cried, "Oh, mother! See what you have done. I have told you a thousand times and yet you continue to be meddlesome and divert my attention from cooking. Now you will have to eat this burnt chapati. And I want you to get out of the house this very minute and stop carrying tales."

I was so angry that I got up and stomped out of the kitchen for good. I then plumped down in the living room and began to swot India's exports, "Mumbai, Ahmedabad, Coimbatore", I chanted...

❑

8

The Decline and Fall of Grandfathers

Looking at the sort of things going on around me these days, I often wonder what the world is coming to. Take for instance the kind of persons who are becoming grandfathers these days. I am well aware that times have changed and grandfathers aren't any more the solidly built, stern, respectable and awe-inspiring persons they used to be. Nor do I expect them to sport ample moustaches and carry thick walking sticks, which lent so much dignity to grandfathers in good old days. But one has to draw a line somewhere and I would unhesitently say that if ever there was a guy unworthy to be a grandfather, it was my schoolmate Visoo.

I am sure, you too will agree with me when I tell you the kind of guy Visoo was. He was constantly scolded by his mother for spilling food from his plate and wiping his nose on his shirt sleeve. He often forgot to bring a pencil to school and then took mine from my school-bag without even bothering to ask. His argument was that as I was his buddy, there was no need to ask. The result was that I was often made to stand up on the bench for not bringing my pencil. My indignant attempts to tell the truth fell on deaf ears and everybody in the class sniggered at me. When we played cops and robbers, he often forgot whether he was a cop or a robber and when we told him who he really was, he endlessly argued with us over the matter. He was so clumsy that he often overturned things or bumped into them. He was particularly dangerous when he ran, for he never looked where he was going. Why, once he even bumped into the rotund stomach of my friend Sachin's grandfather.

"Oi, Oi,!" screamed the old man as he doubled up with pain and then rushed at Visoo brandishing his thick walking stick. Visoo ran like a hare and would have escaped, had he not bumped into Balu's father who held him firmly until Sadu's grandfather caught up with him huffing and fuming.

What was most annoying was that inspite of all these failings, Visoo always wore that silly smirk on his face which seemed to say that he was the finest guy in the whole big world. Why, he even believed that he could sing very well, much to the distress of all of us and particularly our music teacher.

I hope I have said enough to convince you that if ever there was a person unworthy to be grandfather, it was Visoo.

Yet there he was proudly carrying a little kid in his arms and wearing that same old silly smirk that seemed to declare that he was the greatest granddad in the whole world. I was shocked by what I saw and would have liked to slink past him unnoticed.

But he had espied me from a distance and approached me with an ever broadening smile. He clapped me on my shoulder and greeted me so exuberantly and loudly that every one around jerked his head and stared at us.

I was naturally embarassed but not Visoo.

"Guess, who I am carrying in my arms", said Visoo jovially with a fond look at the kid he was carrying.

So I forced a smile and said, "It seems you are a grandfather now."

He smiled a broad self-congratulatory smile and cuddling his grandson said, "Isn't he simply wonderful?"

"Very cute, very!" I responded and caressed the kid's cheek with an even broader smile.

"Everybody says he has taken after me. Don't you think so too?", asked Visoo with a jovial thump on my back.

"Yes! Yes! of course, certainly!" I said, almost choking on my words in my effort to be polite.

"He is certainly very smart. Would you believe it? This kid has a fine ear for music and enjoys it immensely. Don't you, Pakoo?"

"Pakoo? Is that his name?", I asked. It seemed rather a silly name to give to a kid.

"No. No! His real name is Vasant. Pakoo is the pet name I have given him. Isn't it so, Pakoo?"

The kid smiled so heartily that it almost keeled over in his arms.

I rushed to steady it.

"Ha, ha! He has a wonderful sense of humour", said Visoo thumping me on my back.

I moved to a safe distance to avoid being thumped any more.

"And he likes to talk. Don't you, Pakoo? Say something Pakoo", urged Visoo as he fondled the kid.

Pakoo responded enthusiastically with a stream of loud gurgles punctuated with gestures so emphatic that he was in imminent danger of keeling over once again.

"Can you make out what he is saying?", asked Visoo.

I pursed my lips and nodded my inability to do so.

"Oh, you are as dumb now as you were at school", said Visoo with a dismissive gesture and would have thumped me on my back had I not been alert and stepped aside. He then added, "I will tell you what he is saying. He wants you to sing a song for him."

"Me? Sing a song? Here, in the street?", I asked, utterly flabbergasted at the prospect of making a fool of myself in the street.

But Visoo seemed to be totally unaware of the sheer imbecility of the idea. He laughed heartly at my discomfiture and said, "Well Jagu, I know that you can sing no better than a crow can. But Pakoo is used to hearing me sing. In fact he loves it and he therefore seems to think that my friends can sing as well as as I can."

I wanted to tell him to disabuse his grandson's mind of such notions. But before I could open my mouth to say so, he silenced me with a reassuring gesture, and said to Pakoo in baby talk, "No Pakoo. Uncle dumb, can't sing. So I sing nice song for you."

"Right here? In the street?", I asked, feeling embarassed at the prospect of seeing Visoo making a fool of himself.

"Why not?", said Visoo, "This is a free country, isn't it?"

I gulped and then said in a hurry, "Visoo, I have an appointment to keep."

"This will take only five minutes. I want you to see how appreciative my grandson is of music. Here, hold him", he said.

"Hold him? I mean, I mean, you want me to hold the baby?", I asked.

"Of course, I want you to hold him. I can't sing holding a baby. Can I?"

"But..."

"Raghu, don't tell me you are so dumb that you can't even hold a baby", he said and shoved the baby into my arms. I had no option but to hold it.

Visoo then moved a little to a corner, cleared his throat and began to sing. Initially, his voice was low, but as he warmed up it became louder and people in the street began to stare at us.

It is not easy to suggest to somebody by gestures that he should lower his voice and certainly not when one is holding a slippery baby. But I did manage to do so.

But Visoo ignored me completely and began to sway as he sang, much to my embarassment.

After a while the baby too began to sway and move its arms and it seemed to be in imminent danger of slipping out of my arms.

I was scared out of my wits but Visoo was totally unaware of my predicament. On the contrary he thumped me on my back and said, "See how he is swaying and smiling and appreciating music. He promises to grow up into a very talented musician. Don't you think so?"

"I certainly do", I said hastily shoving the baby back into his arms.

"And..."

"Of course, certainly. He is a wonderful kid. But Visoo I have to go now", I said and turned to leave.

But Visoo gripped my arm and said, "Do you really have to go now? I am sure you can spare a few minutes."

"Oh no, I have to go. I am getting awfully late", I protested.

"Well! In that case, I won't detain you. But before you leave, I must show you something else that my grandson is good at."

"And what is that?"

"He is very good at punching people on their noses. Come on, Pakoo. Punch him on the nose. Show him how good you are at it." Visoo punched me lightly on the nose to let his grandson know what his granddad wanted him to do.

That light punch made me sneeze and made Visoo's grandson burst into peels of laughter. Egged on by his grandfather, he punched me on the nose too.

I was certainly glad when I walked away in a hurry and decided to keep as far away from Visoo as I possibly could, until his grandson grew up.

I was itching to tell my other friends what a fool Visoo was making of himself on becoming a grandfather.

So the following weekend I called on Sadu to tell him about my eventful encounter with Visoo.

It was Sadu's wife who opened the door for me and she seemed to have considerable difficulty in holding back her laughter.

I went in wondering whether I had smut on my nose.

I found Sadu lying prone on the floor. He was utterly absorbed in watching his granddaughter who was extremely busy with her toys. She was biting the head of a camel which she held with one hand and she was busy smashing to pieces an elephant with the other hand.

I bent over Sadu and asked, "Whatever is the matter with you Sadu? Why are you sleeping on the floor?", I asked.

"Sadu looked up at me with a smile and said, "Oh no! Nothing is the matter with me. I am lying prone on the floor because that is what dogs do."

I stepped back without meaning to and asked, "And why do you want to do things that dogs do?"

"Because that is what my granddaughter has asked me to do", said Sadu and laughed heartily. He seemed to thoroughly enjoy playing the role of a dog and it seemed to me that at any moment, he might start barking.

I was stunned by the change that had come over Sadu. Visoo was a little weak in the head ever since he was a boy and I was therefore only mildly surprised by the change that had come over him on becoming a grandfather. But Sadu was a very sober and responsible person ever since I knew him as a schoolboy. In fact he was considered to be the embodiment of propriety and responsible behaviour in our class. Year after year he was appointed the monitor of our class by our class teacher, and it was he who every Thursday garlanded the picture of Lord Datta. Moreover, when he distributed the prasad of sweets to all the boys, he never took more than his due share for himself. I was therefore expecting him to grow up into a respectable grandfather who would inspire respect in the grandchildren and be a model to all of us who were rapidly becoming grandfathers.

At that juncture Sadu's little granddaughter rubbed his head. That seemed to give him immense pleasure and he began to bark. While he barked he lifted his feet by bending them in the knees and shook them vigorously.

"What did you do that for?", I asked, bending low so that he could hear me.

Sadu looked at me and cried, "Can't you understand such a simple thing?"

"No. I don't", I confessed.

"Goodness, Raghu! Even after all these years you are as dumb as you were when we were at school. Well, I am a dog now, am I not? But the trouble is that while every dog has a tail, I don't have any. I therefore cannot wag my tail as a dog does. So for the time being, I am using my legs as a tail and wagging them vigorously."

"I see!", I said but Sadu did not notice the rebuke in my voice.

Instead he said, "I think I do a good job of wagging my tail but I don't feel that my bark is upto the mark. Perhaps your bark will be more authentic. Give it a try. Will you?"

"I don't think my bark would be even half as good as yours", I said hastily.

"Oh shucks!", said Sadu in disgust, "Well, if you can't do that, do something much easier. Be a cat."

"Be a cat? What for?"

"To keep the baby entertained."

"You see, the baby's parents have gone to see a movie and the baby's grandmother and I have to look after her until they return. The grandmother is busy cooking the big Sunday meal. So I have to look after the baby and keep her in good humour." Sadu seemed to think that he had explained the situation satisfactorily.

"But aren't you doing it already by pretending to be a dog?", I asked.

"Well. I have done this for nearly an hour and I can see that my granddaughter is getting a trifle bored with my barking and tail wagging", explained Sadu.

"I see!", I said, sensing danger and then quickly added, "But I am no good at pretending to be a cat. Your granddaughter won't even look at a cat like me."

"I know Raghu that you are no good at doing such things. But all that you have to do is to pretend to be a cat. I will do the rest", said Sadu confidently.

"What do you mean, you will do the rest?", I asked, not at all liking in the least what I was being called upon to do.

"It will be like this", said Sadu expansively, "The moment you become a cat, I will snarl and pounce on you. We will then have a fight after which you will run and I will pursue you."

"Well! The way you put it, it sounds very easy. And I would have loved to do it. But I remembered that I have an engagement to keep and I seem to be getting late", I said and got up to leave.

"Hell! What kind of a friend are you? Can't you ring up that guy and tell him that you will be late by half an hour or so?", asked Sadu in a surly voice. I could see that he was very cross with me.

I was reminded of the adage we had learnt at school, 'A friend in need is a friend indeed'. So I said to Sadu, "I can't postpone the appointment; but I think I can spare a few minutes. So let us get this over and done with."

So I got down on all fours and mewed as best as I could. Sadu responded with very excited barks and crawled after me in pursuit. He then pounced on me and I mewed very vociferously.

All this noise and hubbub alarmed Sadu's wife, who rushed out of the kitchen to see what was going on. When she saw us both engaged in a fight, she cried, "What on earth are you two doing?"

We both sorted ourselves out and stood up. I soon realized that a lot of explaining needed to be done and Sadu was far better placed to do it. So I mumbled, "I have to go now. I have an appointment to keep and I am already late."

I then left in a hurry and decided that it would be unwise to call on my friend Sadu, until his granddaughter grew up.

I was more than a little worried by what was happening around me. My friends were becoming grandfathers one by one and what that was doing to them was not very nice. I thought that those guys needed to be told that it was not necessary to go so completely overboard on becoming grandfathers. I pondered over the matter and concluded that my classmate Chandu was the man most suited to do this job. He had worked all his life in the income tax department and retired as Commissioner of Income Tax. Long years spent in the midst of tax files had made him as sober and down-to-earth as a brick. Intricacies of tax laws had not baffled him and he had not been taken in by the most artful tricks of tax dodgers. He had remained unmoved by tearful pleas of leading movie actresses and he had a ready answer to the most clever arguments of tax lawyers. Such a man, I thought, would not do anything silly because of the laughter, tears or sweet babble of a grandchild.

It was therefore with considerable hopefulness that I went to Chandu's house to induce him to give sound, sensible advice to grandfathers who were being swept off their feet by the arrival of grandchildren in their families.

I was greeted at the door not by Chandu but by his wife who was carrying a child in her arms. I surmised that it was her grandchild.

When I enquired after Chandu, his wife told me, "He is not well. He is in bed."

"Whatever is the matter with him?", I asked with concern which I naturally felt for an old friend.

"He has fractured his leg."

"And how did that come about?", I asked. I had a sneaking suspicion that an offended tax payer had lost his temper and hit him.

"He fell off a tree", said his wife.

"Fell off a tree? How could that happen? He is now past sixty. This is not an age when people climb trees. What made him do that?", I asked.

"It was the kite", explained Chandu's wife.

"Kite? What kite?", I asked wondering why a kite should come into the picture.

"He was flying a kite. The kite got caught in the branches of a tree. So he had climbed the tree to disentangle it and that was when he fell off the tree", explained Chandu's wife with admirable patience.

That baffled me completely. I asked, "Do you mean to say that Chandu, at this advanced age, has started flying kites all over again? Has he gone off his rocker?"

"It is Babdu, this grandson of ours, who made him do it. He loves kites and struggles to fly them all the time. If he can't do it he gets very upset and cries. My husband gets quite upset if he sees tears in his grandson's eye. This boy is the apple of his eye", said Chandu's wife and affectionately mussed the baby's head and kissed it too.

"Good heavens!", I cried and stared at her open-mouthed. A sudden demand to pay forthwith a tax of a million rupees wouldn't have stunned me more. I never expected a stern, hard-headed Income Tax Commissioner to fall to such abysmal depths. When I had recovered from the shock sufficiently, I asked, "But why on earth did he climb up a tree to salvage a kite? Was that really necessary? Couldn't he have bought another kite and flown it for his grandson?", I asked, wondering why anything so obvious had not occured to an erstwhile Income Tax Commissioner who could spot tax dodging by a cursory perusal of a tax return.

"Certainly", said Chandu's wife sweetly, agreeing with me and then added, "But our Babdu would have non of it. He wanted the same kite that had got entangled in the branches of the tree."

"Your Babdu seems to be a very stubborn little boy", I observed. It was not a compliment but Babdu seemed to think it was, for he responded with a very big smile.

I ignored the kid pointedly and followed his grandmother into Chandu's bedroom. His leg was encased in plaster and he lay in bed like an uprooted lamp post.

I gingerly touched the plaster on his leg and said. "Nasty business this! Must be pretty uncomfortable to be immobilized like this."

"Very!", said Chandu, who seemed to be considerably agitated and sore.

"It must be impossible to even to go to the toilet on your

own", I said, although I felt that a chap who makes such a fool of himself deserves no commiseration.

"Yes! It is a pain in the neck. I mean, this business of hobbling on crutches. But do you know what peeves me most?"

I nodded in the negative.

Chandu clenched his fist and thumped his bed in frustration. He then said, "What upsets me most is that I can't fly a kite any more for Babdu and that makes the kid miserable. He whimpers and cries all the time. My heart melts for the poor kid. I asked my wife to fly a kite for Babdu until I got better. But she is no good...utterly dumb when it comes to flying kites. I scolded her. Asked her why she cannot do such a simple thing as that. But you know how women are!"

All that I could do on hearing this was to shake my head sadly.

Chandu, however, was totally oblivious to what a spectacle he was making of himself. His face suddenly broke into a very broad smile and he began to tug at my sleeve most enthusiastically.

When I gave him a questioning look he said very eagerly, "I have got a bright idea."

I was in no mood to listen to bright ideas of chaps who had become wacky on becoming grandfathers. But Chandu was in no condition to notice the frown on my brow. He tugged even more vigorously at my sleeve and said, "It is all absurdly simple. You, Raghu, can do it."

"Do what?", I asked.

"What else? Fly a kite, silly! I am surprised it didn't occur to me right away, when I saw you", said Chandu.

"Oh no! I don't think I will be able to do that", I said hurriedly.

"What do you mean, you can't do it? I remember you were very good at flying kites when we were at school", said Chandu, who seemed to be annoyed with my lack of enthusiasm.

"That was years ago. I haven't handled a kite in the last fifty years and I don't think I will be able to fly a kite any more", I was polite but quite firm.

But Chandu would have none of it. He laughed and said, "That is what I thought too. But these skills are never forgotten, and it took me no time at all to send a kite soaring in the sky. So don't worry. Come over every day and fly a kite for Babdu. You have retired from service, haven't you? So you must have time on your hands. So come over and have a lot of fun every day. You will have to do it only for a month, until I get well."

I stared in amazement at Chandu and then vigorously nodded to tell him that I would have none of it.

But Chandu slapped me on my back and said, "So, it is all settled, eh!" He then looked at his wife and said to her, "Don't you think it is an excellent idea?"

She kissed the baby in her arms and said, "Certainly! It would make Babdu very happy? Isn't it, my tinny winny darling?"

"You can start right away, Raghu", said Chandu.

I realized that it was impossible to argue or persuade Chandu out of this proposition. So I decided to make good my escape in another way. I said to him. "Certainly, Chandu. I would love to fly a kite for your grandson. But I am afraid I can't do it right away. For I have an engagement at Borivali and I will have to leave right away to reach there on time."

Chandu frowned and said in a surly voice, "Must you go right away? Can't you do it after flying the kite for an hour or so?"

"I would have loved to do it and make Babdu happy. But I am afraid that I have to leave right away." I glanced at my watch and with a gesture of helplessness left in a hurry.

Well! That settled it and I thereafter kept away from all friends and acquaintances who had become grandfathers.

As I ponder over what is happening to chaps who become grandfathers, I cannot but feel deeply distressed.

My memory takes me back to the kind of grandfathers we had when we were kids and when I compare them with the grandfathers of today, I cannot but hang my head in shame.

Grandfathers in the good old days were a very impressive lot. They used to be stern, sturdy and burly. They had ample moustaches which gave their faces a lionine hauteur. Among them the most impressive was the moustache of my classmate Janu's grandfather. The two ends of it were like handle bars on which one could have hung a jacket. Visoo's grandfather did not have moustaches that were that big. But they were groomed and twisted to look very pointed and intimidating. The moustaches of Sadu's grandfather travelled round his lips to form a bracket. While Chandu's grandfather's moustaches so completely covered his mouth that he always seemed to drink his tea through them. No grandchild would have ever dared to ask Janu's grandfather to pretend to be a cat or Visoo's grandfather to fly a kite. And none of course would have ever dreamed of asking a grandfather to sing.

The long ropes of hair which hung at the back of their shaved heads used to be equally impressive. When Jagu's grandfather shook his impressive rope of hair after a bath to shake off the water in it, it made a sound like a loud clap. Nanu's grandfather used to tie his rope of hair in a tight knot and it curled up at the end like the intimidating tail of a scorpion. Chandu's grandfather was extremely short-tempered and his very cleanly shaved head used to glow menacingly when he lost his temper.

The clothes those grandfathers wore used to be equally impressive and intimidating. They wore long jackets that reached down to their knees and were buttoned all the way upto their necks. They wrapped shawls around their broad shoulders and wore bright pugrees or big intimidating turbans on their heads. They wore blood red shoes, which were jauntily curled up in front. They all carried gold or silver watches in the inside pockets of their jackets and gold or silver chains of those watches stuck out of one of the buttonholes. To watch a grandfather take out and consult his watch thoughtfully and solemnly used to be an impressive experience. And when they sallied out of their houses on some weighty errand, women and children scurried to get out of their way.

Everything they did used to be highly impressive. The way Visoo's grandfather snarled and gargled when he cleaned his mouth every morning used to be a memorable event in our chawl. He did it so noisily and for so long that the entire chawl woke and listened with bated breath to the variety of sounds he made. Jagu's grandfather opened his snuff box, took a pinch of snuff out of it and delicately pushed it in his nose, with such calm deliberation and dignity, that we kids watched it in awe and waited fearfully for the loud sneeze that followed. It used to knock down little babies who were learning to walk and they screamed and bawled so much that it took quite a while to pacify them.

Grandfathers in those good old days wielded considerable authority and never hesitated to exercise it. Nanu's grandfather used to get extremely annoyed if proper preparations were not made for his morning worship of the family deities. It was the responsibility of his newly married daughter-in-law to make the preparations. Scared of offending the head of the family she used to make the preparations with a great deal of care. But every now and then something went amiss and Nanu's grandfather lost his temper.

"Soonbai", he bawled.

On one occasion it scared the daughter-in-law so much that she dropped on her foot the heavy bucket of water she was carrying. The poor girl limped for many days thereafter. But she had learnt her lesson so thoroughly that she never made any mistake ever again.

Sadu's grandfather used to be equally demanding. If Sadu made a mistake in reciting his numbers tables, he was administered a whack so loud that it could be heard in the neighbouring households. Visoo's grandfather was very devout. Every evening he recited hymns to gods. He did it so loudly that they could not fail to reach the ears of the gods in heaven. They also incidentally so clobbered the ears of people in the vicinity, that nobody could carry on any conversation as long as his prolonged recitation continued.

Everything about these grandfathers was highly impressive. Their worship of gods used to be so elaborate that it lasted for hours on end. And nobody could eat his or her lunch until the worship was over. Everybody and particularly we kids suffered acute pangs of hunger while we waited for hours for our lunch. After the lunch, the grandfathers had their afternoon siesta which lasted for an hour or two and nobody was allowed to make any disturbing noise during their siesta hours. Everybody had to talk in whispers and the women had to do the chores in the kitchen, particularly clean copper and brass utensils, without making any noise.

After the siesta grandfathers had their afternoon tea and then they went out to do the usual shopping and pay a visit to the temple. As all old people went to the temple in the afternoon, they could also meet their friends.

It was the grandfathers who held the purse strings in the good old days. The sons who earned money were expected to hand over their monthly salaries to the grandfathers who took all the decisions and made all the purchases.

It would have been gross impropriety for a daughter-in-law to ask for anything. It was for the mother-in-law to assess what she needed and if she was kind-hearted she asked the daughter-in-law whether she needed anything. The grandmother then told the grandfather the needs of the household and it was for him to decide as to which of those deserved to be met.

We children had to tell our grandfathers about our scholastic needs, and I can tell you it was not easy to get out of him anything at all. If one asked for a pencil, the grandfather eyed one suspiciously and asked, "Didn't I buy you one last month?"

One then said, "Yes, granddad. But it got used up."

"Used up? How come it got used up so soon?", asked grandfather in a thundering voice.

The wisest thing in such a predicament was to keep silent and leave it to Almighty to persuade grandfather to buy a pencil. He generally did so, but one couldn't be too sure about it.

Generally, after one had mumbled what one needed, grandfather fixed one with a stare and that was a warning that the dreaded question would be asked.

"And what is your rank in the class this month?"

"Seventh."

"Seventh? As low as that? And you have the temerity to tell me this with a straight face? Aren't you ashamed of yourself?" These angry words were generally accompanied by a stinging whack on the back.

That made one burst into tears. But as that was likely to annoy grandfather more and invite another whack, one tried hard to hold back the tears.

This generally brought grandma to the door of the room. That meant protection and one was spared the second whack. But obviously grandfather would still be quite annoyed. So he demanded, "Now, let me have a look at that pencil."

One would then show him the stub of the pencil.

Grandfather inspected it and said, "Well! It looks as if it would do for a week more."

That made one quite nervous. Because one couldn't write a neat hand with such a small pencil and one got scolded for that by the teachers.

Here again grandma offered help and protection. She said, "Maybe, we should buy a pencil for that boy."

"Ha! It is this kind of talk that spoils the kids", cried grandfather angrily.

"The lead of that old pencil was breaking every now and

then. It seems the shopkeeper didn't give us a good pencil. We might ask him to give a better pencil this time", grandmother said evenly.

"That is enough. I don't want to be told what to do by women in my house. Let your wisdom stay in the kitchen near the stove", retorted grandfather angily and walked off in a huff.

But more often that not he bought for me a much better pencil than he had done before.

It was our good luck in those old times that all of us kids had grandmothers. I shudder at the prospect of what would have happened to us if they had not been around.

We had a brief respite while the grandfather was away shopping and visiting the temple. But that had to be used to complete the homework given by our teacher. For everyday, without fail, a grandfather checked whether the homework had been done to his satisfaction. Thereafter we had to recite the ten times tables without making a single error or slip.

The ten times tables had to be recited for numbers ranging from two to thirty and also for quarter, half, three quarters and so on. Our throats ran dry due to the prolonged recitation, but the recitation had to be completed without a break or pause. Errors were rewarded with whacks and however much we tried, we used to fumble and err while reciting the difficult tables for figures like nineteen and twenty-three.

There was no respite even after the recitation of times table for thereafter we had to recite Ramraksha, the long hymn in Sanskrit in praise of Lord Rama.

Grandfather was generally inclined to make us learn by heart more things. But at this juncture Grandma again appeared at the door and said, "Isn't this enough for the day? The children must be hungry and their evening meal is getting cold."

This would annoy grandfather but generally, after some angry words, he let us off.

We had to take our evening meal under the strict eye of our grandfather. We had to avoid spilling food or eating it messily. To ask for a serving and not to finish it was a serious misdemeanour which invited instant punishment.

During the meal, searching question were asked regarding our performance at school. Poor performance brought instant reprimands or worse, but good performance did not earn an appreciative pat on the back or words of praise. Grandfathers in those good old days firmly believed that words of praise spoilt children.

If one stood first in one's class, grandfather would say, "Standing first in a class of thirty children doesn't count too much, does it? If a boy stands first in the entire school, that would be something."

Occasionally one of us did stand first in his standard in the entire school. That earned some grudging appreciation, but the boy was quickly reminded that his school was but one amongst many in the city or the province and really noteworthy achievement would be to stand first in the entire province in the school leaving examination.

At this point grandma again appeared in the doorway and said, "The boy stood first in his school, didn't he? Why not give him a new set of clothes for his performance?"

Such words used to upset grandfather greatly and he cried, "There you go again. With such pampering, the kids are going to be thoroughly spoiled."

But one did get a new set of clothes and sometimes grandma managed to persuade grandfather to send us to the movie.

However, the next day grandfather used to be more stern to ensure that his grandchildren were not spoiled as a result of being pampered by their grandmother.

Those were the kind of grandfathers we had in the good old days and we looked up to them. No wonder, I do not think much of today's grandfathers, who to please their granddaughters, crouch on the floor like dogs and wag their feet in the air, because they have no tails. ❑

9

Tiff Over Watermelons

It was an annoyed, impatient and insistent ring of the doorbell that summoned me to open the door. Guessing who was at the door, I rushed and opened it with alacrity. I had guessed right because it was my wife who confronted me when the door opened. She was tired, perspiring and surly. This was not surprising because she carried a big watermelon in one hand, while the other hand was weighed down by two unwieldy and heavy bags. Her fat purse hung awkwardly from the hand that carried the watermelon.

I was all sympathy and commiseration and said, "Oh really! You shouldn't carry such heavy loads. And you shouldn't have walked all the way from the market to the house carrying all these things. You should have jumped into a taxi. Oh, you poor thing."

"Stop oozing sympathy and do something. Take something off my hands", snapped my wife.

I hastily tried to take the huge watermelon.

"Don't", cried my wife tightening the grip on the watermelon. "You are sure to drop it and ruin it. Take the bags."

I suppressed with some difficulty the urge to protest against this brusque and peremptory response to my expression of sympathy and proceeded to take off her other hand the two bags she carried.

They were quite unwieldy and I dropped one in the process of carrying them. The sharp look that she shot at me went right through me. 'I knew you would do that', it said and many more things, too many and too unpleasant to enumerate.

Words of protest naturally rushed to my lips but I swallowed them and put the unwieldy bags neatly in a corner.

This was eyed with disapproval and after putting the watermelon and the purse on the diningtable my wife lifted those bags and put them in what she considered to be their proper place.

I again swallowed my protest. Because I could see that she was in quite a temper and my protest would have made sparks fly.

It was quite some time before my wife calmed down and could engage in reasonably civil talk with me and the children.

She looked with satisfaction and pride at the watermelon she had brought and asked, "What do you think of that watermelon? Isn't it really big and nice?" She spoke in an even voice but there was an edge to it which warned, "And don't you dare to disagree."

I took the hint and looked at the watermelon as appreciatively as I could and said in a honeyed tone, "Of course, it is! It is really big and promises to be sweet, juicy and luscious."

My smile was as broad and appreciative as I could make it. 'If you can offer no help in household work, you could atleast show some appreciation for what others do'. That is what my wife used to say atleast four times a day and I always dutifully tried to follow this eminently sensible advice.

"You know what! You always talk endlessly of the big watermelons your father used to bring home from the market. I therefore said to myself, "I will buy and carry home an equally big if not a bigger watermelon. I will do that even if it breaks my arm."

It was not fair to suggest that I expected her to buy a watermelon so big that it would break her arm. But I ignored that dig and said with a broad smile, "You really ought to have taken a cab when carrying such a big watermelon."

"Come, come!", said my wife, "Nobody hires an expensive cab to carry home groceries and watermelons."

I could see that there were gaping logical flaws in this argument, yet I again pursed my lips and swallowed that dig. I did not want any breach of peace and tranquility in the house.

But it seems that my wife was itching to needle me and score a point. So she said in a teasing voice, "Now, isn't this one as big as the ones your father used to bring? Let us hear what you have to say about that."

That was a claim much too tall to swallow.

However, determined as I was to avoid an argument, I pursed my lips and said nothing. But there was an involuntary nod of my head and a knowing smile escaped my lips.

Looking as she was very intently at me, my wife noticed that nod and smile and cried, "This is absolutely the limit! Are you suggesting that the watermelons your father bought were bigger than even this one?"

There was a sense of outrage in her shrill voice and flashing eyes.

I, however, kept my cool and said nothing. In fact, to avoid giving offence I didn't even look at her. But that seemed to annoy her even more.

"Are you suggesting that the watermelons your father bought were bigger than even this one? Are you?", cried my wife, "Take a good look at this watermelon and swear in the name of Mhalsa, our family goddess, that the watermelons your father bought were bigger than this one."

I could take it no more. I said quietly and firmly, "As you have brought our family deity Mhalsa into the picture, I must tell you that the watermelons my father bought used to be much bigger. They were that big."

Here I showed how big they were by the spread of my hands.

My wife too spread her hands to match the spread of my hands and cried in an exasperated, jeering voice, "That big, did you say? Pooh! Rubbish! Watermelons that big just don't exist. I think it was a pumpkin he brought and you mistook it for a watermelon."

I could take it no more and I cried, "Are you suggesting that I am such a nitwit as to mistake a pumpkin for a watermelon?"

"Don't you put words in my mouth. In our family, we children were taught to be polite always. All I said was that watermelons that big simply don't exist", said my wife, tilting her chin with an air of determined finality as she appreciatively fondled with her hand the watermelon she had brought.

I shot a contemptuous glance at that watermelon and bringing my fist heavily down on the diningtable cried, "That is what you think and that is because you have so far seen only the measly watermelons that grow in nearby Alibag. But much bigger and sweeter watermelons grow in Dharamtar and those are the ones my father used to buy."

"And what makes you think that the watermelon I bought grew in Alibag? Is it written on it?" asked my wife eyeing me belligerently as she spoke. To drive home the point conclusively she banged emphatically the brass utensil she was about to put on the stove.

"Such things don't need to be put in writing. A mere look is enough to tell that this measly little watermelon is from Alibag", I asserted with a contemptous dismissive look at that watermelon. I wanted her to know that when it came to watermelons, I knew what I was talking about.

"Ha ha! You can make that out, can you?", my wife cried at her venomous best.

"What do you know about watermelons?" I cried, "I used to accompany my father when he went to the market to buy fruits. And he was an expert judge of watermelons, if ever there was one. Why, he merely tapped a watermelon gently with one finger and could make out whether it would be red, sweet, luscious and juicy."

"Is that so? A mere tap and that revealed whether the watermelon was red, sweet and luscious too? Why then don't you ever accompany me to the market and choose for me a good watermelon with the expert tap of your finger?", said my wife with an unnecessary and offensive tilt of her chin.

"There you go scoring points by mixing up and confusing issues as usual. I never claimed that I could do it. But my father certainly could. He was in a class by himself. Why, I haven't see any other father who could hold a candle to him when it came to watermelons", I said and nodded my head emphatically several times.

"No. Spare me. I don't want to hear that again. I concede that there never was a father comparable to yours. Now let us cut and eat the miserable and puny watermelon I have brought. The children are eyeing it and licking their lips", she flounced into the kitchen and picked up a big knife to cut the watermelon.

I don't know what your experience is. But I have observed that whenever a woman takes it on herself to cut a watermelon, she ends up butchering it.

I kept my lips pursed and hands folded as I watched the watermelon being butchered. But after a while I could take it no longer. I cried, "Why are you butchering it so? One can cut a big watermelon into two with a deep thrust and circular sweep of the knife. That is how my father used to cut a watermelon."

"I wonder why those remarkable skills were not inherited by the son even a wee bit. I could then have had at least a few of the household chores off my hands", said my wife. She was so preoccupied with butchering the watermelon that she had no time to express her annoyance more sharply and eloquently.

"Well! I don't seem to be able to convince you about it. But my father was good at a lot of things. Let us forget about cutting a watermelon which is relatively easy. But breaking open a hard coconut is a different proposition altogether. I have seen you do it. You keep it on a hard grinding stone and hammer away at it with a thick kitchen scythe. Eventually it breaks, but what a mess it is. But whenever my mother had to break open a coconut, she called my father and placed the coconut before him. He held it firmly in his hand and then dealt it a sharp blow with a kitchen scythe. And with that single blow the coconut broke neatly into two in his hand. He then held it so that the water in it never got spilled. I always used to sit next to him when he did that. So holding the two pieces of coconut tightly together, he would ask me to look up and open my mouth. When I did, he opened the broken coconut so neatly that its sweet water fell straight into my mouth."

My little daughter who was listening to me in wonderous awe, cried, "Dad, tomorrow would you break open a coconut like that and pour its sweet water in my mouth?"

My wife guffawed, "Ha, ha! Your Dad! He would break open a coconut, would he? Well! If you look up hopefully and wait with open mouth for the water of a coconut to neatly fall into it, you will have to wait till you are an old woman for that to happen."

She had now finished butchering the watermelon and was separating its juicy flesh from its thick hard skin. Having done that she cut the flesh into pieces and put it in plates for our children to eat.

They soon got busy eating it and wiping their cheeks smeared with the juicy flesh.

My wife asked them, "Well! Is it sweet and luscious?"

The children nodded appreciatively and dug with their teeth into bigger morsels of flesh.

My wife also pushed a plate in my direction, but didn't care to ask my opinion about how the watermelon tasted.

It was good that she did not do so. Because although it was a decent sort of watermelon, it wasn't half as sweet, juicy and luscious as the watermelons my father used to buy. Its flesh wasn't as firm as it should have been and it was only moderately sweet. I remembered the out of this world taste of the watermelons my father used to buy and felt sorry that I would never eat the likes of them again. But mind you I never said a word. For I knew that people and particularly women, do not like to be told unpleasant truths, particularly about themselves.

I therefore ate without any complaint the rather insipid watermelon my wife had brought home. Even after I had eaten, I didn't say a word about that watermelon or about watermelons in general. In fact, I changed the subject altogether and said, "Now let us do something different and buy mangoes for a change. Let me warn you though, that people often make the mistake of judging mangoes by their colour or by their size. They don't know that a mango may look very yellow and may be quite big and yet it may not be particularly sweet and may have a poor flavour too. On the other hand, a small mango with a reddish-yellowish colour can be very tasty and have a very distinctive flavour. I must say that my father had an uncanny knack of judging mangoes by merely looking at them and smelling them. And you know what! He never bought them by measly dozens as people seem to do these days, but by basketfuls. And they had a wonderful taste. Eating them used to be a feast fit for the gods."

I closed my eyes and nodded my head ecstatically as I remembered those days when we children used to gorge on those divine mangoes to our fill.

When I spoke thus, I never even suspected that I was saying something that would offend my wife. In fact, I had changed the subject to avoid any such eventuality.

Yet she was almost livid with rage. She screamed, "Enough is enough. I can take it no more. I admit once and for all that I will never be able to buy anything which is even half or a quarter as good as those wonderful things your father used to buy. I concede that I won't be able to do it not only in this birth but in my next seven births. But don't din it into my ears whenever I buy anything at all. It drives me crazy."

I stared open-mouthed at her explosion of anger. For I had never expected that my innocent words would be so grossly misunderstood. So I smiled apologetically and bent my head low to seek pardon and said, "Please don't misunderstand me. It was not my intention at all to run you down. Not even a wee bit. On the contrary, I deeply appreciate all that you do to run this household. I merely wanted to point out how mangoes should be judged. It is a special knack you know. Why, let alone mangoes, take an ordinary thing like cucumbers. One should never go by the look of them. It is not the big fat ones that are tasty. It is the thin and long ones, with a famished look, that are the tastiest of them all. My father as usual always spotted them right away and they used to be so tasty that we ate them with tremendous relish. Oh, ho, ho, ho! They used to be divine."

Even the memory made me feel ecstatic and I closed my eyes and shook my head several times as I remembered the good old days.

You will agree that I had said nothing at all to offend my wife. But for no reason at all she threw a fit, banged on the dinner table the plate she had in hand and walked away clutching her head and screaming.

No dinner was cooked that evening and I heard bags being packed and the children being asked to get ready to leave.

I could see that she was getting ready to walk out of my house and go and stay with her mother.

There really was no reason to be so upset. But women will be women and they have to be humoured.

But she rejected my overtures with flashing eyes and cried, "I have had enough. I will not step into this house of yours ever again."

When she said that the children protested and rebelled. They insisted that they wanted to stay in their own house and they liked their father who took them out to nice restaurants and let them eat all that they wanted to eat.

Luckily my elder sister turned up at that juncture. She sized up the situation and firmly took matter in hand as she was wont to do. She had a long talk with my wife and persuaded her to unpack her bags.

She then scolded me and told me not to mention my father ever again in the house.

She added, "If you want to talk about our father come over to me, sit in a room all by yourself and sing praises of father to your heart's content."

That was both unfair and unkind. But women being what they are, I responded with an ambiguous grunt, which was interpreted as agreement.

In any case, to avoid unpleasantness, I kept my father out of domestic conversation. But there were occasions when I couldn't help mentioning him.

Many years elapsed thereafter. Our children grew up and went abroad for studies. It seems they had taken after my father for they performed very well in their examinations. My daughter found for herself a husband too in those foreign lands, which sorely upset and disappointed my wife, who had spotted several good young men, who would make excellent husbands and nice sons-in-law. But, the daughter was eventually forgiven as children generally are by their mother.

My daughter being very affectionate came back loaded with gifts for all of us. She knew what her mother would like and her younger brother and sister had written to her and sent long lists of the things they wanted. She brought for them all the things and some more.

I, therefore, was the only one who posed a problem for her. What gift to give to a father is somehow always a problem for children. They know him as a provider of all the things they and the entire family needs and they cannot imagine that such a powerful person would be needing anything at all. So she ultimately settled for a light sweater made of very fine English wool.

She gave it to me with a warm smile and an affectionate hug. I must say that unlike her mother she admired her father as a big strong man, who protected her from nasty street dogs and sometimes even an angry mother.

I took the gift with a warm smile, inspected it and said, "It is soft and light. In fact, it is just the thing I wanted."

"Oh Dad! How can you say that without even trying it on? Come on, put it on", said my daughter.

"Oh! He won't do it. He is just contrary", said my wife eyeing me disapprovingly.

"He will do it, won't you, Dad?" said my daughter.

"Of course, I will", I cried warmly and shot a sharp look at my wife.

I then removed my glasses, took off the big loose flowing zabba I used to wear at home and tried on the sweater.

I have always found getting into sweaters a troublesome operation. They are generally tight and I find it difficult to put my head and shoulders through them. But happily I found no such difficulty with the sweater my daughter had brought for me. Putting it on was a smooth and painless operation. So I said appreciatively, "These Britishers certainly seem to know how to make sweaters. See how easily it slid over my head and shoulders."

After I had put it on, it did not grip my chest like a vice but hung loose comfortably over it. That made me happier still and I said, "It certainly is a nice sweater. It is just the kind that I wanted."

But instead of nodding their heads and agreeing with me, all my family burst into peals of laughter.

I was quite surprised and asked, "What on earth is the matter? What makes you laugh?"

But when I looked down at the sweater I was wearing, I realized that it was several times too large for me. Why, I could hardly get my hands out of the sleeves and the sweater reached down below my knees.

While I was surveying the sweater my wife propelled me in front of a mirror and I found myself clothed in an enormous sack, rather than a sweater.

My poor daughter felt very embarassed. But others continued to laugh and the one who laughed the loudest was her husband.

He said, "I was all the while trying to convince her that the sweater was far too big and persuade her to buy a sweater of a more reasonable size. But she wouldn't listen. She kept on saying, "My father is a very big man. He has enormous shoulders. Why, he used to carry me on them. I am sure he needs a very big sweater."

My wife again broke into peals of laughter. She said, "Your daughter seems to have taken after you. You all the time remember the glorious deeds of your father and keep on saying, 'Oh, ho ho! He was wonderful'. That is exactly what she is doing now. Like father, like daughter."

She could have done much worse than that, I thought, but wisely desisted from saying so.

❑

10

Uncle Nana and Bricks of Gold

It was our uncle Nana who inspired the greatest admiration and awe in us children. So great was our awe that the mere sound of his footsteps on the stairs silenced us and the women in the house engaged in high pitched chatter also lowered their voices to scared whispers.

Uncle Nana was in every way worthy of such respect and awe. He had an imposing presence and even his big round belly somehow seemed to add to his formidable stature. The sternness of his expression was heightened by his copious overweening moustache. He wore glasses with a gold frame and we cowered with trepidation when he fixed any one of us with his stare. Particularly, it made me shake with fright because he used to ask me impossibly difficult questions about the fractions time-table. How much is three quarters of seventy-nine, he would ask and I had to give an answer right away. I could never do that. That to him used to be incontrovertible proof that I had been remiss in swotting my times-tables and I was made to recite them all in his presence. That used to be an exhausting labour of more than thirty minutes, punctuated by sharp reprimands for errors.

Nevertheless, in spite of the scare and fright uncle Nana inspired in me, I had, like all others in our family, a deep respect for uncle Nana and his formidable capabilities. How could one have anything but respect for a man who could instantly tell how much three quarters of seventy-nine was! The respect was greatly enhanced because he could, as it seemed to us, single-handedly run a bank which dealt in millions. I had learnt that he had to write huge cash books and ledgers, which were too big to be lifted by one man and send telegrams as far as London and Amsterdam. I couldn't therefore but be overwhelmed by his capabilities.

What bowled me over completely was the fact that the bank he ran single-handedly was not a mere Indian bank but a foreign bank. Uncle Nana was extremely proud that he ran a bank that belonged to white foreign sahibs and so were we. He had nothing but contempt for Indian banks, which were being formed in those days.

"These things", he used to say contemptuously, "are they really worthy of being called banks? They are no better than nine day wonders. They would sprout today and vanish the next day. Running banks is an extremely difficult business way beyond the capabilities of our Indian people. Only the white sahibs can do that."

He never deposited his money with Indian banks. He deposited it with either a foreign bank or with the post-office savings bank which was run by the Government. He sternly made all his relatives do likewise. When one patriotic young man in his family stubbornly refused to be guided by him and opened an account with an Indian bank, uncle Nana berated him with such scathing words, that on hearing them, we children had to rush to the toilets in panic.

Uncle Nana had never told us in so many words that he single-handedly ran the white sahib's bank. But it was easy to surmise that from the way he conducted himself. He was never rushed or flustered, but did everything with calm deliberation and confidence. From the way he spoke we could gather that he had to do enormous amount of work at the bank and carry immense responsibilities on his shoulders. It therefore seemed to us only natural that he should relax in an armchair when at home. He, however, kept an eye on all that went on in the house and got a whole lot of things done from members of the family, dependants and servants. In fact, he kept them on their toes, that is, when they were not running around to do his bidding. Whenever he went out he was greeted respectfully by people who met him in the street and shopkeepers smiled sheepishly and stood with folded hands when he entered their shops.

He never lost his cool and did everything with calm deliberation. This was brought home to me, vividly and impressively, on one occasion when his daughter Yamu's fingers were caught in the joint of the door and the door frame. Poor Yamu screamed and everybody rushed to get her fingers out of the door joint. Poor auntie was in such panic that she began to scream and cry. But the fingers were stuck there and efforts to take them out only caused acute pain to Yamu without accomplishing anything. I got so scared and flustered that I ran back and forth like a headless chicken.

Uncle Nana, however, sat unperturbed and cried in his booming voice, "What on earth has happened? What is all the fuss about? Wouldn't somebody come and tell me what is going on?"

Uncle Nana was held in such awe by everybody that on hearing his booming command, poor auntie forgot for a while the urgent task of pulling poor Yamu's jammed fingers out of the door joint and ran out to tell Nana about the accident in the house.

She was so worked up and so incoherent that uncle Nana had to admonish her and ask several searching questions to find out what had happened.

Having learnt that, uncle Nana thoughtfully digested what he had heard and then got up with his usual deliberation and began to walk with his usual unhurried gait towards the scene of the accident. Poor auntie was so anxious about Yamu that she found it very difficult to follow him at the same unhurried pace, while Yamu continued to scream. But being a dutiful wife, she had to.

We were all scared stiff. But Visoo, a young college student, who lived next doors, showed the audacity to rush past uncle Nana to the source of the screams. He then quickly moved the door a wee bit and gently pulled Yamu's crushed fingers out. He then asked auntie to bring some antiseptic and also a bandage.

Uncle Nana, however, silenced him with an intimidating look. He then took Yamu's crushed fingers in hand, examined them and then administered such a whack on her behind that she fell over and then ran away, screaming.

The college student stared in amazement at uncle Nana and walked out of the house. I, however, could not but be overawed by the calm, unhurried manner in which uncle Nana had handled the situation. If my children get into any similar trouble, I try to emulate Nana. However, I do not inspire the same respect and awe in my family and instead of being admired and obeyed I am berated and run down for my timidity and incompetence in handling domestic crisis.

Nobody ever dared to run down uncle Nana and we in the family continued to look upon him with respect and awe even after the episode of Yamu's crushed fingers. He was considered the final arbiter in all matters big and small. Thus when auntie prepared savoury shira for him, she waited with bated breath when he put its first morsel in his mouth and asked timidly whether she had added salt and spices to it in the right proportion. Uncle Nana would then slowly munch and savour the shira to make a careful assessment of its taste. He did this with the same deliberation and care which he probably exercised when writing his ledgers and cash books. While engaged in this serious assessment he would gaze at the ceiling. I always wondered why he did that until my friend Bapu told me that gazing at the ceiling helped concentration. Poor auntie used to wait with bated breath to hear his verdict. Eventually, when she was almost in tears, he would give his verdict saying, "I think it needs just a pinch of extra salt. Mind you, only a small pinch. Otherwise you would spoil it as you did last Sunday."

Auntie would lower her head with guilt written all over

her face and then add that little pinch of salt to the shira with considerable trepidation. When I saw her doing that, I felt kind of relieved that it was not I who was called upon to add that pinch of salt.

Uncle Nana did everything with great deliberation, be it putting a cap on his head, sandals on his feet or winding his gold pocket watch. I used to be particularly impressed by the solemnity with which he produced his gold clipped pen from his pocket and removed its cover. He did it the same way as the owner of a perfumery shop opened the small bottle of a very expensive perfume for a very special customer. And I used to be utterly overwhelmed when he produced a wad of currency notes from his pocket and counted them, wetting his finger on his lip from time to time. In those days, hardly anybody I knew carried such a big wad of currency notes in his pocket.

The awe in which we children held him used to be heightened, every time we saw lesser men cringing before him with sheepish smiles on their faces.

Getting a job in those days was not as easy as it is now. Even a young man, who had graduated from the University in the first class, had to wait and struggle for a year to land a decent job in the Government service. And I shudder when I think what lesser mortals went through before they landed jobs that gave them as little as forty rupees a month. Mind you though, forty rupees was a lot of money in those days.

It was in such difficult times that uncle Nana had managed to provide three of our relatives with jobs. He had even given the brother of our domestic servant the job of a peon in his bank. Our servant was so overwhelmed by this kindness that he used to spend all his spare time dancing attendance on uncle Nana.

This business of persuading uncle Nana to find a job for the concerned person used to be a long, arduous and exacting operation that often took as long as an year or even more. The needy relative never dared to approach uncle Nana directly for such a great favour. He first went into the kitchen carrying a gift of a small packet of pohas brought from Konkan. That gift was worth very little but its value lay in the fact that it was brought from Konkan. Our family hailed from Konkan and anything brought from there struck a chord of affection and love particularly in the heart of our grandmother and also her daughters-in-law. Having thus established his credentials as a son of Konkan and made it known that he was our not too distant relative, the man got on the right side of our grandmother. He then gave her a detailed account of all the relatives and neighbours in Konkan as well as the cows and bullocks in our cowshed. The mango tree, that stood on the edge of the backyard and gave the most luscious mangoes, was not forgotten. That made the milk of human kindness flow from grandma's bosom, which in any case was always full of it. Thereafter the young relative began to run errands for grandmother as well as my mother and auntie. Later on he made bold to exchange greetings and small talk with my father who was younger than uncle Nana. Like all people who hailed from Konkan that young man was poor and perhaps the eldest son in a large family. His grandmother was a playmate of my grandmother in the good old days and also distantly related to our family. Grandma naturally felt very sad to learn that her playmate and her family were so poor. She told uncle Nana the sad story of her playmate's family and said, "Can something be done for the young man? After all he is a close relative and son of Mathu, my childhood playmate."

Everybody was expected to respect his elders and particularly parents and grandparents. Our grandma's word, therefore, was the law in our house. But such was the awe in which uncle Nana was held that even grandma used to be hesitant and somewhat deferential when talking to him.

Uncle Nana would then nod and grunt and observe with a wry smile, "Jobs aren't so plentiful as to be picked up from dirt as one walks along the street."

When he said that, he did not even deign to look at the young man, who stood with bent head and quaking heart to hear his words. Hearing these words, I used to conclude that there was no hope whatsoever for the young man and feel sorry for him. However, others put an altogether different interpretation on these words. The grunt and smile and Nana's dismissive words were generally interpreted as offering ground for hope. Thus encouraged, the young man tried to be useful around the house even more diligently. Now he made bold to run errands even for uncle Nana and was often scolded for being dumb and doing the wrong thing.

After about a month or two of such diligent service, the matter of a job was mentioned once again by grandma.

"We will see", said uncle Nana laconically and that was considered one more step in the right direction and also a signal to the young man to redouble his efforts to please uncle Nana.

The young man at this juncture got a sort of promotion and began to enjoy the privilege of giving uncle Nana his box of snuff or his cap or accompany him bag in hand when he went to the vegetable market.

Another month or two had to elapse before the matter of finding a job for the young man was mentioned yet again.

On this occasion uncle Nana deigned to look at the young man and scan him critically from head to foot and growled, "The matter will have to be looked into and then some khatpat will have to be done. It is not going to be easy though. Times are hard."

I always wondered why these words, which seemed very discouraging to me, were heard gleefully and considered by the young man as a firm assurance that uncle Nana would find a job for him. He, therefore, proceeded to dance attendance on uncle Nana with redoubled vigour.

I never quite understood what 'khatpat' meant and what difficult moves and manoeuvres it involved. But when I saw the wrinkles on uncle Nana's brow as he talked about it, I could surmise that 'khatpat' was something way beyond the competence of ordinary mortals. Sometimes uncle mentioned in hushed tone how severe and demanding the white sahibs or Indian Shetjis were and auntie repeated it in even more hushed tones to her relatives and neighbours. Sometimes there was mention of one Mr. Joshi who seemed to be a sly and mean fellow who always tried to put spokes in whatever uncle Nana wanted to do. All of us in the family used to await with bated breath the outcome of the 'khatpat' uncle Nana was engaged in.

Eventually uncle Nana triumphed and the young aspirant for a job was called for an interview. So he went to uncle Nana's office wearing a new set of clothes specially stitched for the occasion. Sometimes a single interview used to bring success, while on other occasions the poor chap had to present himself for interview twice or thrice before he was appointed. Initially, the appointment used to be temporary and the salary used to range between forty and fifty rupees.

In the evening the young man called on us carrying a big packet of a seer of sweet pedhas. He fell at uncle Nana's feet, who blessed and also admonished him to do his work honestly and diligently so as not to tarnish uncle Nana's fair name. He also fell at grandma's and auntie's feet and smiled while we ate the pedhas. Auntie teased him saying that the pedhas were no good. The poor chap then felt guilty and rushed to buy a new packet of pedhas. Auntie then stopped him, saying it was all a joke and forced him to eat a couple of pedhas himself. This he did after a great deal of persuasion and with a very shy and guilty expression.

The young man's appointment continued to be temporary for a long time, which sometimes extended to even two or three years. During this period he lived in constant dread of losing his job. He, therefore, continued to dance attendance on uncle Nana. Uncle Nana accepted or rather tolerated this attention as if he was conferring a great favour on that young man.

He kept a close eye though on how the young man did

his work at the bank or at the office of one of bank's customers, where he had been given employment. If he was found remiss or less than diligent in his work, uncle Nana scolded him loudly and harshly in the presence of everybody. The poor soul heard it with bent head and a guilty expression. This enhanced immensely the admiration and awe in which uncle Nana was held by all around him.

Uncle Nana assessed the performance not only of the lower order of employees but also of powerful leaders and distinguished men in all walks of life. Thus when Hitler declared war against the British, uncle Nana unhesitatingly asserted that Hitler was a damned ass if he believed he could defeat the English sahibs. He also condemned with equal contempt Gandhiji's efforts to win independence by launching satyagraha movements. He used to ask everyone contemptuously whether independence can ever be attained by getting one's head broken for a handful of salt. He was firmly convinced that the British, who were our rulers, were the most powerful, clever and resourceful people in the world; and it would be in our interest to live under their benign and wise rule. It would be a disaster, he believed, if power was ever transferred into the hands of our foolish leaders.

While he had only contempt for Hitler, Mussolini and Gandhiji, he had nothing but admiration and awe for the British rulers and of course the British sahibs who ran his bank. He used to talk often and at length about the many victories the British had won and also about their many achievements in diverse fields. He did this with such conviction, that we in his family had not the slighest doubt that what he said was utterly and completely true. Such was his devotion that he used to be distraught if one of his British superiors at the bank so much as caught a cold. In fact, he expected every one in the family to be equally distraught and auntie thought it wise not to prepare any sweets on such a day even if it happened to be a day of religious festival.

What distinguished uncle Nana from lesser mortals was the fact that he had won the trust and confidence of the British sahibs who were incomparably powerful, wise and resourceful. We often heard the stories of how much the British sahibs trusted him and deferred to his advice. And that constantly enhanced our awe and admiration for him.

That he was in a class apart was proved beyond all doubt when we saw with our own eyes, what we had heard all along.

It all started with a casual remark auntie once made. She said, "There may be bricks of gold in the Lanka of the demon Ravana. But what good are they to us? We can never lay hands on them."

Uncle Nana happened to hear these words and he then indulged in one of his extremely rare humorous sallies. He smiled in his ample moustache and said, "Bricks of gold can be found not only in Ravana's Lanka, but also in our bank."

We all smiled as we were expected to when uncle said anything humorous. But we thought that what he said was no more than a joke.

When uncle Nana was in one of his rare humorous moods, small liberties could be taken with him and auntie proceeded to do so. She said, "We all know that the sahib's bank is very rich. But how can it own bricks of solid gold?"

Uncle Nana replied with a loud guffaw, "Are you suggesting that I am telling a lie?"

Auntie winced fearing that she had transgressed the limits. Then she said timidly, "I didn't mean that. But I thought..."

Uncle Nana cut her words midway with a even louder guffaw and said, "Well! I will take you to the bank and you can then see the gold bricks with your own eyes."

We almost fell backwards when we heard those words and stood gazing wide-eyed and open-mouthed at uncle Nana.

Thereafter we children so forgot ourselves as to cry, "Please take us along too, uncle Nana."

A moment later we realized the enormity of what we had done and shrank and cowered in fear of receiving the verbal lashing we expected. But uncle Nana that day was in a very happy and generous mood. He smiled, patted us on our backs and said with a broad smile that filled his ample moustache, "All right. If that is what you want, I shall take you along too. But it will take some time for all the arrangements to be made."

These words lifted us off the ground and we floated in the air for the rest of that day. The story of our wondrous good luck spread among our relatives, neighbours and schoolmates. Naturally, we were inundated with requests to be taken along with us for seeing bricks of gold. We had to turn them down, which we did with broad smiles and with a certain pity for those lesser beings, who didn't have an uncle like Nana and who therefore never could see bricks of gold with their own eyes.

It took fifteen days, which appeared to us as long as a millennium, for the arrangements of our visit to the bank to be made. Ultimately on a Saturday morning, when the bank worked for only half a day, we got ready to visit the bank. The lucky ones included auntie, mom and us four children in the family. We wore our best clothes and we children were admonished to be on our best behaviour. Auntie and mom wore their gold jewellery and wore sarees which had gold thread in them.

Uncle Nana had sent one of his assistants home to escort us to the bank. He hired a victoria in which we all sat feeling very important as numerous envious eyes saw us depart. The victoria ran through the streets so fast that we thought it almost flew. When it reached the downtown Fort area, we were overawed by the tall stately buildings, which had big signboards written in golden letters and doormen, in liveried uniforms, standing at their huge polished doors. Those doors had heavy brass fittings shining like gold.

Our victoria stopped at the entrance of one of those buildings with a sign board which announced the name of uncle's bank in golden letters. I had then spent a year in a middle school where English was taught. I was therefore the only one who could read that name. I read that out to auntie and mom and told Damu that those letters looked like done in real gold. Damu quickly nodded agreement.

I was initially scared of the liveried doorman who was a hefty Pathan with a big turban. But he ushered us into the bank with a courteous smile, which further convinced me of how big a man our uncle was.

We sat on a bench for a while. But soon uncle came out. We being on our best hehaviour stood in a neat row. Uncle took us inside the bank, where he made us stand near his office table and went inside into the sahib's room.

I and Damu had half a mind to take to our heels, if the sahib was in foul temper. This was because uncle Nana had told us that this sahib had a bad temper and scolded people very harshly. However, the sahib came out of his room smiling. He then touched my cheek playfully and said, "You want to see gold bricks, don't you?"

I couldn't make out what he said but guessed it and said, "Yes, yes."

I felt very proud then that I knew English and so did my mother and auntie.

The sahib then went to the strong-room, turned a number of knobs and wheels and opened its thick heavy door. All this while our uncle had asked us to stand at a distance. When the door of the strongroom opened, the sahib invited us into the room. There, to my amazement, were gold bricks stacked in a corner. They weren't quite as many as I had thought they would be, but they were quite a few. All of us gazed at them in wonder and awe.

"Let us ask the sahib if we can take away one of them", I whispered to Damu. I didn't mean it of course. It was just a joke.

In that quiet strong-room, the whisper sounded louder than what I meant it to be and everybody heard it. My auntie and mom were quite alarmed and even Damu became uncomfortable and tried to snub me with his eyes.

Sahib asked uncle what I had said. Uncle eyed me sternly and then told the sahib with a smile what I had said.

The sahib laughed uproariously and said, "Certainly you can, provided you can lift one of them and carry it away."

I couldn't make out what the sahib said with his incomprehensible pronunciations. So I asked uncle and when he told me what the sahib had said, everybody felt relieved and laughed loudly.

I remembered that I was supposed to be on my best behaviour and indicated with a nod that I wouldn't do it.

But the sahib continued to laugh and insisted that I should give it a try. So uncle too laughed and told me not to be afraid and try to lift a brick of gold.

So ultimately I tried that and discovered that the brick was heavy far beyond my expectations. In fact while trying to lift it I almost lost my balance and my toes barely escaped being crushed by the brick falling on them.

Both uncle and the sahib laughed at my discomfiture and invited my cousin Damu and my auntie to lift it.

But they were too shy to make such an attempt.

The sahib touched my cheek when we were leaving and I very boldly shook hands with him saying, "Good morning."

"Good afternoon", he said and laughed again. I too responded with a cheerful laugh.

This bold deed of mine once again impressed mom and auntie and Damu too.

On our way home we ate some sweets that uncle bought for us.

It was a truly memorable event in our lives and I felt very proud of my part in it.

Moreover, that even put a seal of finality on our conviction that our uncle was a very great man. So great was he that his greatness extended from the toes of Lord Rama to his crown and there was nobody else equal to him in the world. ❑

K.MARX.

11

Chandu in the Brave New Socialist Order

Propriety demanded that Uncle Nana's eldest son should seek appointment and eventually take his place in the bank which Nana had served with such distinction. But Damu disappointed him and became an engineer instead. There would have been nothing wrong if the second son had become an engineer or even a veterinary surgeon. But Damu shouldn't have done it. Moreover Damu had not observed the proprieties, which hurt Nana deeply. Later on, instead of asking his parents to find a wife for him, he fell in love with a girl belonging to another caste and married her. This was a stigma that as good as blackened Nana's face and he disowned Damu completely. He didn't allow even Damu's name to be mentioned in his household.

Mothers, however, cannot bring themselves to disown their children, and Indian mothers particularly so. So Damu's mother began to refer to him as Lord Vithoba and made it a practice to visit Vithoba's temple quite often and she took with her laddus and other sweets as offerings. Thus Nana's pride was not hurt and family ties were not broken.

The eldest son having disappointed him, uncle Nana expected his younger son Chandu to join his bank. Chandu did take up employment with a bank. It was, however, not uncle Nana's foreign bank but an Indian bank. He contended that he had much better chances of going up the promotional ladder in an Indian bank than in a foreign bank. He said, 'We are now an independent country. So it will be our banks that will expand rapidly and not the foreign banks.'

Uncle Nana was furious when he came to know of Chandu's decision. Having grown up in the heyday of the British Raj, he had the highest respect for things foreign, particularly British, and thought very poorly of things Indian. To avoid confrontation and exchange of bad words, Chandu avoided being around when Uncle Nana was at home. That made Uncle Nana feel bottled up and ultimately he gave vent to his fury by berating Chandu's poor mother.

He said, "Mind you! That bank will fail and he will soon find himself on the street. If he comes whining to my door under those circumstances, I will throw him out. Mind my words, he will land out there on his ear."

One of the things an Indian woman has to do is to quietly suffer such talk from the husband and other elders in the family. That is what Nana's wife did with firmly pursed lips.

She knew, however, that Uncle Nana's forebodings wouldn't come true, and that was what happened. Instead of finding himself in the street, Chandu got promoted quickly and became a junior officer at the bank.

That might give the impression that Chandu was a smart and competent chap. Well, he was, but not particularly. His promotion was rather the doing of the bank employees union, which had suddenly become enormously powerful in socialist independent India. The union had insisted that atleast fifty percent promotions to officers' grade should go to the clerical staff, who were building up the bank by the sweat of their brow. The employees struck work, organized huge demonstration and screamed frightening slogans, which made the management quake in their shoes. Chandu, who was then a clerk shouted the loudest in the true spirit of a socialist revolutionary.

"Down with the capitalist criminals! Down with the management! Down with the thieves and cheats!", he screamed.

Even I used to get scared to see him carrying on so. I feared that Uncle Nana's forebodings would come true and Chandu would soon be on the streets. Uncle Nana himself didn't have the slightest doubt that this would happen. He looked forward with grim satisfaction to Chandu falling at his feet, admitting his errors and begging for forgiveness. He would then show Chandu the door. Poor Chandu having no other recourse would fall at his feet again and would again be shown the door unceremoniously. Chandu's mother would then beg for forgiveness for her son and after telling her a few home truths, Uncle Nana would at last relent and find a job for him in his foreign bank.

Unfortunately for Uncle Nana things turned out quite differently. Instead of being sacked, Chandu was rewarded for his militant leadership by his union and recommened for promotion to officer's grade. The management accepted all the demands and recommendations of the employees' union on bended knees. Chandu was soon sitting in an air-conditioned cabin and ringing a bell to summon a peon. He was given a nice two bedroom apartment to live in and a car was only a few promotions away.

This was quite embarassing for Uncle Nana. For even after serving his foreign bank dutifully for thirty-five years, he had never managed to progress beyond the post of supervisor, and the poor man had never sat inside an air-conditoned officer's cabin. His highest achievement had been to enjoy the privilege of sitting, in his capacity as a supervisor, almost at the door of the cabin of the General Manager. He had no doubt progressed beyond a wooden chair without arms to a wooden chair with arms. But it had no cushions and was not a swivel chair either. He had improved matters a little by buying a cushion for the chair with his own money.

As against this, his son Chandu now enjoyed the privileges of an officer. He had a cushioned swivel chair, which could also be tilted backwards for comfort. He had a big steel table with a nice glass top. And his salary cheque was so fat that Uncle Nana was stunned when he learnt how fat it was. That was not surprising because in those days, even when he was on the verge of retirement, Uncle Nana earned much less. Later on when he learnt that the bank gave Chandu a bonus equal to two months' salary, Uncle Nana got utterly disgusted. He turned away from worldly affairs and began to spend his time in reading the holy scriptures.

But stories of Chandu's good fortune continued to reach his reluctant ears. Chandu's wife also got employed in a bank and both of them earned so much money that they right away bought a refrigerator, an air-conditioner and spent a month's vacation in the bank's luxurious holiday quarters at a hill station. Such luxurious lifestyle had been the privilege of only the white managers of Uncle Nana's foreign bank. And now Chandu enjoyed it in the early stages of his career. Even though Uncle Nana had withdrawn his interest from worldly life, this was too much for him to swallow.

Uncle Nana had, in a huff, completely broken off relations with Chandu. But his family gravitated more and more towards him, attracted by the loving and lavish hospitality of his wife and the comforts and luxuries his home offered. The grandchildren provided excellent excuse for Nana's wife to visit Chandu. To love and pamper grandchildren was the prerogative of a woman and even tradition considered it improper for her lord and master to deny it to her. Children were considered exempt from family feuds and tiffs and the rest of the extended family would not have approved if Nana had been unkind to them. They began to visit Nana's house to meet their grandmother and be pampered by her and soon enough they began to run around in Nana's den and even climb up his knees. Uncle Nana tried to stay grim and be stand-offish but couldn't do it for long.

Hindu religion can be of great help in breaking down barriers. When a pooja is performed in a household, all the relatives are expected to visit and bow to the god or goddess being worshipped and it is considered improper to allow anger or hostility to stand in the way. Nana's wife performed such poojas often and Chandu and his wife visited Nana's house on such occasions. Soon enough they began to stay for the festive lunch and Nana could not object to it. He tried to be grim and aloof but that was ignored by the rest of the family.

Soon it becâme difficult for Nana to be in a huff whenever Chandu and his family visited him. After a while Chandu's wife arranged a pooja in her house and she and her husband called on Nana, fell at his feet and sweetly invited him to perform the rituals. Nana couldn't refuse and invoke the anger of the gods and that put paid to his efforts to stay grimly aloof. He wasn't unhappy about it either. For he too had got tired of refusing to share the togetherness of the family.

Nana saw Chandu enjoy the comforts and luxuries which only his white sahibs could enjoy in the good old days and soon he began to enjoy them too. We, the close relatives, were also happy that the family feud had ended and enjoyed the lavish hospitality Chandu's sweet-tempered wife extended to all of us. But while we recognized that Chandu was far more fortunate than Nana ever was, we all felt that there was a lacunae somewhere. Chandu didn't enjoy the awe and respect in which Nana was held in his days of glory. It was true that Nana never rose beyond the lowly position of a supervisor in his 'foreign' bank. But his ample moustache, his haughty demeanour, his self-assured, confident gait and the deep growl in his voice put him on a high pedestal altogether. Our noisy house used to fall silent the moment his heavy steps were heard on the stairs and if he raised his voice, not only the children but even the women in the house got so scared that they dropped the pots and pans they had in their hands. In those days Uncle Nana's subordinates stood with bent heads and folded hands in his presence and ran with alacrity to obey his commands. In our eyes he enjoyed the status of a Maharaja of a small kingdom.

Poor Chandu, it must be confessed, never enjoyed anything even remotely comparable to that. He had a fridge and other fancy gadgets in his house. But his wife talked to him with familiarity on a first name basis and asked him to attend to household chores which were considered demeaning by men in the good old days. Why, I have seen him bathing his children and even helping them in the toilet. I had seen his little son playfully pulling his ear and his little daughter scoffing at him for his inability to comb her hair to her liking. Both the children were convinced that their mother was a far more capable person than their father and didn't hesitate to tell him so. Their mother, I noticed, made no efforts at all to change this perception of theirs. They therefore believed that mothers in general were more capable than fathers and this they considered to be true of grandmothers and grandfathers too. They went so far as to tell Uncle Nana so. It made me wince but Nana suffered this indignity quietly. That things should come to such a pass, seemed to me terrible. To my amazement I found that women in the household including auntie Laxmi were not in the least bothered about it. I could therefore only shake my head in distress.

Things change with the passage of time. Over the years I too have experienced that. My wife now expects me to help in the kitchen and berates me for being clumsy and my children are amused when she does that. But that does not matter too much, because I never enjoyed the royal authority Uncle Nana did in our family. But to see Uncle Nana suffer indignities used to make me wince. I remembered the old days, when panic gripped the house on hearing Uncle Nana raise his voice in anger.

Maybe Uncle Nana's days of glory were over. But Chandu who rose rapidly up the promotional ladder didn't seem to enjoy a comparable high status and glory in his office. I never saw his subordinates visiting his house and standing with bent heads and folded hands to obey his commands. On the contrary, Chandu once gave a party to his subordinates and I saw him dancing attendance on them to keep them happy.

I asked him, "Well, Chandu! What is the occasion for this party?"

Chandu looked at me sheepishly and stuttered, "Oh nothing in particular! Just an occasion to meet and enjoy in a friendly spirit."

I raised my eyebrows in surprise and looked at him curiously.

Chandu gave me a meaningful look and said, "Well! I know it is difficult for you to understand. But that is the sort of thing one has to do these days."

In those days, I was a lecturer at a college and the trade union movement had not yet reached the portals of colleges. So I couldn't quite make out what Chandu implied when he said that. Getting curious about the state of affairs in banks, I once went to Chandu's bank.

I found a number of red flags fluttering militantly all around the bank's premises and big cloth banners were strung up at various points which in big screaming letters denounced the management of the bank as a bunch of reactionary exploiters and thieves. When I entered the premises, I saw big paper posters being pasted on the walls and doors. I looked at one of them, and I found that it carried a charter of demands. I furtively read and counted the demands and I found that they were twenty-two in number. I must confess that I was quite overawed by the sweep and boldness of those demands.

In the old days when I studied economics at the college, we had to study the great controversy of the nineteen thirties about whether the exchange rate of the rupee should be one shilling and four pences or one shilling and six pences. Our learned professor had given us a list of eleven reasons in favour of the first option and a list of an equal number of reasons in favour of the second option. That had aroused in me profound respect for the learning of our professor which I continue to feel to this day. I felt the same deep respect for the union leaders when I read that detailed and comprehensive list of demands.

It was with a respectfully bowed head that I approached the liftman and asked him on which floor was the department located in which Chandu worked. The response was an angry stare and stony silence.

Fearing that I had been unwittingly rude, I smiled sheepishly and asked the question again most humbly and apologetically. That made the liftman thaw a little and he imperiously pointed his finger at a board, which listed the various departments located on different floors. I noted that Chandu's department was located on the third floor and thanking the liftman profusely stepped into the lift with appropriate humility. The liftman made me wait until there was a full compliment of five passengers in the lift. He then got into the lift and banged its door shut. He made it amply clear to me that he considered visitors, who made him operate the lift, an unmitigated nuisance. I could guess right away that in the next charter of twenty-two demands one demand would be that the liftman should not be called upon to operate the lift more than once every hour. I realized that I had to be very careful not to offend the bank employees in any manner whatsoever.

When I got off on the third floor and entered Chandu's department, I found that the atmosphere there was very relaxed, laid back and informal. Quite a few chairs there were empty indicating that the occupants had gone out to attend to some work or more probably to have a refreshing cup of tea in the canteen. Some were perusing papers and ledgers with furrowed brows. One of them banged a ledger shut so noisily that it made me jump. Some others seemed to have finished their work for they sat in a bunch and chatted and laughed.

In the midst of this general atmosphere of bonhomie, I saw only one man working with a great deal of concentration and diligence.

Uncle Nana would have been shocked had he witnessed such a scene on entering his bank. In his bank, the clerks worked diligently at their tables with bent heads from morning until they left the office premises in the evening. They hardly exchanged any words and nobody had ever heard any laughter on those premises. Hard work, obedience and respect for authority constituted the culture of the establishment.

The bank employees seemed to think that the change from that grim back-breaking culture to the new culture of a relaxed easy-going workstyle was an improvement and it would have been unwise to disagree with that view. I wondered what things would be like if this new culture invaded the educational institutions where already a relaxed atmosphere prevailed.

I realized that it would be impertinent to interrupt the happy bonhomie of the employees by asking them where I could find their boss. So I walked up to the table of the gentleman who was diligently at work and asked him where I could find Chandu.

He looked up, his brow furrowed and he shot an angry glance at me and then came a curt reply, "Inquire with the Inquiry."

I was about to ask him where the Inquiry was, but realized that that inquiry would also have to be addressed only to Inquiry.

So I moved away with an apologetic bow and began to look around for Chandu's air-conditioned cabin. After a while I located his nameplate and gingerly pushed open the swinging door and peeped in. I was greatly relieved to find Chandu sitting there and walked in.

Chandu had really a very comfortable cabin. He had an upholstered revolving swivel chair. But instead of leaning back in it and dictating to a secretary, he sat hunched over the table amidst piles of files.

He tried to extend a warm welcome to me. But his smile

was thin and lifeless and his effort to pump my hand warmly wasn't particularly successful.

I knew that he was trying his best to be nice to me and said sympathetically. "You seem to be frightfully busy."

He nodded and said, "Yes indeed! And the impending strike has added to the usual heavy burden. We have orders from the top to finish off as much work as possible before the strike gets launched."

I nodded in appreciation of his difficulties and then offered, what I thought was, a constructive suggestion. I said, "I appreciate your problem. But why are you doing all this work yourself. I see that you have quite a few subordinates. Why don't you ask them to share the burden?"

Chandu responded with a wan smile. It seemed that there was a great deal he wanted to say but he swallowed his words with great difficulty and said, "Oh, they have done their work. But as a manager it is my responsibility to ensure that it is done properly. So I am doing it all over again", he sighed and continued, "Well! You are a professor and I know that you teach people how to manage businesses, So you might find it a little difficult to understand what goes on here."

He shook his head morosely several times and heaved a big resigned sigh.

I couldn't make head or tail of what he was saying but I realized that it would be unwise to discuss the matter any further. But what I saw around me made me blurt out, "Do you want me to believe that these people have completed this mountain of work? I see none of them bent over his table. They are talking and giggling like carefree larks."

Chandu swallowed hard and said, "Well! It is like this. The bank acknowledges that they are overburdened with work. So it allows them to work overtime and pays them at double the normal rate for the extra hours of work. So the employees are conserving energy during working hours, so as be able to work longer and earn more overtime."

I found this very complicated and confusing and after

thinking hard for quite a while, gave up the effort to comprehend it.

I remembered, however, that I had seen one chap working hard on my way to Chandu's cabin. So I asked Chandu, "I saw one man bent over his table and working very hard. He was so busy that he had no time to answer my question. In fact he was offended by the interruption and growled at me brusquely."

Chandu almost jumped out of his seat in fright and stammered, "I hope you haven't been rude to him. Better be careful, otherwise you will cut my throat from ear to ear. The strike will be launched and if that guy is offended, they will shout slogans denouncing me as an enemy of the working class and as a running dog of thieves and bloodsuckers."

I was shaken by this frightful prospect and cried, "Goodness me! I didn't know he was such an important personage. Who is he?"

Chandu bowed his head and said in an awed whisper, "He is the union leader in our branch. A very powerful man indeed - very powerful!"

I was glad that I hadn't said anything offensive to that chap and said in an equally awed whisper, "I have heard that union leaders don't do much work in the office and also dissuade others from doing work. But this gentleman was very diligently at work."

"Ha!", Chandu cried, "Well! Now that the union is about to launch a strike, he naturally has a lot of work to do."

"Do you mean to say that this union employee is a very conscientious employee and was trying to finish his quota of work before he went on a strike."

Chandu opened his mouth to laugh and then stifled it quickly. He then indicated with a sweep of his hand that I was barking up the wrong tree. He explained, "He wasn't doing the bank's work, silly. He was doing his union's work."

That confused me even more and I asked, "Union work?

Here? How can he do union's work during the working hours of a bank?"

"Of course, he can. That demand was conceded by the bank at the conclusion of the last successful strike of the employees. Not only can a union representative do union's work during office hours, he can use all the communication facilities at the bank for that purpose. Why, he can even travel by plane at the bank's expense to do union's work." Chandu watched with amusement as my mouth fell open in astonishment at what I was hearing.

It took me quite a while to recover from my stunned astonishment and when I did so, I asked, "Let me get this straight. Are you telling me that your bank gives free of cost all the facilities needed by union leaders to organize a strike for demanding higher wages?"

"Precisely!", said Chandu, "Don't forget that we are now a socialist country and in a socialist country there can be no conflict of interest between the bank and its workers. The bank feels that a stong union serves its interests best."

Uninitiated as I was in the principles and practices of a socialist dispensation, I couldn't make head or tail of what Chandu said. I stared at him uncomprehendingly.

To help me understand, Chandu explained, "This is how things are done in socialist Britain and we are following in their noble footsteps."

That put my mind completely at ease. After all it was socialist Britain that gave us freedom and our leaders had taken their lessons in socialism at Cambridge and the London School of Economics too. I was therefore gratified that we were following in the footsteps of profound and seasoned socialists.

In the midst of our conversation, a person entered Chandu's cabin carrying with him some files.

Seeing him I realized that my throat had gone dry due to all this excitement and I said to Chandu, "Can this man get a glass of water for me? Will you please ask him to do so?"

Chandu shot out of his seat when he heard what I said. He then clamped his hand on my mouth and said, "No. No. Of course not! He then turned towards the peon and said apologetically, "Please don't misunderstand, Ganpatrao. I know how insulting such a request is. This friend of mine is imbued with the old ways and doesn't know what a gross impropriety he is committing. Please forgive me and ignore what he has said."

The peon stopped for a moment to make up his mind whether he should be wildly angry and make a scene or large-heartedly ignore these remnants of bourgeois habits. Eventually he decided to be large-hearted and walked away.

Chandu heaved a sigh of relief and clutching his head collapsed in his chair.

I felt quite alarmed and guilty at the enormity of my error and apologized to Chandu profusely. "Forgive me", I said, "But to avoid the repetition of similar faux pas, let me know where I went wrong. To me it seems that it was a grave error to address him in a first person singular rather than in a respectful plural."

Chandu said, "Well, that was one serious error but not the only one. What was most offensive and insulting was to ask him to bring water for you to drink."

"Oh, is that so? I didn't realize that", I said, still not quite comprehending where I had gone wrong.

"Well! Please get it clearly in your head, that it is not the work of a peon to fetch a glass of water. It is demeaning to him to be asked to do so."

"But that has all along been a part of the work of a peon", I said.

"Not any more", said Chandu in a sharply admonishing voice, "A separate and a slightly lower class of workers is now employed to do that work. They are called, 'water boys'."

"Oh, I see", I said, "I presume they also do other lowly work like sweeping and cleaning."

"No! No!", cried Chandu, "You are now making another

error which wil greatly offend the water boys."

"Good Heaven!", I cried, feeling that I was picking my way through a minefield.

"There is", explained Chandu patiently, "another category of employees who sweep the premises. But cleaning the toilets is not their job. It is done by another set of employees."

"My God!" I cried. As I brooded over the matter, I realized that a new socialist caste system was being evolved in the brave new socialist dispensation.

Chandu felt that I had not fully grasped the ramifications of the division of labour in the banks. So he explained, "The categorization of work and its distribution among different classes of employees is a very elaborate and intricate arrangement based on very fine and subtle distinctions. For instance, a peon assigned to deliver cheques will not deliver bills of exchange. A clerk writing one ledger would not touch another ledger. Nor will he hand over the ledger to a colleague seated nearby. That will have to be done by a peon. As a consequence no employees are overburdened with work as they used to be in the old capitalist order.

I nodded my head appreciatively. All doubts in my mind were cleared as it had happened to Arjuna when he heard the Bhagwat Gita from the lips of Lord Krishna. I said, "Wonderful! This is a most benign and wonderful scheme of things. With such an elaborate and clear distribution of functions, there can be no confusion, no frictions and nobody will be overworked. Stress will cause no illness and so many people will get jobs, that unemployment will almost vanish. For as I see now three men are employed to do the work which in the old days was done by one or rather half a man."

Chandu expressed agreement with an emphatic nod of his head and cried, "And let me add that the problem of poverty also gets sorted out under this new and benign socialist dispensation. For now, the peon gets double the salary he earned in the old days."

"Yes", I cried with tears of joy in my eyes, "That is truely the socialist dream come true."

Chandu could do no more than mutely nod agreement.

As I happily pondered over this new socialist dispensation, I noticed another benefit built into it. I said to Chandu, "I must say that in keeping with our noble tradition of blending the old and the new, this system brings about a happy combination of our old caste system and the brave new socialist order."

Chandu nodded agreement again and added, "I only wish that we in the management cadre are not as overburdened with work as we are now."

I nodded agreement and pondered over the matter. But soon I found a solution to the problem and said to Chandu, "I realize that in this system at present, you are getting a raw deal. You have to do all the work and don't get paid overtime."

Chandu nodded sadly.

I said, "There is a solution to this problem. You in the managerial cadre should organize a union of your own and submit a charter of not twenty-two but forty-four demands. You are not at present allowed to do so. But if you organize morchas, shout slogans and go on hunger strikes, you will be given the right to form unions, submit charters of demands and go on strike."

Chandu smiled and said, "You have hit the nail on the head. That is exactly what we propose to do."

"Ha! Then all your problems will be solved", I cried, clapped him on the back and departed cheerfully from that temple of socialism.

❑

TODAY'S SPECIAL
AMLET....
RICE PLAT...
BRED.BUTTER
TOSS
MISAL
BESAN
LADDU
COPI.TEA
DO NOT
SPIT

12

The Big Silver Rupee

"Here is something for you, son", said my father. My palm opened automatically when he said that. My father was in a very cheerful mood, because one of his clients had given him a thickish wad of currency notes.

That something was so heavy that my palm was weighed down. Had I not been alert and clutched it firmly in my hand that something would have slipped to the floor and rolled away under the table or a chair.

I lifted my palm and opened it. I couldn't believe my eyes when I saw what was in it. Why, it was one whole big shining silver rupee. Rupees are a dime a dozen these days, and they are generously given to kids in tens or even twenties by their doting parents. Things were, however, pretty different when we were kids. A rupee was pretty hard to come by in those days, when salaries could be as low as twenty-five or thirty-rupees a month. Moreover, fathers in those days were not the pliable lumps of clay that they are now. They were stern, unbending and grim. They never made the mistake of pampering their children for fear of spoiling them and avoided as far as possible giving any money to their children so that they would not get into the bad habit of spending it.

I have only to cite the instance of my friend Sadu who had the temerity to ask for one nickel anna (sixteen annas made a rupee in those days) from Tatya, his father.

Tatya stared at Sadu and cried, "You are a small boy no bigger than a man's thumb and yet you have the temerity to ask for money? What on earth do you want it for? You get food to eat twice a day and you have clothes on your back. What else does a boy need? In any case if you need anything ask for it. If it is something that a boy must get, I will bring it for you. But I will certainly not give money in your hands. If boys can lay hands on money, they get into bad habits. They buy halwa and other sweets at will and they are even tempted to place bets on playing cards at street corners. That, my boy, is the beginning of a short and quick journey to penury."

Sadu pleaded, "But, please listen to me, Tatya!"

That threw Tatya into a rage. He shouted, "You are talking back, are you? Do you know what I will do. I will break your leg to teach you to behave yourself."

Sadu was a sensible boy with considerable experience in dealing with an angry father. The moment he heard the raised voice of his father, he took to his heels and remained out of Tatya's sight for quite some time.

That little episode will tell you what fathers were like in those old days. They were particularly prone to threaten to break the legs of their errant offspring. If no legs were broken the credit must go entirely to us clever boys, who could sense danger well in advance and had strong and nimble pairs of heels to get away from it pretty fast.

My father was an exception to this general run of parents. He used to give me a nickel anna every day so that I could buy some snacks and sweets in the mid-day break at school. Sometimes, when he did not have change, he even gave me a two anna coin. All the boys in my class envied me for having a father like that. Their parents, however, would shake their heads and mutter about the dire consequences of such misplaced generosity. These feelings of theirs were promptly conveyed to my father by my mother, grandmother and others in our household. But luckily my father just tossed his head, guffawed and continued to give me one anna every day. I must mention, if I am to be truthful, that there were some other fathers too who used to give a copper paisa or two to their sons.

However, even my father had not until then gone so far as to give me one whole big shining silver rupee. That really would have been much too much. A rupee was a very substantial sum of money in those days. If my mother went shopping with a rupee tucked in the fold of her saree, she could buy a bagful of groceries and sweets and still have a few copper paise left in her hands. Why, the whole family could go to the ferry wharf in a horse drawn victoria for less than a rupee. We did that every year when we went to our village in Konkan in the summer vacation. No wonder I was taken aback when my father put in my palm such a huge amount of money. In fact, I felt quite certain that he had made an error. I did not want to be blamed for not pointing it out to him. So I said to my father, "Baba, what you have given me is a whole big rupee."

"Is that so?" said my father with a great show of surprise and laughed loudly. Being a shrewed boy, I immediately made out that my father really meant to give me a rupee. I was so overjoyed that I ran all over the house, leaping around with raised hands. That was not enough to express my jubilation so I cried, "Victory to Mahatma Gandhi! Victory to the great King Shivaji!"

You may wonder why on earth Mahatma Gandhi and the great Shivaji came into the picture. Well! Those were the days of Gandhiji's non-cooperation movement. People organized big processions and marched through the streets shouting slogans. The most popular slogan was "Victory to Mahatma Gandhi." We would walk out of our classes at school and shout, "Victory to Mahatma Gandhi!" whenever a call was given to organize a general strike. We looked forward to such calls because they meant extra holidays. No wonder we had become great patriots and shouted "Victory to Mahatma Gandhi" whenever we wanted to express jubiliation.

It was, however, unwise, as I soon learnt to run around shouting slogans in the house. Mother immediately came to know that father had given me a rupee. She expressed her strong disapproval to father and wanted to confiscate the rupee right away.

She cried, "Hand over the rupee to me, will you. I will keep it for you safely in the steel almirah."

I knew from bitter experience that whenever I gave money to my mother for safe-keeping, I never saw it again.

So I shook my head and said, No! I shall not give my rupee to you. Once you take it, you never give it back to me."

My mother said, "Your money is all there sitting safely in my box. It is yours and it will be spent for you. What I have in mind is to buy a gold ring for you when there is enough money."

I did want a gold ring to wear on my finger during marriage ceremonies. So I was half-inclined to give the rupee to mother. But alarm bells began to ring in my ears and I pushed away her extended hand. I took as stubborn a stance as I could and said, "No. I don't want a gold ring."

"In that case, I will buy you a silver tumbler in which you can drink your milk" said mother with sweet persuasiveness.

It is almost routinely impressed on the mind of every Indian boy and girl that the best thing in the world is to own silver and gold. I was no exception. But I had discovered that one had to sacrifice far too many good things one craved for in order to get a gold or silver trinket, in some distant future. Over the years, I had been convinced that it made no sense to deny oneself so many things. So I took an even more stubborn stance and said, "I don't want gold and I don't want silver."

"What then do you propose to do with one whole rupee?" asked mother.

"Well! I will buy sweets, eat bhelpuri and even buy chocolates which the white sahibs eat!"

"Death be on you, you brat", shrieked my mother, "do you propose to eat one whole rupee worth of bhelpuri and sweets and such other things? Your stomach will burst, if you do anything so foolish."

I said defiantly, "Well! If my stomach is going to burst, let it burst. It is my stomach, isn't it? Don't you worry about it. I will stick it together with gum."

"Never in my life have I seen a boy as perverse and wrongheaded and nasty as you," cried my mother in disgust.

"All right! Let good boys give their rupees to their mothers for safe-keeping. I prefer to be perverse, wrongheaded and nasty. What do you have to say about that?" I said with a real nasty smirk. In fact I gave my lip a wicked twist and narrowed my eyes in a devilish manner to show my mother how terribly nasty I could get.

Mother got quite mad. I could sense the menace in the air. She advanced towards me and I could see her hands itching to twist my ears. I wasn't a fool to let her do that. So I ran out of the house and went over to Sadu, my bosom friend who lived in the neighbourhood.

I made sure that his father wasn't around and then beckoned him in a hushed voice and with loud gestures. I then walked out and stood at the street corner to wait for Sadu. He soon found a suitable opportunity to slip out of the house and joined me there.

Sadu looked at me and said, "Why? You seem to be mighty pleased with yourself."

"What makes you think that?" I asked trying to look very innocent and surprised.

"Well! You are walking as stiffly and haughtily as a wrestler who has won a bout."

I looked at Sadu with disdain and said nothing.

"And, why on earth are you leaning so much to your left and clutching your pocket on that same side?"

"What else do you expect me to do? Do you know how heavy a whole big silver rupee is? It is not easy to carry a rupee in one's pocket without supporting it with one's hand. Why, the pocket may get torn." I explained with even greater disdain.

Sadu's eyes became so big that they almost started out of their sockets. He cried, "Did I hear you right? A whole silver rupee, did you say? I guess your mother needs some medicine very urgently and has sent you to buy it, as there is nobody else around."

"Nonsense!" I cried, "Do mothers ever give a rupee to any of their children? A copper paisa or two or a nickel anna, is the most they are prepared to trust a boy with. Why, if my mother gives me a small four anna silver coin to buy something for her, she admonishes me umpteen times not to lose it. Would she ever give me a rupee to buy something for her?"

Sadu nodded assent, because that was his experience too. He asked, "Who was it then that gave it to you?"

"My father gave it to me," I said proudly, "and I can do what I like with it. I must say I have the nicest father a boy can ever have."

Sadu stared at me. He felt very sore about the injustice of it all. He protested angrily. "This is as unfair as can be. I go to the temple of Lord Ganapati every day. I devoutly walk round the idol of Ganapati not less than five times and beseech him to put Tatya in a generous frame of mind. Yet Ganapati does not put a drop of generosity in Tatya's mind while he pours a bucketful of it in your father's mind. It is not fair."

Sadu certainly had excellent reasons to feel sore. But there was nothing that I could do about it. In any case, I was too eager to talk and make plans about my rupee. So I said, "Sadu don't you want to see my rupee? It has Emperor George the Fifth on it."

Sadu asked, "Did you test it by dropping it on a stone? The rupees of this emperor are sometimes fake. Tatya had got one such fake rupee, when he went to the market. It was quite some job to pass it on to somebody else. The rupees of Queen Victoria are, however, always genuine."

My face fell. I had never imagined that a big bearded emperor like George the Fifth could be a cheat. It would have been a terrible disappointment and humiliation if my precious rupee had turned out to be fake. I said in a tearful voice to Sadu, "No. I didn't test it. Shall we do so right away?"

I took the rupee out of my pocket so hastily that it fell out of my hand and dropped on the footpath paved with stones. It rang loud and true and went rolling straight towards the stormwater drain hole. If Sadu hadn't been around, that rupee would have fallen into the drain and I wouldn't have seen it ever again. But Sadu pounced on it and grabbed it just on the brink of the drain hole. He then slapped me on my cheek and said, "You fool!"

I deserved the slap. I even deserved being punched on my back with a clenched fist. I wiped clean the rupee with the loose end of my shirt and said to Sadu, "Well! Now you better do the testing."

"Idiot!" Sadu cried. "Didn't you hear it ring true when it dropped on the pavement? There is no need to test it again. In any case rupees are too precious to be tested on the pavements of streets."

"It did ring true, didn't it? Are you absolutely sure?" I asked anxiously.

"Yes, yes. I am absolutely sure. And you are not supposed to discuss your rupee loudly in the middle of a busy street. What do you think will happen if thieves overhear our talk? They certainly would steal it from us. Don't you know that thieves always roam around in the streets looking for things to steal?"

That scared me out of my wits. I hastily pushed my hand into my pocket and clutched the rupee firmly in my palm. I then walked on in constant dread of a thief pouncing on me.

No wonder, I jumped high in the air with a scream when somebody clutched my shoulder. Luckily it wasn't a strong burly thief who did that. It was one of the residents of our neighbourhood. He eyed me suspiciously and asked, "Aren't you the son of Gopalrao, the lawyer?"

I smelled what was coming. So I said sheepishly, "Yes, I am."

"Why are you playing about with money on the street? Don't you know that good boys aren't supposed to do that? I saw that you were playing around with a silver rupee. How come, you have so much money with you?"

In those days all the parents in our neighbourhood had some kind of a secret pact. They kept a sharp eye not only on their children but all the children in the neighbourhood and any parent could scold any child found doing anything wrong. The parents of children so scolded did not protest but warmly thanked those that scolded their offspring. In fact they were told "Do not hesitate to give the boy a stinging slap if you find him doing anything wrong."

I was therefore quite scared when that man shot at me all these questions. In fact, I feared that he may go so far as to confiscate the rupee and hand it over to my father.

I mustered all my courage and said, "My father gave me the rupee. You can ask him if you like."

"I will certainly do that", said the man fixing me with a stare. He added, "I will also tell your father that it is not advisable to give so much money to small boys."

I felt relieved when he stopped at that. I knew of course that my mother would soon come to know about me playing with a rupee in the street. What she would do therafter, was unlikely to be pleasant. I sighed and braced myself for things to come. Yet I was quite happy that the rupee was still there sitting in my pocket.

Life was pretty hard for us boys in those days of unionized parents. Things, however, have greatly changed since then. Now people say nothing even if they see their neighbour's son smoking cigarettes or drinking liquor.

When the neighbour walked away, Sadu caught hold of my arm and punched me on my head. He cried, "I haven't yet seen a bigger ass than you. If you carry on like this, soon somebody will go and tell tales about us to Tatya.

Thereafter as soon as Tatya sets his eyes on me, he will give me a thrashing."

I could see that Sadu's Tatya was not only prone to break the legs of young boys but also to thrash them. That scared me quite a bit. At the same time I developed a greater respect for Sadu who could live with a father like that.

I told Sadu, "You can tell Tatya that it was I who was dropping rupees on the pavement."

"I certainly would do that. But that would not do me any good. Our Tatya administers a resounding slap to begin with and then asks questions", said Sadu with admirable calm.

I, however, squirmed with fright and asked, "In that case what is the way out?"

"Well! In any case I am likely to be thrashed. So I may as well make the best of a bad bargain by joining you in eating snacks and sweets that the rupee can buy," said Sadu with fortitude, with fright and asked, "In that case what is the way out?"

"Well! In any case I am likely to be thrashed. So I may as well make the best of a bad bargain by joining you in eating snacks and sweets that the rupee can buy," said Sadu with fortitude, resignation and down to earth good sense.

I cast an admiring glance at Sadu and said, "I can see some chewy sweets in the grocer's shop across the street. Let us go and buy some."

Sadu once again thumped me on the head. He said, "You are really an ass if ever there was one. We don't know that grocer, do we? Supposing he takes the rupee and does not return the change, what will you do?"

"How dare he do that? If we give him a rupee to buy the sweets, he jolly well has to return the rest of the change," I said in righteous indignation.

"Supposing he says that we never gave him the rupee, what will you do?"

"What do you mean, what I will do? I will scream at the top of my voice and tell all the people around there that the grocer is a big cheat and a crook." My righteous indignation had now reached boiling point.

"Well, you can certainly scream as much as you like. But will the people believe that a mere boy had a whole rupee of his own? Or will they believe the grocer?" asked Sadu looking straight into my eyes.

My jaw dropped and stayed dropped for a very long time. I was flabbergasted by the enormity of the dirty tricks that people play on simpletons like me. I gazed at Sadu with growing admiration. Here was a boy, I said to myself, who would be able to outsmart all the crafty grocers and cunning thieves in the world. I was glad that he was around to take good care of me and my rupee.

My eyes still glittered with admiration when I said, "Really Sadu, I do not know what I could have done without you. But for you my rupee was as good as lost! Well, I now know what to do. We shall go to Nana Mehendale's shop and buy sweets there. He is the grocer of your family and mine. He certainly will not cheat us out of our rupee."

Sadu bent low and bowed to me with feigned reverence. I was not such a fool as not to realize that Sadu was indulging in biting sarcasm. I asked, "Now what have I done wrong?"

"Well!," he said, "Nana Mehendale will certainly not cheat us, but he will certainly tell Tatya that he saw me with you and that we were squandering money on sweets."

"Oh God! I hadn't thought of that. But what then shall we do?" I asked.

As far as I could see, we were in a nice pickle. We couldn't buy sweets from a grocer we did not know, nor could we buy them from a grocer whom we knew quite well. Having a rupee to spend seemed to create far more problems than I could imagine.

But luckily Sadu was with me and he could find a way out of any pickle. He pondered over the problem for a while and said, "Here is what we will do. We will go to Nana Mehendale's shop and tell him that your mother is suffering from a stomach ache and she asked you to buy for her a copper paisa worth of ginger and another paisa worth of ova."

"Let us go", I said. But a little later I stopped and asked, "But wouldn't Nana Mehendale ask my mother how her stomach ache is when he runs into her next? Wouldn't that expose me?"

Sadu was very philosophical about it. He said, "It doesn't matter a fat lot if you are exposed. After all your father doesn't slap you if he is annoyed with you. Your mother of course would do that. But mothers' slaps and punches don't hurt."

I couldn't quite see eye to eye with Sadu on that matter. My mother too could administer a stinging slap. Moreover, sometimes when she really lost her temper she came, at us children with a big iron ladle or anything else that came to her hands in the kitchen. But I was keen to start spending that rupee. I therefore allowed myself to be propelled into Nana Mehendale's shop.

I stood dumb for a while there because I had forgotten what I had to say. But Sadu said, "Don't you remember what your mother told you?"

At the same time he pinched me without letting anybody see what he was doing. The pinch did the trick and I told the story about my mother's stomach ache.

Nana, the grocer, looked at me suspiciously over the rim of the glasses which as usual had slipped way down his nose. He said, "Stomach ache? Your mother has it? How come I saw her, walking past my shop a few minutes back?"

That rattled me completely. This was something that usually happened to me. In the first place, when it was necessary to lie, I could not think of a good fib. If a fib was suggested to me by a resourceful friend like Sadu, I was immediately found out.

Luckily on this occasion Sadu was with me. He saved the situation very skillfully. He thumped me on the back and said with a big smile that split his face from ear to ear,

"Silly! It is your grandmother who has a stomach ache, isn't it?"

I looked at Sadu with an utterly vacant expression and exclaimed, "Grandmother!"

Sadu again pinched me without letting anybody notice it and said, "Yes, yes. Your grandmother. Don't you remember?"

Once again it was the pinch that did the trick. I nodded my head with great emphasis and said loudly, "Yes, yes. Of course, my grandmother. She wants a copper paisa worth of ginger and a paisa worth of headache."

"What?" snapped Nana Mehendale. Sadu gave me a nasty look and then broke out into loud laughter. He explained to Nana, that "His grandmother doesn't certainly want a paisa worth of headache. She wants a paisa worth of ova."

"Yes, yes, of course, a paisa worth of ova is what she wants."

Nana Mehendale eyed me suspiciously while he tied the two things I had asked for into nice bundles. When the bundles were ready, I handed over to him the big silver rupee.

Nana looked at the rupee very suspiciously. He said, "One whole rupee! In the hands of a boy? To buy two paise worth of stuff? How on earth did your mother do a thing like that?"

Sadu did not wait for me to answer that question, because he knew that it was beyond me to improvise an answer quickly. He said, "It was like this, his mother didn't have any small change. So she gave him a rupee and asked me to accompany him to make sure he didn't lose it."

Nana Mehendale continued to eye us both suspiciously. He said, "I an wondering whether I should hand over to you this fifteen and half annas of small change. I think I will rather hand it over to your father, when he goes past my shop in the evening on his way home."

My heart sank, because I thought that the game was lost. But Sadu again came to my rescue. He said sweetly, "But,

Nana, his mother has asked us to buy some medicines from a pharmacy down the street. We will therefore need the money."

Nana eyed us for a while and reluctantly handed over the handful of change to me.

At this juncture Nana's brother interjected, "It was really not necessary to send any money at all to buy things from our shop. Gopalrao has a running credit account with us."

This observation could have given rise to further queries and complications. But as soon as the money was handed over to me, I was propelled out of the shop very hurriedly by Sadu. He didn't let me stop until we were quite some distance away from the shop.

I was scared by the way things were turning out. Moreover, the fifteen and half annas of change made my pocket bulge conspicuously, and the way the change jingled in my pocket made me even more noticeable. Passers-by looked at me curiously when they heard the jingle of the coins in my pocket.

I said, "Sadu, all this is more than I can take. I think I will go home, hand over the change to mother and forget about the rupee."

Sadu thumped me on my back and said, "You crybaby! Is this the time to quit? Why, you have not even chewed a sweet so far."

That restored my courage. Moreover, I realized that I was getting quite hungry and the very idea of eating an assortment of sweets began to make my mouth water. So I fell in with what Sadu suggested and bought two paise worth of chewy sweets. In fact, I spent one more paisa and bought a handful of another variety of sweets.

We both went to the Ganapati temple, sat on the long cement bench in its yard and ate our sweets with great relish. That whetted my appetite and I said, "Sadu! Have you ever eaten the chocolates which the white sahibs eat? They are expensive. A small bar of chocolate costs one whole nickel anna. That really is the sort of thing we should buy when we have a rupee to spend."

Sadu said, "I have never yet eaten a chocolate in my whole life. What does it look like? What does it taste like?"

I had eaten a chocolate not once but twice. I therefore explained to him as vividly as I could what it looked like and tasted like.

Sadu looked all around us with suspicious eyes, he then beckoned me to a far corner of the temple yard and whispered, "Does that thing called chocolate contain eggs? The trouble with these white sahibs is that they put eggs into everything they eat."

We both belonged to Brahmin households and there would have been hell to pay if we had eaten eggs. I pondered deeply over the matter and whispered back in Sadu's ear, "I have eaten a chocolate. My father once gave it to me. But I did not find an egg in it. In any case my father wouldn't have given it to me if it had contained eggs."

When Sadu learnt that my father himself had given me a chocolate to eat, all his fears melted. We looked at each, nodded in silent agreement and went to an Irani shop to buy a one anna worth slab of chocolate.

Sadu looked at it very carefully and removed the silver foil wrapped around it without tearing it. We then carefully broke the slab into two equal parts and ate it slowly so as to relish every bit of it as much as we could.

Sadu seemed to like it immensely. He expressed his deep satisfaction by nodding his head appreciatively several times. He raised both his hands in a gesture of blessing. He said, "It is awfully tasty. It fills the mouth with its delicious taste and goes into the belly smoothly. These white sahibs may be rotten chaps otherwise, but they certainly know how to make truly delicious sweets."

I licked the chocolate which had stuck to the corner of my mouth and asked, "Shouldn't we eat one more?"

Sadu concurred saying, "You have said exactly what I wanted to say. But is it proper to spend money so recklessly?

A slab of chocolate costs no less than one whole nickel anna."

"I don't care" I cried, "I wouldn't be bothered the least bit even if it costs two annas a slab. What do you have to say about that?"

Sadu said, "Well! If it doesn't bother you, why should it bother me? Let us go and get another slab."

That is exactly what we did. Sadu once again divided the slab into two equal parts. He also carefully saved the silver foil, which he gave me as he had kept for himself the first one. Sadu could be scrupulously fair when he wanted to be.

In the Irani shop I saw in a glass jar tiny cricket bats, which contained little silver pills which were very tasty. That bat cost two whole nickel annas. But I was indeed in a very reckless mood. So I said to Sadu, "Let us buy this cricket bat. It contains very tasty silver balls."

"What does it cost?" asked Sadu.

"Two annas."

Sadu thumped me on my head and pursed his lips in disapproval. He said, "Do you mean to say that you propose to spend another two whole annas on this thing? Have you gone crazy? No. I wouldn't let you do that. We shall instead buy lumps of ice bathed in syrup. They cost only one paisa each and one can keep on sucking a lump for a very long time."

Sadu, it seems, had nothing against being reckless once in a while. But he was stoutly opposed to being recklessly reckless. When I thought over his suggestion, I realized that it was quite sensible. So we purchased two lumps of ice bathed in three syrups of different colours and began to suck them noisily with great gusto and relish.

While we were thus enjoying ourselves, Sadu all of a sudden took to his heels and disappeared into a small lane opening on that street. I ran after him and caught up with him. I asked him in a whisper, "What happened? What made you run away like that?"

The brave sagacious Sadu had been transformed into a frightened little boy in tears, "Tatya, my father, is coming that way. I hope he has not seen me. If he has, I am a goner."

We both hid behind a big red post-box standing on the pavement. Our hearts were racing pit-a-pat. We stood there for what seemed like hours. At last Sadu's Tatya walked past the lane we were hiding in. We hid behind that post-box until we felt sure that Tatya had gone a long way down that street. Thereafter we emerged from behind the post box with happy beaming faces. We noticed, however, that a few people around us were eyeing us with suspicion. So we made haste to get out of that lane.

While we were walking in a hurry, Sadu said, "I think I want no more of this. I better go home. I get into trouble in the company of boys like you. Left to myself, I would never have polluted myself by eating a chocolate with eggs in it nor would I have eaten lumps of ice bathed in syrup. It was because of you that I did all these wrong things."

I was amazed at this complete turnaround. I cried, "Now, there! It was you Sadu who egged me on to do all these naughty things. I for one wanted to hand over the rupee to my mother and say quit. But you suggested..."

"Now there, Gangadhar, I shall not take that from you. Who was it that said that we should buy chocolates?" said Sadu staring right back into my eyes.

"Ha, ha; and who suggested that we buy those two lumps of ice bathed in syrups of three different colours?" I stared back at Sadu and stood my ground.

"And who..." said Sadu vehemently.

"But who..." I protested indignantly.

So it went on for quite some time until we ran into Mahadu Shinde, one of the boys in our class.

Mahadu was the son of Dagadu, the head peon of our school. He had entered the school rather late and he was about two to three years older than us.

He put his hands on our shoulders. "What are you

gabbing about? You are carrying on so that you don't even notice friends like me when they are passing by."

I said, "Tell me Mahadu, how can I take it, if Sadu blames me for no reason at all? Why, he says that he is getting spoilt in my company. He says that it is I who make him eat chocolates with eggs in them. He also put the blame on me for making him eat lumps of ice bathed in syrups of three different colours. I must tell you, Mahadu, that it was entirely his idea."

Mahadu firmly caught hold of the collars of our shirts and cried, "You two chaps seem to have a lot of money jingling in your pockets. Where did you get it from? Eh? Did you steal it from your mother's boxes?"

"Nonsense", I cried, "We are not thieves. It was my father, who gave me one whole big silver rupee. We are having a bit of fun with that money."

Mahadu gave such a start that he made us jump too. He cried, "One whole rupee? Oh my mother! If a rupee had come my way, I wouldn't have eaten lumps of ice. I would have gone right away to a big restaurant, and I would have eaten a large dish of spicy minced mutton and bread. I would have washed it down with a glass of bubbly red sweet drink, loaded with ice."

This talk of eating meat made our stomachs churn quite unpleasantly. Sadu, said, "No Mahadu, we don't eat that kind of stuff."

"You gutless Brahmins," cried Mahadu, "All that you eat is rice and insipid stew of alu leaves. Well, it is your rupee. So we won't eat minced mutton. But how about eating a roti or bread dunked in a thick gravy of beans loaded with fiery chillies? Or are you afraid of eating that fiery stuff too?"

I strongly resented this slight. I cried, "Who is afraid of eating chillies? And who minds spending money in a big restaurant. I am not that kind of a chap, Mahadu. I can spend money like Lord Falkland if it comes to that."

None of us had any idea who Lord Falkland was. In fact, we were not sure that such a person existed. But somehow he had come to represent a reckless spender among many other things.

This mention of Lord Falkland greatly cheered up Mahadu. He shouted, "Well, then what is stopping three Lord Falklands from walking into a restaurant?"

I said, "I think Sadu is scared of going to a restaurant."

Sadu protested, "Who is scared? Not I. It was you who were scared when we were in Nana Mehendale's shop, remember? But for me you would have returned home like a sissy and hid behind the pallu of your mother's saree. And do you think that I am scared of the beating I will get from Tatya? Let me tell you I have taken quite a few of these beatings and I am not scared of taking some more. If it comes to that I will enter a restaurant with my chest thrust forward even if Tatya sees me. Come on let us see who is the sissy around here."

Mahadu clapped with a guffaw and entered the restaurant with the air of a Lord Falkland. So did we.

Mahadu then beckoned the waiter with an imperious gesture, "Wipe the table clean," he barked, "and bring three glasses of water with ice."

He thumped the table to add emphasis to his command.

We were quite taken aback and greatly impressed by the grand style in which Mahadu conducted himself in the restaurant. I wondered whether I would ever be able to emulate him.

Mahadu then asked us with a sweeping gesture, "What dishes would you like me to order?"

Sadu said hesitantly "I will eat a besan laddu and shankarpale."

"What rubbish", cried Mahadu. "Nobody shall eat such sweet sissy stuff. Let us eat hot misal. It is so hot that it will bring tears to your eyes. Why, you will remember your mother, when the first morsel burns your tongue."

He then placed an order for three special super hot misal. Soon enough three little mountains of misal steaming in big plates were placed on our table.

"Oh, my father!" I said, "Are we to eat these mountains?"

Mahadu broke into a loud guffaw, thumped us on the back and cried, "You better finish the plateful, if I am to believe all that talk of how brave you Brahmins are."

Confronted with this challenge, both Sadu and I rose to the occasion and fell to digging into that mountain of misal. It was certainly hot but not unbearably so. It was also very spicy and tasty. It contained chivada, shev, usal, potatoes, egg fruit, groundnuts and onions. It had on top a sprinkling of green kothmeer leaves. It was a grand assembly of dozen things all tasty in themselves. Our mouths burned, our noses began to run, but we could not resist the misal. We finished it all sipping cold iced water at frequent intervals to quench the fires raging on our tongues.

At last when those mountains of misal were fully eaten, our stomachs were about to burst. Sadu burped loudly as one is wont to do at the end of a marriage feast. That made all of us laugh.

Mahadu ordered three rose coloured drinks, bubbly and sweet. When we had finished eating, they were placed before us in big glasses which had bouquets of white froth at the top. He told us that each of the bottles cost three copper paise. When he said that, I leaned back and smiled recklessly like Lord Falkland.

It was quite an effort to find room for the contents of those big glasses of drinks in our overloaded stomachs. But we bravely managed to do so. I paid the bill under Sadu's knowledgeable supervision and we walked out of the restaurant with our tummies protruding miles ahead of us.

Mahadu said grandly, "Oh my mother! We must now eat masala paan."

It was a very appropriate suggestion. It is customary to eat pan enriched with various tasty powders at the end of a feast.

We stopped at the paan stall outside the restaurant and Mahadu straightened the collar of his shirt to place the order for three paans in the appropriate grand manner.

But the order was never placed. For while he was straightening his shirt collar once again, Sadu and I saw Mahadu's father approaching us on the sidewalk. Mahadu did not notice him at that time but his father certainly noticed Mahadu. Mahadu's father stopped dead in his track and stared at us in amazement and disbelief. He then rushed at Mahadu and hit him on the cheek with a big, powerful swipe of his arm. Mahadu was a sturdy boy. But so powerful was the swipe that he collapsed. But even in that predicament he had the presence of mind to understand what had happened and to swiftly react to it. He rose from the pavement like a ball on rebound and ran. Nothing stopped him. When a hack victoria stood in his way he crawled underneath the belly of the horse and went to the other side of the victoria.

Sadu and I stood rooted to the ground. Mahadu's father caught us by our arms and said, "You boys! You come from good families and yet you misbehave like this. I will report this to the Headmaster of the school and ask him to give you such a caning that you will never again even think of such things."

A crowd had promptly gathered around us as usually happens in India on such occasions. They all nodded approval of the scolding being administered to us. Dagadu informed them that we were guilty of squandering money in a restaurant.

You must know, that though Dagadu was only a head peon, he had a far more impressive personality than any of our teachers had. The impressiveness was heightened by his uniform, turban and a big moustache. He also carried far more weight and was far more feared in our school than our headmaster. He had been in the school for forty years and had scolded many of our teachers, when they were students like us. He was a strict disciplinarian too. We knew therefore, that his threat was not an empty one. We quailed at the prospect of going to school the next day.

When Dagadu thought that he had scolded us enough and released our arms, we took to our heels. Sadu ran with such alacrity that he dashed into the ample stomach of a policeman.

The policeman caught us both by our arms and said, "Now you boys! I have been watching you for sometime. You have been walking around and hiding behind post boxes. What are you up to? I bet it is not anything good. You look like boys from good families. So I will let you go now. But if I ever see you again loitering in the street, I will lock you up at the police station."

When he let us go, we were shaking all over. When at last I reached home, I heaved a sigh of relief and sank in a quiet corner. No sooner had I done so, then my mother noticed me. She put her hands menacingly on her hips and asked, "What was it that you told Nana Mehendale when you went to his shop?"

Nana Mehendale had certainly not wasted any time in letting my family know what I had been up to.

I am not too keen to tell you what happened afterwards. I need not tell you why.

All I can say is that we young boys had a pretty hard time in those days. But come to think of it, we also had a lot of fun.

❑